HIGHLAND STORM

GUARDIANS OF THE STONE

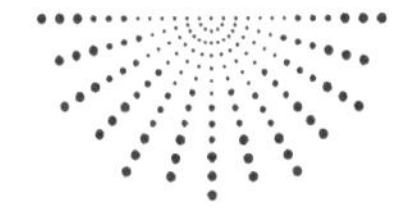

TANYA ANNE CROSBY

0 9 8 7 6 5 4 3 2 1

PRAISE FOR TANYA ANNE CROSBY

"Rich with historical detail and brimming with passion and high-stakes romantic adventure, this newest addition to the Guardians of the Stone series is a spectacular achievement in Scottish romance. The story and characters will enthrall readers from beginning to end. I absolutely loved it."

— USA TODAY BESTSELLING AUTHOR, JULIANNE MACLEAN

"Crosby builds worlds that immediately draw you in, with multi-dimensional characters and rich, detailed story lines. Absolutely riveting!"

— KATHRYN LE VEQUE, USA TODAY BESTSELLING AUTHOR

"Crosby's characters keep readers engaged..."

— PUBLISHERS WEEKLY

"Crosby pens a tale that touches your soul and lives forever in your heart."

— SHERRILYN KENYON #1 NYT BESTSELLING AUTHOR

"Tanya Anne Crosby is a master of her genre …"

— LAURIN WITTIG, BESTSELLING AUTHOR

"Love, honor, suspense, passion... all the good things we love in a Highlander Romance."

— SUZAN TISDALE, BESTSELLING AUTHOR OF ROWAN'S LADY

"Enchanting landscapes, breathtaking betrayal, and heartwarming passion herald Tanya Anne Crosby's triumphant return to ancient Scotland."

— GLYNNIS CAMPBELL, BESTSELLING AUTHOR

GUARDIANS OF THE STONE SERIES BIBLIOGRAPHY

Once Upon a Highland Legend

Highland Fire

Highland Steel

Highland Storm

Maiden from the Mist

ALSO CONNECTED...

THE HIGHLAND BRIDES

The MacKinnon's Bride

Lyon's Gift

On Bended Knee

Lion Heart

Highland Song

MacKinnon's Hope

&

Angel of Fire

ALSO AVAILABLE AS AUDIOBOOKS

THE KINGDOM OF THE PECHTS

THE 7 MORMAERDOMS OF CRUITHNE'S SONS

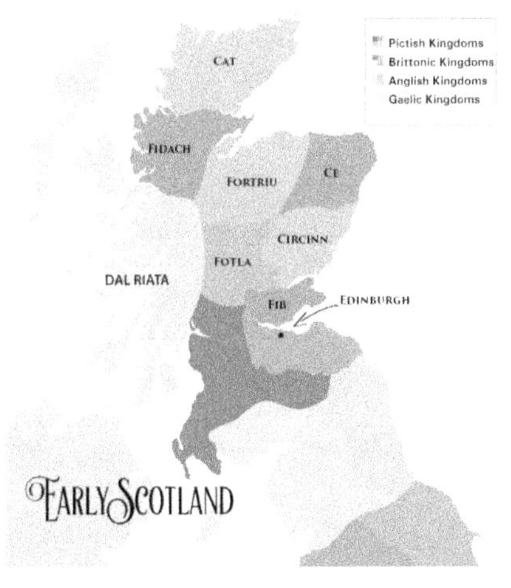

Unless the fates be faulty grown
And prophet's voice be vain
Where'er is found this sacred stone
The blood of Alba reigns

PROLOGUE

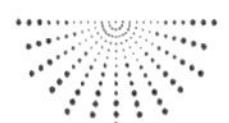

DUBHTOLARGG 1130

The winds of war were stirring in the north.

Casting his eyes on Moray, the eighth son of Malcom Ceann Mor and the sixth of the Margaret-sons made good his threat to conquer the north. Even now, David mac Mhaoil Chaluim was rallying his troops, men who would remain loyal to Scotia's crown.

"I mean to leave," the young man said, and hearing the familiar voice, the old woman halted abruptly before the entrance to the cave.

Turning to face the younger dún Scoti, Una leaned upon her staff for support. The patch over her one bad eye was worn and her skin was withered as a prune. Her coloring held a pallor that made Keane want to stay. "I know," she said, and a smile hovered on her blue-cast lips.

Of course she always knew.

Una had been with their clan for all of Keane's living memory. She was the mother of them all, their healer, their elder. She was the longest living guardian of the Stone from Scone. "Would ye come sit for a spell?"

"Not today," Keane said.

Not tomorrow either, for by then he would be gone.

"Ah, well," she lamented, and seemed to comprehend.

If he lingered now, he might never leave, and his sister Lael had summoned him to Keppenach to help keep her the peace whilst her husband rode to war with Scotia's king.

The old woman eyed him steadily, her green eye shimmering. "I told your Da, your brother as well… a man will oft meet his destiny on the path he chose to avoid."

All men must stand for what they believed in. Keane realized this as well as most. "I am not afraid, Una, no matter what my brother may believe."

She nodded, and the stone in her staff's hilt winked against the twilight. If some part of Keane had hoped she might stop him, the look in her eye only reaffirmed his need to leave. "Will you speak to Aidan for me? Will you tell him why?"

The old woman shrugged. "Your brother is not your keeper, nor is he your king, but if you would give him half a chance, he might surprise you."

Even as he lingered, the sky grew darker still.

"Aidan would never understand," Keane said.

The laird of the *dún Scoti* was not quick to embrace change, neither would he accept Keane's decision to abandon the vale whilst the surrounding lands were so full of strife. Aidan feared the kingdom of Scotia would descend upon Dubhtolargg, when in truth, they were all but forgotten here in the Mounth. At least this way, Keane could make himself useful to his sister. Here, he withered in the role he'd been given.

Una sighed again, the sound as heavy as the Stone

that lay hidden in the belly of their ben. "Ye must follow your own path, Keane dún Scoti. But ye look to your heart, not your head."

Keane nodded soberly. Already, there had been too many words spoken for his taste. What he'd come to hear was simply that he had a right to go, and now that he knew it from her own two lips, he closed the distance between himself and the old woman, embracing her fiercely. Wobbling a bit, she tapped him gently on the back. "Whether ye choose to face him or nay, I ken ye'll know what to do when the time arrives."

"Never fear," he reassured her. "Ye taught us well."

Under the twilight, her one good eye twinkled with unshed tears. "Nay. Ye found your way well enough all on your own." She sounded more stoical then he'd ever heard her sound before, like a mother whose children were abandoning her to the ravages of old age.

"With a bit o' help," he reassured, and reaching out, he shook Una gently by the shoulders to make his point. "None of us could have done aught without ye, Una. Come another day, I will return. Ye have my word."

She looked at him sadly, as though she knew something Keane did not. "Go on wi' ye now," she shooed him. "Be on your way afore I rap ye good upon the head."

She waved her staff to make the point, but the familiar gesture only made Keane smile—not because she wouldn't do it, mind you, but because she had done it already a thousand times before and each time with a heart full of love.

But that was that. Goodbyes were said. Keane gave her a final hug and hurried down the hillside. Under cover of darkness, he packed his bags, and left his sister Cailin to share the news: another wolf of Pechtland had departed the vale.

CHAPTER ONE

DECEMBER 1135

KINNEDDAR CASTLE, AILGINSHIRE

The men of Moray were warriors, the women lovely and fearless, the heart and soul of Moray's men. With eyes the color of honey and hair as radiant as a winter's flame, 'twas said that even the gods above were enamored by their grace and beauty.

But grace was not Lianae's forte, and neither was she the beauty her mother and sister had been. Her hair was more blond than red, and her eyes were the color of dirty *uisge*, not bright and shining like her sister Elspeth's. Nevertheless, she was the youngest of two living females in a long line of Moray queens—the other being her toothless aunt Gruaidh.

Lianae had not been the Earl's first choice, but on the other hand, *he* was no choice at all. So long as she girded her loins there was still a chance the blood of Óengus might rise again. This was the prayer of the Mormaerdom. For all that King David hailed himself a benevolent King, he surrounded himself with blackguards like William fitz Duncan and turned a blind eye to all their evildoings. So this was how he meant to rule —putting others to do his dirty work whilst he donned the cloak of a saint.

Saint David—pah!

Parcel by parcel, the land of Moray was being granted to England's odious barons, and the man seated before her was the most treacherous fiend of all, he who styled himself *de* Moray. *De* Moray, not *of* Moray, because despite that he was the son of a Scots king, he was no better than a Norman usurper himself.

Like his father before him—and King David as well —fitz Duncan had been raised by the English to serve the whims of an English king. Already, through his mother Uhtreda, he was the patriarch of Northumbria, making him one of the richest barons in Northern England, and King David would name him the Earl of Moray as well.

Dressed in pale blue brocade, with a hat and a pair of foppish red shoes that were as pointy as his nose, King David's nephew and son of a murdered king—her sister's murderer as well—ignored Lianae, speaking directly to her brother. "Her insolence will not be brooked," he said, enunciating the words in the Norman accent as he peered down his skinny, beak-like nose.

Much to her dismay, her brother Lulach matched the Earl's diction, eschewing his lilting Moray brogue. "Never fear, my lord… once Lianae realizes her good fortune, she will come to heel."

My lord? My lord! She despised the Norman articulation of her brother's words. The pain in her jaw flaring, Lianae stood abruptly. "I am not a dog! I will not *come to heel!* Ha'e we no' already witnessed what this man would do? Ha'e ye no affection for our sister?"

Never mind her own rising misfortunes! Even as they spoke, Elspeth's body lay above stairs, growing cold, her neck stained with bruises that were put there by the Earl himself. If Lianae had not gone in to see her this morning after the night's celebration, he might have easily concealed his sins—but then neither would she be in this untenable situation.

Reaching out, fitz Duncan's guard shoved Lianae back down into her chair, constraining her by her shoulder, squeezing painfully in warning.

Fitz Duncan cast her an embittered glance. No doubt, half his rancor this morning was due in part to his displeasure in ending with the *wrong* Moray sister. Well, he should have kept his hands to himself! Although now, if he should manage to convince Lulach to accept a new union, Lianae realized he would make her rue the day she came to be his wife. *"Cil-onaidh,"* she hissed beneath her breath.

The man was an *idiot and a fool.*

So *was her brother Lulach.*

"Lianae, please," Lulach begged. After a long pleading silence, he turned to re-address the Earl. "Forgive her, my lord. She is merely frightened. But of course, we did not expect..."

Lianae waited for her brother to finish. *What, Lulach?* They did not expect Elspeth's new husband would strangle her in her marriage bed. *Say it,* Lulach, she begged silently. *Say it. Accept the truth of what has been done. Confess what you would do to me—to your own flesh and blood!*

Forsooth, but if there was any remorse at all for the events leading to their sister's death, there was little evidence of it in the Earl's expression. Cruelty was manifested in his voice, a barely suppressed violence that presented itself as boredom, although Lianae recognized it. It tightened her nerves like the overdrawn strings of a bow. "Frightened, or nay, the girl will learn her place."

The girl?

Lianae was not a *girl.* She was a princess of Moray!

Learn her place?

And what place was that? To step up and be his wife, now that he'd managed to murder the other?

"I will *not,*" Lianae bit out again, but she might as well have never spoken. Neither of the men seated at the long table even bothered to look at her. They continued their discourse, as though Lianae were no longer present.

"Aye, she will," her brother promised, and it was all Lianae could do to hold her tongue. Their land was defiled, her brother seduced by—what? Peace at any cost?

Five years ago, in his quest to control the Highlands, David mac Mhaoil Chaluim finally kept his threat to bring down the Mormaerdom, killing her father during the great slaughter at Stracathro in Forfarshire. Only two of her brothers survived the massacre, and now Lulach, named after their maternal grandfather, was proving himself to be as wretched as his namesake. He was a fool to believe David of Scotia would allow him any boons for this union. It was a contract made in vain, for once Lianae took her vows, she would be trapped, not only in wedlock to a lying, murderous fiend, but in collusion with their mortal enemy. The Mormaerdom would be lost forever—for not only was William Elspeth's murderer, he was also the commander in charge of the very army that had wrested Moray from its rightful heir—her father.

"You must realize, Lulach... there are others I might choose—women who are comelier, and whose gratitude is far more easily won."

Lianae opened her mouth to tell him to shove the pointy end of his shoe up his ironclad arse, but her brother cast her a pleading glance. The Earl's man kept a firm hand upon her shoulder, pinching painfully.

"Aye, my lord," Lulach said, "but Lianae is the last of Óengus's daughters. As such, she may help dissuade a new rebellion."

"Gruaidh is more than willing."

Lianae rolled her eyes at the mention of her aunt.

"Aye, though Gruaidh may not be able to bear your children, nor is she quite so... pleasing."

The Earl flicked a glance toward Lianae. "Neither is your sister once she opens her mouth."

Gritting her teeth, a memento of her own brief time alone with the Earl moments before, Lianae lifted a hand to the bruise on her cheek, urging Lulach to acknowledge it, but her brother refused to look her way again.

Lianae's heart wrenched. *Oh, Lulach,* she wanted to ask, *where has your courage gone? Where now your scruples and foresight?*

"I will make certain she understands her duty."

The Earl flicked Lianae another, more embittered glance. "See that you do."

"Aye, my lord... and if you would but give us a moment alone?"

His face a mask of boredom, the Earl sighed, but he raked his chair back from the table. He stood, acknowledging Lianae with another ill-tempered glance, and there in his gaze she spied something cold and foreboding. He was warning her without words, and she already knew what dangers that entailed. Had her sister angered him somehow? They might never know what happened in that room. Pressing a hand against her cheek, Lianae shuddered over the images that accosted her. Her sister's lips and skin had been as blue as the sapphire gown she'd worn to take her vows. And still Lulach would sell her for—what?

Despair choked away her breath, along with any remaining protests.

Her brother stood, and Lianae made to do so as well —not out of deference, but to leave. Once again, the Earl's guard pushed her down into the chair, biting his strong fingers into the hollow beneath her shoulder, until her mouth parted for a cry of pain she refused to voice—at least not in front of these monsters.

Outliers! Murderers!

The Earl of Moray turned from the table, and only then did his bootlicker release Lianae's shoulder and move away, falling in step behind his master like the dog he appeared to be. Make no mistake, Lianae would *not* marry the Earl, but she recognized the stubborn set of her brother's jaw and she knew he would not relent. It would serve no one to voice another protest. Nay, she must find another way…

Lulach waited until the Earl and his men were gone from the hall before turning to address her. "Lianae," he said quietly. "Ye *must* learn to hold your tongue. If ye would but mind yourself, ye could inherit much, my sister."

Lianae's fingers balled so tightly that her nails dug into her palms.

Once upon a time, she had adored Lulach for his gentle nature. This moment, his gentility seemed more a weakness, and the slender, slightly downturned chin, a tell. The hall doors closed, one by one, and the heavy raucous sound ricocheted off the hallhouse ceiling. To her mind, it had the sound of a cell door.

"I dinna wish to marry that usurper," Lianae said quietly.

Her brother sighed. "Lianae, he won his place the same way the men of Moray all once did, by the grace of his sword."

"Nay," Lianae argued. "He was appointed by King

David, who is nae better than an outlier himself. He was raised under Henry's tutelage. *All* these men were groomed to take our place, and ye give them time and they will quash every last Morayman and woman from this land."

"He is Duncan's heir and bears the blood of kings," Lulach reminded her.

"On his hands!" Lianae said in outrage.

"Ach, Lianae. Be fair. His father was our king for a time."

"Ach, yoursel'!" Lianae said, looking at her brother incredulously. "Dinna ye see, Lulach? King Duncan was murdered by his own brother, and if the rumors be true, William would collude with David even despite this fact! That should tell ye all ye need to know about the mon's character. He would sell himself so easily to his father's murderers. At any rate, he's but a bastard and his mother is an outlier as well. They are all Henry's minions—every one!"

Lulach frowned. "'Tis long past time to make our peace, sister. Óengus is dead—"

Lianae gave a raw little laugh. "No one knows this better than Elspeth!" Tears pooled in her eyes at the images that accosted her anew. Her sister's rent dress, her eyes open and bulging. Fitz Duncan not even had the decency to close her lovely amber eyes. The memory threatened to undermine Lianae's composure in a way that not even the last hour's discussion had managed to do so.

Her brother ignored her tears. "Our brothers, dead…"

"Nay!"

She and Lulach shared a heated look, and Lianae tried to gauge what he knew. Neither Ewen nor Graeme had been spied for many, many months, but Lianae knew they must be out there, biding their time, waiting for the right opportunity. Óengus had taught them well.

"Dinna ye ken, Lianae? We canna fight any longer—not if we are meant to survive."

And there it is.

Her brother's expression was full of fear, and Lianae's heart wrenched for the man he could have been. She knew this was not entirely his wish, to see her wed to a monster. But Lulach wasn't strong enough to stand against despicable men. She wanted to forgive him, she truly did, but she couldn't. He would sell her all too easily. Her sister—their sister—was already dead. Lianae might see the same fate—and for what? For Lulach's self-assurances? To line his coffers? Why?

There was only one way to avoid this fate. It was to allow her brother to assume she would relent. His mind was already made up. "When?" she asked, swallowing her grief. "When would you have me commit this atrocity?"

"Tonight."

"Tonight!"

Tears welled again in her eyes.

"Lianae," her brother pleaded. Despite his youth, there were all-new wrinkles etched in his brow, frown lines that hadn't previously existed. His wife also seemed older than her years, but Lianae couldn't help any of them; but she most certainly intended to help herself. She was not prepared to become a sacrifice. Her body longed to spring up from her seat and run screaming out the door, but she sat.

Peering into the balcony, she caught sight of a figure at the rails, peeping down. William fitz Duncan was not a man who took his chances. No man in the line of succession could rest at ease. Not since the day Kenneth MacAilpín up and murdered the sons of seven Pecht nations had Scotia known lasting peace. Cousins murdered cousins. Brothers murdered brothers. Sisters were naught but chattel to be bartered away.

Her mind grappled for a plan.

The bathhouse was a filthy puddle of sweat, an immodest structure left standing after the retreat of the Roman legions. It was the last place anyone would get themselves clean. But that's where Lianae must find herself tonight… somehow.

Beneath the bathhouse was a tangle of pipes, fed by sweet Highland streams. The pipes were all sealed now, and the bath itself was refilled once a week by a procession of unhappy servants. But Lianae knew how to access those pipes. From there, she could escape into the woods, although she mustn't give rise to suspicion. She must go with the clothes on her back. And once she assented here now, they would return her to her room only long enough to fetch her wedding attire—Elspeth's wedding attire. She cringed, for the thought of taking that odious dress and putting it on her person left her with a pang in her belly that gnawed at her from the inside out. A knot formed in her throat, but she forced words past it, "Very well, but please… at least allow me the courtesy of taking my vows after a bath. As you can see I am filthy."

Lulach lifted a brow.

Does he remember?

She and Elspeth used to enter the pipes from the woodlands, and peek within the bathhouse, giggling with delight over the education they'd received in there—some not so titillating. Forsooth, she'd had little idea how much men liked to pass wind when you put more than two together into a tub.

Lulach stared at her, and Lianae threw up her hands. "Would you have him plug his nose over the stench of me? *Look at me,*" she begged, and prayed he would see the bruises as well. "I have come straight from tending *your* children. 'Tis little wonder he has stared at me all morn as though ye'd put a turd beneath his nose!"

Lulach sighed, relenting at once. "No tricks, Lianae," he warned. "If ye canna find it in your heart to do this for yourself, or for me, then ye must consider your nephews. Alan may yet find a way to make our father proud."

Dressed as a Sassenach? Nay. Never! Óengus would turn in his grave.

Lianae narrowed her eyes. "It is for love of them I did not leave when I had the chance," she reminded him. She loved her brother's children as though they were her own. But Lulach had already pledged his fealty to the new Earl and she doubted fitz Duncan would harm them, not when he needed the people's support. As a rightful born son of Óengus, Lulach was very well regarded. Even to the grave, the people of Moray loved her father dearly.

"Very well, I will arrange the bath."

Lianae's heart leapt with glee. "I thank you. The Earl will thank you," she amended quietly, trying not to squeal as her brother clapped his hands.

The hall doors flew wide and in marched not one, but two burly men to escort Lianae out of the great hall. They plucked her up and dragged her away.

"Remember yourself," Lulach warned. "And dinna tarry."

"Dinna fash yourself, *brother*. I will do my duty," she promised with little compunction.

It was her *duty* to find a way to escape.

Almost at once, the details of her plan began to form in her head. Lianae but needed a few moments alone in the bathhouse—long enough to open and enter the passageway. The entrance should be easy enough to locate, even after all these years. The new Earl and his party could scarce be expected to know the history of these lands, or the structures erected therein. Fitz Duncan had spent his entire life in England and their ignorance would serve Lianae well today.

Out in the corridor, the Earl stepped into Lianae's path. Smiling thinly, he seized her by the arm before she could chance to pass. "Come this evening your brother will no longer have a say over what I do with you, Lianae. Best you find a better use for that soft, velvet tongue of yours."

Lianae shuddered.

Satisfied with her response, he grinned and released her. Heat suffused Lianae's cheeks. But for once, she held her tongue, her heart hammering fiercely against her ribs as she peered back into the hall at her brother. Lulach was watching, unmoved by the plea in her eyes, and she knew in that instant that he was lost to her. And yet she was smart enough to ken that anger wouldn't serve her now. But seduction might. Her mother had been a siren, weaving a spell with every word she spoke, and so she sidled up to fitz Duncan and brushed her tongue across her lower lip. With more bravado than she felt, she said, "Dinna fash yourself, *laird*—" she swallowed over the deference. "—I ken what to do with my saft, velvet tongue. After all, I am a maid of Moray."

Fitz Duncan's pupils dilated, his eyes turning the deepest black. Something bright shone in the depths of his gaze and he smiled a bit as he bent to whisper in Lianae's ear. "Your sister was weak. She had not the fortitude of a queen. But I have always wanted to flay a Moraywoman to her bones... to see what she is truly made of... simply give me cause," he warned, and moved away, stepping out of Lianae's way.

He left her standing in the corridor, a cold sweat seeping into her bones. Fear and doubt paralyzed her limbs. Of course, this man would be unmoved by seduction. He was immune to a siren's charms. He would have his way with her, and she would never have a say. Like Elspeth, who was far more beautiful than she, her life would end by fitz Duncan's hands.

Chuckling deep in his throat, amused by the fear in her eyes, the Earl made his way back into the hall to finalize the wedding plans, and Lianae stood so long that the Earl's man pushed her rudely at the small of her back.

God help me.

She would have but one chance to escape.

And if she failed...

She would not fail.

Lianae didn't look back to see if her sister's murderer and her brother were still watching. Without another word, Lianae of Moray, the last remaining daughter of Óengus the Mormaer, allowed the usurper's men to lead her away.

CHAPTER TWO

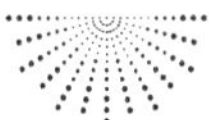

DUBHTOLARGG

Long out of its season, a giant yellow fox moth flittered about the table, lured by the crystal's strong virescent light. With a glower, Una tossed her tartan over the crystal ball, loathe to dwell on the images shimmering behind the luminescent façade. Deprived of the *keek stane's* light, the thwarted moth flapped its overlarge wings toward to the grotto's only torch while Una considered the images revealed.

To all but a few, the *keek stane* might appear to be but a lovely crystal. But for those blessed with *da sheal-ladh—the second sight*—it revealed betimes too much—things to come, things that passed, things that lingered yet in twilight. The trick of it all was to distinguish which of these visions revealed the paths she might yet alter. Today, her visions had been as clear as the faerie pools on the Isle of Skye, which only meant that the future she saw was inalterable now.

Stealing the bounce from her old limbs, a rush of sadness enveloped her. Today, even her skin felt tired; it hung limply from her ancient frame, as though it no longer had the will to remain. She had more aches in her small toe than most suffered in a lifetime. And now time was growing short…

Clach-na-cinneamhain must never be found.

The Stone of Destiny was no longer a blessing to men. Imbued with powers far beyond the faith it instilled in men, the dark-veined basalt rock had once belonged to the Gaels—their holiest of relics, brought to Scotia by way of Erin and blessed by a Pecht priestess. By the power vested in that Destiny Stone, men were doomed to commit vile acts in Alba's name. Having seen the lengths to which they would go for a taste of immortality, Una herself had entombed the Stone and then chosen her guardians well. But to leave it now in mortal hands was to ensure that Scotia's rivers always ran red.

What to do... what to do...

Alas, it was not something she could burden Aidan with, for her prophecy would only serve to breed anger and fear. And worse, if Aidan should discover Keane's part in bringing the Stone's journey to its end, he would blame Keane, and the younger dún Scoti must continue as he should. They did not like to think of themselves as sons of Scotia, but sons of Scotia were what they were—Pechts, Gaels, Scots. These were all merely different names for precisely the same thing. A thorn by any other name was still a thorn.

A thousand cold fingers pricked at her flesh, like a thousand dead kinsmen accusing without words. "I ken," she said with a bit of irritation. "I ken. I will see the stone destroyed. Be still now, and leave me to think!"

As though it merely meant to obey, the fox moth returned to the table, beating its bird-like wings. It landed upon the tartan, atop the crystal and then sat staring at Una, fanning its hairy wings and wiggling its horn-like antennae.

The caves where she made her home were solid throughout, the Stone itself entombed within the mountain's deepest vault. Some years past, Aidan's new wife had fallen inside from a fault line above, but the breach had long been sealed, and now there remained only one entrance into the vault—here through Una's workshop—in the grotto where she now stood. The entrance was accessible only through a trap door that lay hidden beneath her alchemy table. But sealing the door was not proof enough.

Fire was not proof enough. The Stone would not burn, and neither would it score the curse from its basaltic pores. And furthermore, despite the *magik* she possessed, she could never ferret that heavy Stone out alone. But even if she could, it was impossible to remove an object of that size without raising some alarm. The Guardians of the Stone had now been at their task far too long. They would never let it go.

Forsooth, but it was a quandary for the gods—of which Una was most certainly *not* one. She was, after all, only a humble servant of men.

With a wistful smile she considered Aidan's family, the last of the guardians in truth. Lìli, Ria, and the new child Lìli now bore. Young Cailin's path was as yet unknown. And Keane had always been a sweet, sweet lad, though his heart had hardened. Catrìona was the first to leave. She'd wed herself to a second son of the Brodie clan. And Lael too had fled, to wed the laird of Keppenach. And lastly, there was Sorcha... dearest Sorcha...

Soon the guardians would all be free to roam the lands, each aligned to a new clan. Alas, but the paths of men could no longer be altered—not in this age or the next.

Tears pricked at her auld eyes, catching in the folds of her skin. Crow's feet they called them, although after so many years, her wrinkles were nearly as deep as Lilidbrugh's well—that long forsaken place whose visage now loomed from the depths of her crystal. It was there, in that cradle of their clan, that the younger dún Scoti would meet his destiny.

Any day now...

Distracted and weary, the old woman turned from the alchemy table, barely in time to spy Sorcha's long limbs descending into the grotto from the chamber above—searching for Una, little doubt, for Lìli had sent her up the hill long hours before to fetch a poultice for little Ria. Unexpectedly, she'd been waylaid by the crystal.

"Una!" The girl shouted, never bothering to look around.

The fox moth hoisted itself up into the air and flew away.

"I am here, child, please! Save my ears," Una complained, and her gruff voice held a note of defeat.

Hopping down from the ladder, into the grotto, Sorcha furrowed her brow. At twenty-three, the youngest dún Scoti lass was hardly a child anymore, despite what Una liked to believe. Her violet eyes, so like her sister's, were canny and far older than her years. She appraised her young charge through a weepy eye.

"Oh! Am I interrupting?" Sorcha asked, her eyes drawn to the crystal glowing beneath the tartan.

"Nay."

"We thought ye might need help..."

Una lifted a wiry brow. "To carry a poultice down the mount? D' ye think me lame, child?"

Sorcha responded with a crooked smile and Una's staff itched to fly at her, though she stayed her hand. At these moments, she missed Keane all the more. The dún Scoti lassies were all quite hale and sharp of wit, but Una was never inclined to give them a wallop on the head. More's the pity that Kellen was not about, for he made a fitting substitute. Alas, though Lìli's sixteen-year old son would rise up into manhood far quicker than he should, and Lìli would be angered by the decisions her husband had made whilst away at Chreagach Mhor. She blew a sigh, and her despair reared itself in the form of a cold draft that swept into the grotto from the caves above, billowing through Sorcha's blue skirts and fluttering the torchlight so that its flame gave a long obeisant bow. Casting a dubious eye toward the *keek stane,* Una confessed, "I was waylaid, if ye must know."

Despite an overabundance of curiosity, Sorcha knew better than to ask about the lump beneath the tartan, but Una decided that now was as good a time as any to discover what she must know. Leaning on her staff for support, she made her way to the nearest chair and sat down to study her pupil. "How is Ria's rash?" she asked.

"Better, Lìli says, though she is prickly."

"Lìli or Ria?"

Sorcha laughed softly. "Both, if ye must know."

Reaching up for one long plait of hair—a nervous gesture meant to occupy her hands— Sorcha wandered closer to Una's worktable, driven by her insatiable curiosity for the crystal. It called to her now, for she too was a *taibshear*—a *seer.* But it was one thing to possess the *knowing,* quite another to be conscious of it and wish to use it. There were folk who had the natural disposition, but who did not trust their intuition, nor did they keep an open mind and heart…

Even now, seated across the room, Una felt the crystal's energy and knew it longed to be seen by different eyes. The question was, did Sorcha feel the pull as well? Was the lass strong enough to embrace her inner *magik?*

She watched the girl she'd raised from a wee bairn and after a moment her eyes were drawn to a high shelf. "Sorcha, dearling, do ye recall the book we used to read together?"

Made of sheepskin and bound with leather, the volume was painted with ancient symbols that were drawn in blood. It was quite old and delicate, impossible to read, unless ye had the sight. To anyone who did not have *da shealladh,* the pages would simply appear blank. But Sorcha knew them… nearly from the first. Even as a child, she had seen things others had not.

Following Una's gaze to the high shelf, Sorcha said, "Of course. I remember."

Una smiled ruefully. "Promise to keep it safe?"

"I will! But Una—"

"Dùin do ghob somaltag." Hush your mouth, child, the old woman said gently.

Resolved to her task, Una tapped her ash wood staff upon the grotto's stone floor and mist rose like smoke from unseen places. Along with the mist arrived a cold that seeped straight into the bones faster than a wet, cold rain. And yet despite the swirling smoke, the air grew stale—as though before a sweeping fire, sucking oxygen into its flame. Sorcha felt the change, and like a wary doe, prepared to flee.

Only once or twice before had Una revealed herself before men. Each time there had been a wrath to pay. *Next time would be her last.* She stared at her young charge, willing Sorcha to remain.

Never fear, child.

The silky sound of Una's voice slid like an asp through the misty cavern.

Even as she watched, half expecting Sorcha to fly away like the moth, the girl's shoulders began to relax. Behind her on the table, the scrying stone glowed a little brighter, its powerful *magik* seeping beneath the weave like diaphanous threads of light.

Remove the tartan from the keek stane, Una suggested, but her lips never moved.

Startled by the command, Sorcha snapped her head about to peer at the tartan, and turned a wary glance to Una.

Remove the tartan, Una said again.

Blinking, Sorcha's hand lifted toward the blanket as though of its own accord, but cautiously. Una watched patiently as her fingers hovered near the cloth, waiting...

Remove the tartan, she willed once again.

Clearest violet, the girl's eyes were luminous in the grotto's warm light. Her gaze locked with Una's, and Una smiled reassuringly, quite pleased. Sorcha might not realize what it was she knew, but, aye, she knew...

Peer into the crystal and tell me what you see.

Sorcha found her voice. "Truly?"

The old woman tipped her chin but once.

Tentatively, as though she feared it might be a figment of her imagination and that any moment Una's staff would fly at the pate of her head, Sorcha's fingers pinched the tartan. Silently, the old woman rose from the chair to stand beside her pupil at the table, moving more swiftly than her auld bones should have allowed. But if Sorcha sensed her advance, it did not appear to alarm her, nor did she turn to acknowledge the auld woman standing at her side. The *keek stane* now held her undivided attention.

Anticipation became a living, breathing creature in the stone chamber. Una could see the misty tendrils of the *bruadar*—the *vision*—reaching out for the girl, like arms that longed to embrace her. Sorcha's heartbeat ticked like iron tocks, each one in tune with the beat of Una's heart. Una lent her the strength of the *bru-adaraiche—the dreamer.*

Quickly, as though she feared to change her mind, Sorcha tugged the cloth and the tartan slid off the *keek stane,* revealing a concave crystal from whence all the mist in the room seemed to emanate. All that remained trapped within the crystal shifted violently into desperate shapes.

Una waited patiently for the energy to be harnessed, and then demanded, "Tell me what you see."

For a long moment, Sorcha's gaze was inscrutable, and then, curiosity silenced the beat of her heart, and she slipped past Una, around the table so that she might better peer into the ancient *keek stane.*

There inside the crystal, shapes began to coalesce… but this *bruadar* was not for Una, so she kept her eyes affixed to Sorcha. Illumined by the changing light of the crystal, the girl's dark hair appeared as violet as her eyes. Her skin took on the translucent hue of a pearl. After a moment, Sorcha lifted her eyes from the crystal and met Una's gaze.

Una's brows wiggled with amusement. "Speak. Tell me what you see."

"I-I canna be certain," Sorcha said.

"It is better to see without certainty than to yield to blindness."

Long accustomed to Una's enigmatic lectures, Sorcha peered down again into the *keek stane,* staring into the swirling eddies. She swallowed perceptibly. "I see a broch."

Una's brows lifted. "A stone tower?"

Sorcha nodded.

"Of the Norman type, or rather those erected by our ancestors?"

"Not Norman."

"What else?"

"A wolf and a blue four-legged bird."

"What else?" Una snapped.

"I canna be certain," Sorcha said, nipping at her lower lip.

"Ye must remember that certainty is the death of dreams. Hurry, child, tell me what more ye see."

The images faded irretrievably and Sorcha shook her head. "I dinna see aught more," she said, looking confused.

Annoyed, Una clucked her tongue. "'Tis too late now!" She lifted up the tartan from the table, tossing it irritably over the *keek stane*, concealing the crystal.

"What does it mean?"

"It means what it means."

"What is that crystal?"

"There is an unseen life who dreams us, Sorcha... one who knows our fate. The crystal provides a glimpse through Cailleach's eye. But the *bruadar* is yours alone to decipher."

Sorcha's gaze lifted to Una's face, to the patch that hid Una's one missing eye. Disappointed, Una turned her face. "Go on, take my book back to your room."

"Why?" Sorcha argued. "I dinna ken how to read it."

"But ye will."

"Una... I mislike the way ye're speaking—as though ye mean to leave us."

The chords of Una's neck and shoulders tightened. The strain was taking a toll. Another winter would be her undoing. She needed a long rest. At the moment, even the thought of making her way down the hillside did not appeal.

"Tha mi cho sgìth ri seann chù," she said. *I'm as tired as an old dog.* Slowly, as though her bones might break with the effort, she moved back toward the chair and

sat down once more. "Take the poultice down yourself, Sorcha."

Sorcha's brows slanted unhappily. "But why, Una? I dinna ken."

"Ach, child! Go! Ye ha'e nae need for an auld woman's trembling hands to apply a simple poultice—not when ye're strong and capable yourself."

"But—"

"There is no *but*, Sorcha. Take the poultice to Lìli. She will know what to do with it. And take my book as well. Guard it with your life."

Frowning, Sorcha's gaze moved to the high shelf where the book was supposed to be, and gasped in surprise, finding it vanished. Now, it lay beside her upon the table. Dumbfounded, she brushed her fingers across the old leather binding, and a long overdue weariness settled into Una's bones. "Tell Lìli I will come later."

"Very well," Sorcha said, relenting.

"And tell her to set two more plates at table in time for the evening meal."

Sorcha hugged the book to her breast. "There will be guests?"

"Not precisely."

Sorcha shook her head. "Ever with the mysteries," she complained. "Very well, Una. I shall tell her, and I will make certain she makes a tonic as well. Ye're no' looking so verra well." And with that, she picked up the book and came to kiss Una lovingly on the forehead. The kiss was sweet and filled with love and Una lifted grateful eyes. Up close, the evidence was indisputable, even through her tired old eyes. After peering into the *keek stane*, one of Sorcha's eyes had turned the color of a leaf in spring, the other remained clearest violet. So many words teetered on the tip of the old woman's tongue, but she kept her mouth shut, swallowing a wave of emotion that bobbled up like an apple in her throat. She patted her young charge on the arm. "Go. I will come anon."

With her arms wrapped about the ancient grimoire, Sorcha gave a nod. And keeping it close, she made her way toward the ladder. As she lifted herself out of the grotto, the torch in the room guttered, leaving Una seated in the darkness. The fox moth returned, fanning the air before Una's nose, before finding purchase on the stone in the hilt of her staff.

"We must prepare," she said, and the fox moth went perfectly still.

CHAPTER THREE

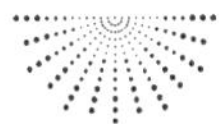

Gauging his position against Càrn Dearg—the highest peak of the *Am Monadh Liath*—Keane dún Scoti sidled his mare as near to the edge as he dared to go. The wind ruffled his black hair and the fur of his heavy cloak tickled his chin.

Nestled between the red hills and the grey, hidden by the pinewood forest below, *she* would be easy to miss. But the closer he got, the more fervently *she* whispered to his soul.

Anticipation quickened the beat of his heart. Horseflesh tensed between his muscled thighs. Beithir's right front hoof clipped the rock and a smattering of loose stones trickled down the bluffside... but then he saw *her*.

Lilidbrugh.

Huddled beneath the half-light exchange between the sun and moon, she lay strangling in weeds, brambles clawing at her stone. The ancient ruins lay at the edge of the great boreal forest, where his ancestors had once battled Roman legions. Blackened, not by age, but by ash that had been scoured now by nigh on two hundred years of Highland wind and rain, she stood, battered and bruised, clinging to her berth.

Until her doom, she had been the ancient seat of Fidach, the heart of his kinsmen, back when their lands all bore the names of Cruithne's sons—Cat, Fidach, Ce, Fotla, Circinn, Fortriu and Fib. One by one, all seven Pecht nations had fallen to the Scots or to the Gaels, with the final blow being dealt five years past to Fortriu, elsewise known to the Scots as the Kingdom of Moray. As he'd claimed he would do, David mac Mhaoil Chaluim brought down the Mormaerdom, wresting the North from his brother's allies and heirs. Against all odds, the youngest son of Malcom Ceann Mor was now the one true king of all of Scotia.

Tendrils of pink and violet wove their way through the dark silhouettes of evergreens, like fingers threaded through a lover's mane.

Their priestess once said the dawn of their people was past; the sun was setting now, and soon, no one living would remember from whence the dún Scoti had come. They were the last of the painted ones—those men the Romans once called Pechts. They carried the heartbeats of their ancestors in their blood, and the song of their people in their hearts. But like the light of this day, their song was fading fast.

Downwind, by the burn, Keane could hear his men chattering endlessly, none of them overly concerned about being overheard. For his part, he was so entranced by the ruins that he never even heard his friend approach. "What is *that?*" Cameron asked.

"Lilidbrugh," Keane replied, and his tongue made love to the name.

"Lilidbrugh?"

"Aye." The White Lily of Fidach, named after the rare stone from which she was hewn, the white quartz that had been culled and hauled from the lands near the River Ness. And there, in the courtyard had once stood a lavish fount, fed by sweet Highland springs. The fount was drained now, dismantled piece by piece, its keystones chipped away and filed into jewels for the curious.

"Ye're ogling it like a woman's arse! Is this what draws us to this god-forsaken place? Tis naught but a pile of rubble, Keane."

Keane smiled and said nothing more. Like the Stone of Destiny hidden in their vale, some things were not meant to be discussed. "Where are the others?" he asked.

"Stopped to take a piss in the burn."

"*All* of them?"

"*All.* Of. Them. Dirty bastards."

Clearly, his friend's mood was sour, and unlike Keane, the vision below improved it none at all. But then, Cameron MacKinnon, like his kinsmen of Chreagach Mhor, was far removed from this past. They were more Scots now, if the truth be known. Though if Keane meant to discard every man and woman who'd strayed from the auld ways, he would be left with no friends at all. He and his folk were the outliers now. Dún Scoti was their name for his clan—*hill Scots*—a profanity used to describe the handful of men, who'd fled into the Mounth after the death of King Aed, some two hundred fifty years past.

"Bastards are all like to be down there comparing cocks!"

Keane tried not to picture some thirteen grown men, all standing with their cocks out, pissing in a tiny burn, but his shoulders shook with mirth.

Cameron responded with a disgruntled growl. "Seems to me those *eejits* would question the wisdom in pissing in a brink where their mouths will drink."

"Laggards," Keane said, though without much heat.

And now he came to the root of his problem. "David

has pit us against one another, like fresh-faced lads at a priory full of girls," he groused.

"Lead and they will follow, Cameron."

"I have tried."

Like a carrot dangled before a mule, the king's promise of payment was meant to be fought over betwixt the two, but Keane had little interest in squabbling for titles. He studied his co-captain, his good friend now going on ten years. Despite that they hailed from different clans, circumstance had made them brothers. Cameron was a McKinnon, a cousin to his chief, and Keane was a younger son. Although Keane ranked higher by blood, he had come lately to David's service and David trusted him not at all.

The feeling was mutual.

On the other hand, while Cameron had been the longest in the king's service, he was far more apt to brood than stir himself to change what he did not like. Alas, but the man needed a spine. Case in point: For more than ten years now, Cameron had coveted Keane's sister Cailin, and still, all these years later, he'd yet to ask for Cailin's hand. Instead, he spent his nights lamenting the fact that Keane's brother would not take it upon himself to find Cameron worthy. That was never bound to happen.

"Tis simple enough for you to say," Cameron complained. "They wadna test ye the same way."

Only because the men were half afraid of him, Keane knew, for they, like so many, believed him to be little more than a dún Scoti savage. Little did they realize he'd learned the Church's language by the age of three and his histories by the age of seven. He knew more about Scotia's *politiks* than most of the principals involved, and merely because his clan kept themselves apart, did not mean he did not know the lay of this land.

But, of course, some of the fault was his. He might have dispensed with the braids and woad long before now, but it served him well enough to keep them. Besides, conforming hadn't earned Cameron all that much to speak of.

With a sigh of longing, he peered down at the ruins. Although little remained of the old fortress, Keane saw her, not as she was, but as she could be in the future and his heart stirred like an untried youth's. To hell with all of Scotia—including the vale—if he could but rest his head for the remainder of his days, right down there…

What if he could rebuild? Raise the guard towers one by one? Build a wall? Her bones were still good. He envisioned her restored to her former glory, the towers rising as high as the bluff, the well restored and the white stone washed until she glistened…

Mayhap she could be his reward?

Though what about Cameron?

Staring down below, Keane hardened his heart. He'd given Cameron numerous opportunities to rein in their motley crew. Their good-natured rivalry could easily make a sour turn. Friendships had been torn asunder over women far and wide… it just so happened that Keane's lady should be made of stone.

"Di' ye see that?"

Despite his distraction, Keane's eyes registered the movement below and he automatically plucked an arrow from his quiver.

"Someone's down there," Cameron said.

"I see him," Keane replied.

"Could it be?"

"Perhaps."

They had been following a pair of scouts in hopes of luring out a marauding band of rebels that remained loyal to the Mormaer Óengus, but only he and

Cameron had been told as much. The rest of his men all believed they were merely en route to Dunràth to deliver the king's message to its steward. Dunràth was but a small manor house, though David was apparently reluctant to give William fitz Duncan yet another thaneship, for it remained without a laird since the battle at Stracathro in Forfarshire.

They'd lost sight of the scouts about midday, although Keane had not yet witnessed any attempts by his men to seek anyone out, nor any quiet trepidation over the prospect of spies being caught. For all that he could tell they seemed perfectly oblivious to any intrigue, and for the most part, they were a soft-hearted bunch of dafties, with little purpose in life but to fill their bellies and piss under the stars.

But even if it were the scouts they'd been following, there was no way to know whether the insurgent sons of Óengus actually existed. By all accounts, the sons of Óengus had not been seen now in five years or more. They lived only in whispers, around campfires, and at the bedsides of little children—like faeries, brownies and the like.

And yet, some faerie's tales were true, for until this moment, Lilidbrugh too had been only a tale from the lips of an auld woman…

He saw a flash of silver in the waning light and positioned his bow, nocking the arrow. Beneath him, Beithir remained motionless, taking her cues from Keane's form. Betimes the animal knew him better than he knew himself.

Beside him, Cameron slid off his own massive beast, with its lumbering limbs and great hairy hooves, and patted the animal's rump, urging it back down, toward the burn, taking a ready post. Slithering down the mountainside was a steep, rock-strewn path. If by chance Keane should hit his mark, they would needst fly down and Cameron would travel better on foot, while Beithir had been bred to the Mounth.

"I see but one man, not two," Cameron said.

Keane's gaze followed the figure in the sights of his arrow, wondering who it could be. Lilidbrugh was not a place where men were wont to come. Most folks turned a blind eye to the ruins, seeing only what it had become. As far as he knew, no one ever ventured there anymore. It lay forgotten upon a remote piece of earth where mortal men dared not go, rumored now to be a place where faeries lay in wait to curse the unwary soul.

But *someone* was there...

Keane couldn't make out the features, but the figure was slight, half swallowed by a bright blue cloak. How dull-witted was that? To wear a rich coat, especially with the coming snows. If the man had but cloaked himself in common colors, he might not seem worth the trouble of descending for the spoils, but by law, no peasant ever wore such a garb. The fool might as well have waved huge sacks of gold.

At the moment, his target remained a good three hundred yards away.

Keane was not the greatest of archers, but he was not the worst. A lifetime of competing with his ruthless sisters had greatly honed his skills. Inasmuch as Lael was a master with her blades, Cailin was an expert with her bow. She could nail a mark from two hundred fifty yards. Keane's best effort was twenty yards' shy of that. He was far better with his sword. Still, with the downward trajectory, he could do it, although his target seemed far more pre-occupied with someone—or something—following behind... so he waited to see who else would come.

No one did. The man was alone.

He waited for the perfect opportunity as the idiot

scuttled along a half wall. At last, when he flattened himself against a spot and went perfectly still, Keane's eyes honed in on a small ruby purse in his hand—and he smiled, for the purse afforded Keane a perfect mark. Whatever that purse held would be valuable enough for the man to carry naught else. Cailin would call it an impossible shot, but Keane was not a man to back down from a challenge. It was never his intent to harm the man, nor did he particularly intend to frighten him. Very simply, he wanted him to stay put, so he set his sights on the purse and let the arrow fly.

THERE WAS little familiar about her surroundings but Lianae knew the place. More to the point, she knew the fear it inspired in the hearts of men.

Her breath came in soft pants as she stole across the bramble-covered ruins, tripping as she went and wincing when her cold, bare feet encountered jagged edges.

It was warm enough for the month of December. Until now, the lack of shoes had merely been a nuisance, but now she longed for her shoes—not those frilly slippers she'd abandoned in the bathhouse, but her own sturdy leather boots. Her feet hurt, and it was getting too dark to see, but she was nearly certain her feet were bleeding now as well. It couldn't be helped. Better that her feet should bleed than the rest of her.

Poor Elspeth.

Only now that she was alone, with no sign of pursuit, did she dare allow her anger to morph into grief. The ache in her heart manifested as a lump in her throat, threatening to cut off her breath. She swallowed past it, looking beyond the painful memories into the night's shadows, studying her surroundings.

Abandoned.

Cursed.

These were the ruins of Lilidbrugh—the last known seat of the sons of Fidach. Encroached upon by the woodlands, long, lean pillars encircled what appeared to be a long, forgotten courtyard. Detritus fell about the crumbling bases like women's fallen skirts. Cobbled in places, the yard itself was oblong and in the center was a gaping hole—an open maw, waiting to be fed. The sight of it gave Lianae a shudder, for it was here that folks supposedly brought their changelings to leave for the faeries.

She'd met a mother once who'd been so certain her bairn—who merely would not sleep through the night, and who suffered a constant malaise of the belly—was a changeling, that she'd abandoned her child here. The next day, the child had surely vanished, but with no babe left in her place and the mother was disconsolate. Lianae only hoped the wolves did not discover the poor babe, or that she did not fall into that deep, dark well. Instead, she prayed some good woman had found the child and carried her home.

Swallowing the sun sooner than its sister peaks, Càrn Dearg rose before her, black and foreboding against a twilight sky. Like quivering wraiths, the surrounding pinewoods slid into shadow, and the growing darkness left Lianae feeling colder than she'd felt only minutes before. It was said that the weather in these parts was as fickle as a Highland lass, sweet and sunny one minute and raging the next. She felt a storm brewing. She felt it down in her bones. Shivering yet again, she resisted the urge to pinch her cloak together, far more concerned at the instant with finding a place to hide for the night. Shadows were falling swiftly and the snows had begun.

Her gaze returned to the well. Not down *that*, for

certain, although she was far more amenable to that possibility than she was over the prospect of ending with the Earl of Moray. His men were out there, likely not far.

Catching her breath, Lianae stood, waiting for the beat of her heart to still. All the while shadows played havoc with the jagged edges of Lilidbrugh's walls. The stones themselves shone with a curious light—a trick of the pale white stone and a fresh dusting of snow, no doubt, but it was unnerving enough for her to reconsider the wisdom in coming to such a place. She was not immune to superstition, after all, only more practical than most.

Faeries be damned.

Curses be damned.

She but needed to spend one night here—until the Earl's men tired of searching. And she was certain they would never dare enter these ruins. Forsooth, but if men would not dare, they would never presume a mere lass would ever find the nerve. But she was quickly losing what mettle she'd earned as the skies overhead darkened to the color of a bruise.

Swallowing her grief and a new wave of fear, Lianae found a bare spot along the wall and laid back her head, listening for telltale sounds, and trying to gauge whether anyone was near. An ageless, abiding silence was her only response—a silence that lengthened and seemed to be swallowed by the White Lily herself.

Up on a half wall, a murder of crows sat, opening their fierce little beaks, but their squawks were silenced by a rising wind. Even her own panting breath came silently, evidenced by a fine grey mist that hovered near her lips, but there was no sound to be heard. Inching her way carefully along the wall, she surveyed the courtyard, one finger toying with the satin cord that held her purse cinched. And then suddenly, without warning, the crows took flight. It was a bad sign.

Before she could shove away from the wall, to run, she heard a hiss and then a whack at her side. An arrow narrowly missed imbedding itself into the flesh below her thumb.

Flittering above her, the crows all beat the air with shining black wings, their shrieks now unleashed and Lianae's gaze skidded to the blufftop, where she spied two men rushing down the steep path—one on horseback, the other making his way more slowly on foot. She tried to run, but the arrow had found purchase in a fat stalk behind her silk purse.

Her heart stopped. "Oh, nay," she cried, as she heard the men give shout. She gave a little shriek of alarm, and tried again to free the purse to no avail. The arrow had wrested itself so deeply into the petrified wood that she couldn't budge it at all. "Nay!" she cried again. Her cloak was caught as well. It would be easy enough to shrug it off and run, but if she left without her cloak, she would freeze by morning, and if she left without the purse, she might as well go back home.

Home. Dear, God, where is that?

The contents of her purse would buy her freedom and news. It was meant to reunite her with her brothers. Cursing softly in her native tongue, she clasped the arrow shaft, tugging with all her might, wiggling desperately.

The men flying down the mountain were likely not the Earl's, she realized, but that didn't suit her much either. She was no simpering English maid, but she was hardly prepared to deal with mean strangers. With a final, fierce tug, she wrested the arrow free, renting a bit of Elspeth's cloak. The purse split as well, spilling the charm stones onto the snow. Her heart squeezed as they disappeared.

"Oh, nay!"

Hurrying to scoop up as many as she dared, she realized there were but seconds left to spare. Abandoning the ones that rolled beneath a bramble bush, she grabbed what she could and ran, hoping to come back later to retrieve the rest.

Behind her, she heard the clatter of hooves and to her dismay, she spied the rider close upon her heels—a black-haired, blue painted fiend galloping on a snow-white beast, churning up the ground beneath its hooves.

Lianae bolted across the courtyard, toward the well, uncertain what she meant to do, but at the instant, that well, seemed the far lesser of evils.

CHAPTER FOUR

He was pursuing a woman.

It wasn't until he nearly overtook the lass that Keane realized, and his shock must have been evident in his form. Beithir reared back as he reached out to sweep the girl into his arms. Dropping her cloak —and something else—she elbowed Keane in the temple, and hurled herself back out of his arms with a profusion of curses, narrowly missing the opening of the well. She landed on a snow laced, dirt expanse of courtyard, cursing as she rolled free of Beithir's hooves. *"Thoir ort!"* she screamed. *Begone! "Mac bhàdhair fhuileach!"*

She spoke the old tongue—quite well, Keane surmised, as she blistered his ears. Stunned by the ferocity of her temper, he rubbed at his bruised temple as the woman glared up at him, scarce able to form words of his own, much less respond to her angry curses.

Down in the midst of the ruins the gloaming light appeared surreal, defying the darkness that waited beyond the citadel's borders. Sprawled on the ground as she was, her golden red hair spilled behind her and her sapphire blue gown stood out sharply against a thin mantle of snow.

"Ye could ha'e killed yourself," he admonished.

Not to mention, she might well have made him daft with the blow from her elbow. His ears were ringing even now, and not merely with her curses.

"Me?" she returned. "*You!* You might have killed *me*! Bloody damned Scots," she said, and curled her lip like a she-wolf.

Seated atop his mare, Keane frowned at the girl, at a loss for words. Her dialect was distinct, but not entirely familiar, and yet, he clearly understood she had no love for the Scots.

Nor did he, in truth.

But that was neither here nor there.

Arriving belatedly on foot, Cameron made his way into the courtyard and Keane took one look at the girl's dress—the way her breasts spilled from the lavish bodice—and had the sudden yen to wave him away. "I'm no Scot," he reassured.

"Nay?" She tilted Keane a dubious glance. "Then why do ye wear the *King's* livery? And ye must think I'm daft because I wear a dress?"

"Dress?" Keane argued. "Ach, lass, ye're barely wearing aught at all. That's a nightshift at best."

Her brows twitched and her expression quickly turned from one of fear to one of disbelief. She lifted herself up on one elbow, snow clinging to her strawberry curls, her face flushed pink. "I'll have ye know this gown is made of fine Flemish silk."

Keane screwed his face. "Silk?"

"The *f-finest*," she repeated, her teeth beginning to chatter now that she was without her cloak and sprawled in the wet snow.

"Aye, well that'll keep ye warm on a cauld night," Keane said acerbically. "What's wrong with good Scot's wool?"

Annoyance flickered behind her honey-colored

eyes. "And ye'll forgive me for not dressing to please ye." Her tone took on airs now as she smoothed down her dress, pulling it down to cover her ankles. "I wasna expecting company, dinna ye see."

Now it was Keane's turn to tilt her a disbelieving look, for she'd appeared, quite to the contrary, to be expecting *someone*—unwanted though her guest might be.

"Are ye certain about that?"

"Ab-bout what?"

"Well, it seems to me that ye're running from someone—mayhap your groom by the looks o' ye. And ye must have angered him plenty to go stealing away without your shoes." He lifted a brow as he nodded at her bare feet.

She shivered ferociously, and gave Keane a narrow eyed glare. "I was running from *you,* ye blundering knave! 'Tis a woman's plight to save herself from defiling men."

Smacking himself upside the temple to stop the clatter in his ears, Keane slid out of his saddle and gently pushed Beithir out of harm's way. The girl's limbs seemed quite prepared to deal the animal a sturdy blow—or anyone else who might be stupid enough to venture near. God's truth, she looked more like a wildling, with those *uisge*-colored eyes filled with liquid fire. "Relax yourself," he assured. "I've no mind to be defiling anyone today—even as lovely as ye be."

She watched him warily. "Nay?"

"Nay, lass."

Well aware that Cameron was nearly upon them, Keane bent to retrieve her cloak before Cameron could chance to see her quite so... *exposed.*

Lined with ermine, the sapphire velvet was new and properly sewn. It matched her gown rather nicely. But he was pretty certain their spy wouldn't be a woman, although she certainly had more mettle than ten men. However, she was a woman of substance.

Where had she come from? And more to the point, what the hell was she doing here in Lilidbrugh? He held the garment out for her. "You must be cauld?" he asked dryly and tossed the cloak at her. "Dress yourself, afore ye freeze, lass."

Who did he think he was?

Lianae flashed the stranger a look of disdain as she caught her cloak, relieved to find that he meant to keep his distance.

God's truth, it had never suited her overmuch to be told what to do. Her father would never have done so—nor would her brothers, save Lulach—and Lulach, not until the day he'd sold his soul to the Scots. But, aye, she was bloody cold—cold enough that her teeth were banging like drums behind her shivering lips.

Clenching her jaw to keep her teeth from chattering, she scooted backward, and tried to stand as the man's mail-clad companion came skidding to a halt. Belatedly, Lianae realized that her ankles—and the bruises thereon—were exposed and she drew her feet beneath the folds of her gown, concealing them from prying eyes. She was far less concerned about her cleavage than she was about her bruises. The cleavage could prove to her advantage; the bruises would merely decry her weakness—not that it made any difference to a man who answered to his todger. The newest Scot to arrive was also dressed in David's livery, and she eyed them both with no small measure of contempt.

It was all because of David mac Mhaoil Chaluim that she was in this untenable position. Before David, she and her family had lived a quiet, peaceful life, dutifully tending their manor. No matter that her lineage had been disparaged and that her kinsmen's' arses no longer stood a chance to warm that stupid stone at Scone, they'd all been quite content to live their lives in peace. Now Graeme and Ewen were both at large and Lulach had his nose so far up the Earl of Moray's arse that Lianae doubted he could smell aught more than dung.

"Ouch," she cried as she tried to rise. Pain shot through her right ankle—though not because of the bruises. This ache was new.

What a *craidhneach* she was coming to be!

Wretched though she might be, she somehow found her way to a standing position, dragging the cloak up with her and swinging it about her shoulders.

Blood tinged the snow beneath her toes, but Lianae pretended not to see it. Her knees felt scraped as well, though she daren't complain about that either as she drew the heavy cloak around her shoulders, brushing off the snow, and praying to any God who would listen that these men would give her no cause to run.

She had a dagger strapped to her thigh. She kept it with her always, and no one ever knew it was there, unless she undressed before him, and that she had yet to do for any man, although the earl had come dangerously close on the morning he'd murdered her sister. If Lulach had not stopped him and convinced him to wed her first, she would have plunged her dagger into his back whilst he'd tried to put his manhood in a place it did not belong.

"Well, now," said the new arrival. "What have we here?" In his hand, he brandished a great sword that was nearly as tall as Lianae.

In one swift motion, Lianae reached behind her, beneath the hem of her dress, plucking her dagger out of its sheathe. She held it before her and warned both men. "Your worst nightmare if ye dare to touch me."

For a moment, both men remained silent, staring at her stupidly, and then, the black haired demon with the braided hair and the woad on his face and neck, dared to laugh out loud and Lianae shot him a baleful glare. "Rude mon! Most wee ones outgrow the need to paint pictures on themselves by the time they reach the age of five. Di' ye never outgrow it, or are ye one of those cod biters I've heard tell about?"

Cod biters?

It took Keane a full moment to discern what it was she was talking about—and more, why any man would wish to bite a pillow. And furthermore, aside from his own kinsmen, he had never met any man who'd ever painted their flesh, save for a handful of priests, and, to the best of his knowledge, they didn't own any pillows. They slept on bare cots. A man could only bite a pillow with his arse in the air, and—

Cameron beat him to the realization, guffawing loudly. He tossed up his arms in obvious glee. As for the paint, she must be referring to his woad, the blue tincture he wore to remind himself from whence he'd come—that no matter how high he rose in David's service, he was still but a simple man, far removed from the vices of David's court. Aside from scaring the hell out of his enemies, the woad also helped to prevent infections. But as for the pillow biting—this was not something he knew about firsthand. "Amusing," Keane said drolly.

Cameron continued to laugh and Keane ignored him, unconcerned with the girl's silly barbs. Rather, he had a sudden, overwhelming desire to prove to the lass that the dún Scoti men were not the savages most folks believed them to be. Considering the English style of dress she wore, she was probably a lady of the house of

Moray. And despite his original intentions, there was enough blood shed here already. He eyed the spots she'd left in the snow and offered the lady his hand. "I dinna mean to harm ye, lass. We thought ye were a spy from Óengus's camp."

Something indecipherable flickered behind the honeyed gaze and Keane took it for fear. "Óengus of Moray is dead," she said quickly.

"But not his sons, or so they claim."

"Aye, well, I am *not* afraid of Óengus's sons!"

But she was; Keane could see the fear in her eyes—a look of distress that was unmistakable. "Ye may keep the knife, only gi' me your hand."

Still, she eyed Keane's proffered hand as though it were a poisonous asp rearing its head from the grass, and then she hobbled backward another step. "I would sooner see ye go," she said. "I dinna need help from a *Scot*."

To Keane's amazement, there was little diminished about the girl's demeanor, nor did she cow from him even now. Injured and cold, bruised and limping, her gaze burned as brightly as the strange light they'd encountered amidst Lilidbrugh's pale stones.

But she *was* injured; he could see the pain register in her face when she took a step backward, even if she didn't intend to confess as much. More dark red spots appeared in the snow wherever she stepped and his nostrils sniffed for the tinny scent. "You're hurt," he insisted.

"No thanks to ye." She waved the knife at Cameron, who was no longer laughing. "And ye."

The look in her eyes returned to fear—but not the fear of a hapless lass, rather that of a caged beast. Even a sweet baby rabbit could do serious damage with its teeth when it was afeared.

Brandishing his sword, Cameron cut an imaginary

line into the air. "This is no place for a woman to be all alone," he argued, clearly scaring her even more, for she took another step backward, wincing again as she did so.

Unlike Cameron, Keane left his sword in his scabbard, where it belonged, and cursed Cameron for a witless fool. "We're men of honor," he assured the lass. "Dinna worry. We'll see ye come to no more harm."

"Put away your knife," Cameron demanded.

With more temper than he meant to display, Keane spun about to face his old friend. "Go! Tell the men to come down the hill. I will deal with the girl!"

Cameron lowered his sword in surprise. "You want them *down here*? Why?"

"Why not?"

"But shouldn't we take her *up there,* where we can keep watch?"

"Nay," Keane snapped.

The girl was watching to see what Cameron would do—probably measuring to see which of them was in charge. She was in no condition to walk back up the bluff, and Keane wasn't inclined to force her onto his mount. She didn't trust them, and who could blame her? "I said *go,*" Keane demanded of Cameron, this time more firmly. "*Now.*"

Cameron screwed his face. "Ach, Keane, these ruins are—"

"Cursed?" The girl asked with a bit of a smirk. She peered from Cameron to Keane and then back again, clearly challenging them both—*because she knew.* She knew precisely where she was, and so it wasn't likely she'd stumbled here after losing her way. Nay, she was hiding from somebody.

Cameron re-sheathed his sword, but there was bitterness in his tone. "If I've a say in the matter, I—"

"But ye dinna," Keane said.

The two friends locked gazes, and to the girl's credit, she realized enough to know that underlying tensions were now coming to head. She took another step backward, clearly unwilling to be caught in the middle of two men butting horns.

Keane's gaze returned to the girl. Even bedraggled as she was, she was quite lovely—more so than any lass had a right to be. With her attitude, she was no doubt high born, and would have been offered to a man with equal standing. Her dress was too fine to be aught but a bride's gown. So that meant she'd fled either *after* taking her vows... or *before*... either way, someone would be quite pleased to see the girl returned.

Grateful enough to reward him with a pile of stones?

His gaze swept over the ruins of Lilidbrugh. Even in her decrepit state, she was a far greater treasure than any land he might wish to hold. Something dark and covetous swept over Keane in that instant, something he longed to deny, though he could not—not whilst he stood surrounded by the birthplace of his kin.

"So that's how it is?" Cameron asked between clenched teeth.

Keane tipped his chin. "That's how it is," he agreed. His eyes narrowed in warning. "Go on now."

A muscle ticked at Cameron's jaw. His easy stance vanished, replaced suddenly with a rigid back and clenched fists. "Very well," he said, nodding as he turned to go.

He walked away without another word, and Keane watched him leave. But what his friend didn't say, he carried in the set of his shoulders. It was a message Keane could hardly mistake. Regrettably for Cameron, this was how it was always meant to go. There was no point prolonging the inevitable. Keane was in charge now.

CHAPTER FIVE

As the night lowered and twilight passed, the woodlands beyond the ruins grew black and foreboding, cloaked in mist and surrounded by shifting shadows. The sound of bog-bush crickets grew louder.

Lianae shivered, drawing up her cloak, protecting her nape from a biting wind. Her feet were nearly frozen but there was little to be done about that right now, save to block the wind with her gown. She was fortunate enough that the warmer weather had endured so long. But now there was a bite in the air that foretold a change. Winter had arrived at long last.

Her gaze returned to the dark-haired stranger. She found herself both drawn to and repelled by him at once. Forsooth, but there was little civil about the man. If his crew appeared more English than Scots, *he* was something else—a specter from Lianae's past. Unlike the others, he wore no mail at all, no coif. He had no shining helm tied to his saddle. His long hair was braided at the temples and otherwise left free to bluster in the wind. He wore a leather hauberk, with a threadbare grey tunic, but his cloak was crude, unlike the ones his counterparts wore, and it was fashioned mostly of grey wolves' fur, thickly padded about his shoulders. And yet despite that he looked nothing like them, it was clear to Lianae who was in charge.

He was.

Standing arms akimbo, his dark hair lashing at his face, he watched Lianae's every move, though he kept his distance, now and again barking orders at his men.

Whilst he stood guarding her, the mangy band of Scotsmen marched down the bluffside and set about to making camp for the evening, settling horses beneath a makeshift tarp, checking shoes and gathering tinder for a fire.

All of his men wore the *king's* colors, some over leather hauberks, others over mail. None looked so much like a Scotsman—more like Sassenachs, if the truth be known, with all their silver coifs and shining metal helms covering oily black heads.

Strangely, Lianae wasn't afraid of *him*—not in the least—despite that she sensed his own men were inclined to be. Every last one of them did the man's bidding without a word of complaint, despite that they seemed leery of this place. She could see the apprehension writ upon their bodies and in the way they peered over their shoulders at the surrounding woodlands, starting when anyone came near. It was almost comical to watch—grown men afeared of their own shadows.

In fact, Lianae had the sense that, given their druthers, not a one of them would remain in this place, but even the man who'd challenged the woad-covered leader no longer seemed inclined to protest. Instead, he kept himself apart, brooding all alone by the fire, watching it burn. Whittling furiously at a long limb, he tossed his shavings into the pit, and every great once in a while looked up to study his commander with narrowed eyes.

There was tension between the two men. Lianae

filed the information away, to be used later should the need arise.

But, time and again, her gaze was drawn to the braided one, feeling his regard as surely as she felt the charm stones calling to her from beneath the brambles and the snow.

She'd dropped a few where he'd seized her into his arms—strong arms, wider about than the trunk of a small tree. He was strong, but quick, and he'd lifted her with little effort—something she'd never seen any man do—not even her father when she was three.

To this extent, she counted his strength as a blessing, for as yet, no one had dared approach her. So she continued searching for her stones, staying near the spot where she'd dropped them. Her feet were half numb, but she could still feel the soft, round pebbles beneath her toes. Time was of the essence; for now, the snow was barely half an inch deep. If it continued to fall at this rate, by morning, there would be two feet or more, and then her stones would all be lost. Limping along, she discovered two of Uhtreda's stones and snuck them into the pocket that was sewn into the hem of her gown. She continued to search, stooping now and again to lift up a bit of refuse, merely to discard it, lest they suspect she was hoarding something else. If they should happen to learn what treasure she possessed, there was no guarantee they would allow her to keep them, and Lianae didn't believe she'd been gifted the stones only to lose them quite so easily. Fortunately, most of the men paid her little mind... save for *him*.

Trying not to think about *him*—or the Earl's men who were still out there—Lianae mentally recounted the stones she'd already recovered—three in all—less than half the number that were originally in the purse.

A few remained by the wall where *he'd* put an arrow through the purse.

At one point, she watched him saunter over, pluck out his damnable arrow and then stand by the brambles, inspecting his fletching. She held her breath as he then stooped to pick up something from the ground—presumably the remnants of Lianae's purse. He eyed her pointedly and then replaced the arrow into his quiver—mayhap to re-use the fletching later—and then tucked the scrap of her purse into his belt. But then afterward, he didn't bother to search the ground at his feet, and Lianae let out the breath she'd been holding as he made his way over to attend his mare.

For long moments, she watched him brush the animal's flank with a loving hand. Moving forward, he stroked the mare's muzzle, and then seemed to whisper in her ear. Mesmerized by his gentleness with the beast, Lianae gave up looking for her stones and sat atop the steps of a ruined hall to inspect her feet, trying to determine in her mind's eye where the remainder of her stones might be.

How many did she pick up before she ran? She hadn't had the chance to count them yet. Mayhap she had them all by now and the rest would be over beneath the brambles, where the king's men placed their tarp.

But she told herself not to worry. Even if they should happen upon one of her stones, most of these Sassenach-loving *eejits* wouldn't know what they were. That fact gave her a modicum of relief—more so than the state of her poor feet.

Despite the rising cold, the bottom of one foot continued to bleed from a cut beneath her toe. Briefly, she considered ripping up the hem of her gown in order to wrap her feet, but the gown was protecting her legs from the wind. It wouldn't behoove her to weaken the barrier of her dress, so for the time being she would simply sit on her feet in order to warm them, and then, come morn, she would consider a new solution.

There was no doubt that she must flee, but she was going nowhere before morning, and in the meantime, she sensed these men would provide very little threat—far less than what would be awaiting her *out there* with the Earl's men. Aye, for now, she would bide her time. And if the Earl's men should chance to spy the glow from their campfire, they would be far more apt to stay away.

Regardless, Lianae was no longer afraid. Long before Lilidbrugh had become a haven for the faeries, it had belonged to simple men. There was a legend told of a relic the dún Scoti absconded with the day they'd fled into the Mounth. No one knew precisely what it was, but Lianae had her suspicions.

Once lost amidst the Sìol Ailpín—the Highland Clans who all claimed blood lineage to the first king—the sword of the *Righ Art* was only recently found. According to legend, that sword had been gifted to Kenneth MacAilpín on the day he was crowned. The sword vanished about the same time as the coup that took King Aed's life. But, then, ten years ago that same sword resurfaced and was re-gifted to David of Scotia by a lowly Scotsman from Chreagach Mhor—a man named Broc Ceannfhionn. And, of course, once he had possession of it, David used the sword of the High King and Chief of Chiefs to further press his claim. In fact, he'd wielded it that day at Stracathro in Forfarshire, wherein four thousand men of Moray died, including Lianae's father. Word of Óengus's death traveled swiftly and it was grief over the news that killed her mother, particularly when her brothers Graeme and Ewen went missing thereafter.

Of course, David mac Mhaoil Chaluim had named

them both cowards, stripping them each of their birthrights, awarding their titles to men like William fitz Duncan.

And Lulach, who was only fifteen when her father and brothers went to war, took for himself an English bride. The rest was history, or so they said.

Her heart filled with longing as she thought of her brothers, Graeme and Ewen. She had not seen either of them in more than five years, but one day after her mother's funeral, she'd discovered a white lily on her grave. It wasn't Elspeth or Lianae who'd placed it there, and it certainly wasn't Lulach, who, rather unfortunately, rarely thought of anyone aside from himself. It was here the lily had led her, to Lilidbrugh, to the White Lily of Fidach...

Lianae sensed her brothers were here... *somewhere.* She could feel it in her bones, the same way she felt the presence of Uhtreda's stones.

How she would dearly love to see the Scots ousted and William fitz Duncan returned to England where he belonged. More than that, fitz Duncan deserved to die, but Lianae was loathe to offer him good Moray soil to lie beneath. Rather he should take himself back to England. She would rather freeze to death in the hands of these *eejit* Scotsmen than leave and find herself at William's mercy. They were no doubt still searching hill and dale, if for no other reason than to retrieve Uhtreda's charm stones. Like a godsend, the purse had been abandoned in the bathhouse last night. The Earl's shrewish mother oft used the old baths, and in their rush to secure it for Lianae before the priest arrived, they must have ushered the old woman out. The purse would have been left by one of her servants, and once Uhtreda discovered them missing, she would no doubt rage, for 'twas said she used the stones to hide her age. The very notion made

Lianae roll her eyes. More like than not, whatever *magik* Uhtreda possessed, it was rather due her father's purse. After all, she was the daughter of the Earl of Northumbria and the consort of a king. Fitz Duncan's sire would also have left the woman with means.

Lifting a finger to the sore spot on her cheek, she wondered where a man like fitz Duncan had learned to be such a fiend. As injuries went, the bruise was inconsequential—more so than the pain in her heart. But betimes she could still feel the blow of the Earl's fist after she'd told him she'd rather die than wed a traitor like him. That was when he'd shoved her down... on the bed... next to her sister... And he would have taken her there, save that Lulach's wife walked in on them and ran to tell and her brother had come running.

He'd asked fitz Duncan to wait.

To wait?

To wait!

Well, he could wait until the end of his days—until he turned cold in the ground and the worms feasted upon his dirty todger. Come what may, she was never going to wed that odious man—and damn Lulach for a greedy fool.

She was in the midst of repositioning herself, crossing her legs and tucking the gown and cloak beneath her like a tent, when the "wolf man" came to offer sustenance. He held the meal in his hands, wrapped in a napkin.

"What is it?"

"Food," he answered simply, responding as her mother might have.

Lianae frowned. She glanced over at the dark hole in the middle of the courtyard. He was not a very civil looking man. Could it be all those changelings had been left here for him? "Ye dinna eat babies perchance?"

"Hardly." His smile twisted like that of a mischievous boy's. "'Tis merely horse," he said.

Judging by the way he'd tended his beloved mare, Lianae doubted the veracity of that claim, but she peered over at the tarp anyway, silently counting the horseflesh beneath. She counted three heads before she heard him laugh—a rich sound that sent a strange frisson down her spine.

"Horse o' the woods," he clarified.

Lianae screwed her face. "Horse o' the woods?"

"Grouse. They are big and stupid, and slow, but tasty nonetheless—especially given the alternative."

"What alternative might that be?"

"Starving," he replied with a grin.

Amusing. But by damn, Lianae refused to laugh, despite that his smile fairly took her breath away. He was a bit too handsome when he did that. But, aye, she was hungry, indeed. Reaching out for the napkin, she accepted the gift of food, thanking him softly—although she might have said resentfully, but aside from plucking her up from the ground and then tossing her back down, he had done little to offend her. Even that wasn't quite the truth of it, for she'd whacked him aside the head and hurled herself free, after which, he'd merely stared down at her as though *she* had been the perpetrator.

And now he stood there, rubbing his head, peering down at her with that wolfish face, and she had the smallest instant of regret.

Not even his pouty little friend had done aught to harm her. They had simply let her be, whilst they all tended to their business, and not a one save those two had even spoken to her as yet. For all Lianae knew, she had startled them as much as they had startled her...

But it begged the question: What were these people doing in a place like Lilidbrugh? It crossed her mind that perhaps they too might be searching for her brothers... but that wouldn't be likely, now would it?

For a long moment, the wolf man stood, watching her eat and Lianae tried to ignore him—not such a difficult a task, for once the grouse was in front of her face, she was suddenly ravenous. She hadn't had a bite to eat since her sister's wedding two days before. And although they probably would have served yet another "feast" from the leftovers, for Lianae's nuptials, Lianae hadn't remained to see it.

How convenient that must be.

Fitz Duncan murdered one wife and had himself a spare. He would have served two feasts for the price of one.

Ach, but, from the instant she'd left Kinneddar Castle, she hadn't even stopped long enough to think about her feet, evidenced by the sorry state of them now. At one point, she'd feared they might even catch her, but then she'd slipped into the pinewoods, and for a long, long while, she'd followed the stream, covering her scent to elude the hounds. That was probably where she'd cut her feet—in the burn.

Unconcerned with manners, she devoured the food he gave her, thinking to herself that grouse was the finest bird she ever did eat.

Thank heavens they were big and stupid and slow!

FASCINATED, Keane watched the girl tear into the grouse wing as though she hadn't partaken of sustenance for weeks.

What a contradiction she was, dressed in English finery, with no complaints for her bare feet. She ate like a waif and talked like a royal. She had the bearing of a soldier and the diction of a queen. "You should let me look at your foot," he suggested.

She glanced up at him, her lips glossy with grease, and he had the strangest desire to lick them clean—a ludicrous notion, and he wondered if the girl had somehow addled his brain with the blow to his head.

Peering up at him, she held the grouse before her, frozen in her posture, looking like an animal ready to snarl. "Can ye no' see well enough from where you're standing?"

Keane lifted a dark brow. She had a razor sharp tongue—not unlike his sisters. "I meant only that ye should allow me tend to your wound, lass. Your foot appears to be bleeding." He nodded at the surrounding snow, except that with a fresh layer, the spots were very nearly gone. "I dinna need for ye to tend me," she said stubbornly, and returned to her dinner, trying hard to ignore him.

Stubborn lass.

"Ye must be cauld?" he asked, refusing to be ignored. He slid next to her upon the steps, insinuating himself whether it please her or nay. In fact, she reminded him quite a lot of Catrìona, with her flashing eyes and gold-red mane. None of his sisters would ever give an inch, unless you proved to them why they should. The problem therein being that no progress ever could be made, so long as no one ever took a chance. This was something Cameron had yet to learn.

He folded his hands between his knees, well aware that she was watching him from the corner of one eye. But he was not a threat to her and she needed his help, whether or not she wished to admit it or nay—and clearly she did not.

Seemingly oblivious to his presence beside her, she continued to eat, ignoring Keane, and he caught the scent of her hair so near: rosemary and lavender, a heady combination… only a wee bit more so than her supper. His stomach grumbled.

He'd given up his share, unwilling to leave the girl without or to go out and hunt for more. Nor would he ask his men to do so, not tonight. Considering their wariness of this place, if he allowed anyone to leave, they might never return. Unfortunately, now that he and Cameron were divided, if he failed now and allowed anyone to leave, David would demand their heads for abandoning their posts, and their fate would rest upon Keane's shoulders.

As for Cameron... he peered over at his auld friend, watching him whittle away at his stick, trying to make himself a new shaft, though he lacked the skill. Keane had many times attempted to teach him the proper way, but along with a fierce pride, Cameron MacKinnon sometimes lacked a bit of wit. He felt sorry for the man, but whether it was intended or nay, the balance of power had shifted here today.

Something had changed.

Until today, Keane hadn't even considered taking what was offered, and the only thing that had kept him at his post was the simple fact that he no longer had aught remaining for him at home—and for Cameron, who'd hoped to rise to his own fiefdom someday, so Aidan might find him worthy of Cailin's hand. Now he sat in contemplative silence, considering what to do, watching a strange girl eat her food...

Keane was five and twenty and little more than a rover, with no bed to call his own and no chance of ever providing for a wife.

A distant memory surfaced—of a girl he'd once loved... but he was no longer that fresh-faced boy, the simple lad with a pure heart who'd loved a simple girl.

Keane studied the girl seated beside him. For some reason, she made his thoughts wander to places they ought not go... But it wasn't simply her look. She was lovely, it was true, but it was more the fire in her eyes he was drawn to—something poor Meara had never possessed, though his sisters had aplenty. He sensed that, like his sisters, if a man could win the lass's prickly heart, she would make a fine, fine bride.

Alas, she belonged to someone else already…

It was her fine English dress that gave her away.

She shivered a little and Keane longed to put his arms around her to keep her warm. "Surely your mon must be missing ye?" he asked.

She didn't respond, though she hesitated before taking another bite.

What Keane truly wished to know was whether there was someone waiting for her at home. "If ye'll merely tell me where ye belong, I'll see ye safely returned."

She stopped eating and slid Keane a mean glance.

"I *BELONG* NOWHERE," Lianae said, choosing her words carefully. "To *no* mon."

A tiny smirk turned her captor's lips, and she shivered yet again—but not with fear. There was a knowing in his gaze that made Lianae wary, for he missed nothing. His gaze slid over her lavish gown—not so much her form, she realized, for there was something far less lecherous about the inspection, and she understood that he was considering her dress. His gaze returned to her face, lingering on her cheek, and his eyes narrowed slightly.

Wondering if he was looking at her bruise, or even if it was noticeable enough to see, Lianae resisted the urge to touch her face, and forced herself to eat.

"Art certain, lass?"

Her nerves frayed, Lianae turned on him then. "Of course I am certain, ye daft mon! If I belonged anywhere, wouldn't I be the first to ken?"

Furiously, she took another bite of grouse, chewing under his watchful gaze, growing more confused by the instant. It was more the way he considered her that sent her pulses skittering and her thoughts askew. The expression on his face was full of what appeared to be concern, but Lianae knew better than to trust anyone in this day and age.

Go away, she silently prayed.

If she told him who she was and from whence she hailed, he would no doubt return her to the Earl. Or if she confessed herself a rebel, here and now, he might even take her head. If she begged him to take her to Ewen and Graeme, he would know her for a rebel and hand her over to his king. Or worse, he could use her to ferret out her brothers. Alive or dead, the sons of Óengus would be worth more than their weight in gold —certainly more than a handful of charm stones.

Nay, she was better off telling him naught.

Let him think what he will.

Somewhere out there, Graeme and Ewen awaited her. All Lianae needed to do was find them. And once she retrieved her charm stones, she would have the means to buy information.

Tomorrow.

Tomorrow she would find a way to leave—once the Earl's men gave up their search.

"Ach, lass, ye must belong somewhere?" the man pressed. And this time his tone was coaxing—like the will-o'-the-wisp, with their warm bright lights, luring hapless victims unto their deaths. Lianae shrugged and kept on eating, irritated by his presence and hardly knowing why. Thus far, he'd been even so much as kind.

Mayhap it was simply because his face appealed to her—a finely carved face with a strong jaw, and bright green eyes that invited her to let down her guard.

I will not.

After a time, he bent to scoop up a handful of snow and began to shape it between his palms. "I would say ye're well born, by the looks o' ye?" he continued to press.

But he could not know the half of it.

Lianae gave him a cutting look out of the corner of one eye, for there was still a question in his tone—a question she had no intention of answering.

She was a daughter to Óengus of Moray. Her great grandfather MacBeth had been a man of the people. As king, he'd brought Scotia seventeen years of peace—the only such peace her people had known since Kenneth MacAilpín murdered his Pecht overlords. Today, half these earls had been supplanted here by William Rufus, the other half by his brother Henry. They were all minions of the English—which was why MacBeth deposed Duncan. No man of Moray could, in good conscience, follow a dirty Sassenach. So, aye, she was well born, but with her brothers still at large, they would only see her as a threat. And if they could not possess her, or use her against Ewen and Graeme, they would kill her.

"I am but a simple maid of Moray," she said sweetly, meeting his gaze.

But that was a mistake, for her eyes were at once drawn to his woad… to the wolf's maw that peeked out from beneath his tunic. The jaws opened over the cords of his neck, teeth bared over a vein in his throat. Even in the strange twilight surrounding them, she could make out the woad clearly. The sons of Fidach were said to be sons of the wolf…

They were in Lilidbrugh...

Was it a coincidence he was drawn to this place?

But nay, the sons of Fidach were all long gone, or so they claimed. Nevertheless, unnerved, she took another bite of the grouse and chewed thoughtfully, very much aware of the man seated beside her.

He continued to mold the snow between his hands, the muscles of his arms flexing as did the cords of his neck, making the wolf's tattoo move as though the beast were moving its long, powerful jaws. In fact, he was much like a wolf pup, she decided—with large, yearning eyes to tug at her heartstrings, and yet the instant she let down her guard, he would pounce.

It was a curious matter, for no Scotsman Lianae had *ever* met wore the woad of their ancestors. Forsooth, her own people no longer wore the woad of her ancestors! And yet, here was this man, wearing it still… right along with David's livery. And here he was in the lost city of the Pechts. It was a mystery, to be sure.

Confused, Lianae tore her gaze away. "Ye dinna expect a lass to confess herself to a man she does not know?"

He winked at her. "She would if she needed help," he said, and continued to play with the snow in his hand at the same time he swept the toe of his boot over the ground where Lianae had concentrated her search. Even with a new layer of snow, her foraging was perfectly evident. His boot stopped abruptly and Lianae prayed it wasn't because of her stones. They were easy to recognize once they settled beneath your feet, because they were round and smooth.

Finishing her meal, she swiped at her mouth, and then set the napkin aside. She didn't know how, but she knew in her heart there was something beneath his boot. "I have already said I do not."

"But I think you do."

Her gaze snapped to his face, searching for some sign that he *knew… something*. But what she spied there was more questions yet—and some of them mayhap her own. So Lianae called his bluff. She lifted her chin.

"If ye believe it," she challenged. "Then release me and see how long I stay?"

There was a smile in his eyes that didn't appear on his lips.

"You are not a prisoner here."

Surprised to hear him say so, Lianae furrowed her brow. "Nay?"

"Have I restrained you with ropes or chains?"

Lianae shook her head, realizing with a bit of chagrin that he spoke the truth.

"Have I assigned guards to watch o'er ye?"

Once again, she shook her head, for he had not—none aside from himself.

His lips curved into a smile, and he moved his boot and thrust a hand down into the snow, groping, searching for something, and then, seeming to find it, he plucked his hand back up, producing one of Uhtreda's stones.

Lianae's eyes widened.

"Something tells me, lass… if ye meant to leave, ye would already be gone."

CHAPTER SIX

"*That* is *mine*," she said, and reached out to snatch the stone from Keane's hand. Her expression turned to one of outrage when he held it firmly in his grasp, studying her.

While her coldstones might be rare, they were hardly unknown to him. Small and etched with symbols, they reminded him of knucklebones—a game wherein you placed four bleached bones from the ankles of a sheep into a sack. Each bone had four sides, and each side a different shape, each side a different value. Players tossed them from the sack, and the one with the greatest value won, but these coldstones were not quite so easily decipherable, and neither was the end result the winner of a game. Betimes they were rolled and the fates were not so kind. Una kept a purse full in her grotto, hauling them out whenever Aidan wished for her to seek answers from the gods. The only difference between these and the ones Una possessed was that Una's were not marked in the same manner. Regardless, they were valuable enough to steal, particularly if one knew what they were and how to use them. And whether Lianae knew such a thing or nay, she clearly understood the stones' value because she'd fled without her shoes and took the purse, when her shoes might have served her better in this inclement weather.

And by the by, although she could have at least attempted to run away, she'd spent the past hour trolling the courtyard, searching for missing stones. In fact, she seemed far more concerned over the loss of her coldstones than she was about the company of strange men.

Smiling just a little, Keane released her stone, despite his suspicions and she closed her fist possessively about the bauble. Up close, it was perfectly clear there was a bruise on her face, right below the cheekbone.

Did she steal the stones? Were they payment for her favors? A bridal gift?

Somehow he didn't think so.

He plucked a wad of red velvet cloth out of his belt, unwrapping it to show her a second small coldstone that had been caught in the folds of the purse she'd torn. He handed it to her. "Did you steal them?" he asked outright.

"Nay."

Nevertheless, she seemed to blanch over the question, and he didn't let it stop him from speaking his mind. "One must ask oneself why a bonny lass would run away, barefoot, dressed in her bride's gown, with naught more than a cloak on her back and a velvet purse full of coldstones to her name."

She blushed prettily, averting her gaze, her fist turning white over the stones she held in her hand. Keane watched as she placed both stones he'd produced into the hem of her gown. By now her cheeks were bright pink. Was she embarrassed because he'd called her bonny?

Or mayhap she has something more to hide?

Something more than coldstones...

"Why is that d' ye think?"

Keane let his question hang in the air, along with the mist from his breath, until he was fairly certain she would never respond, and then decided to give her a rest —not that he was meant to get anything more from the lass if she didn't wish to give it, for her shoulders were set as stubbornly as his sister Lael's. He recognized a brick wall whenever he met one. Unless he meant to take a harsher stance, he might as well let it go… for now.

On the other hand, if he waited for her permission to tend her foot, she would lose the thing before the night was out. Shrugging off his cloak, Keane produced his woolen breacan, and then, without any explanation for what he meant to do, he ripped a long strip from the end, and then another. Glenna, the weaver, would threaten his manhood for ruining her good cloth, though if he asked her nicely enough, she would make him another.

"What are you doing?"

"Making a pair of slippers."

She sounded stunned. "Why?"

Keane cast her a pointed glance, arching a brow. "To warm your feet perchance?"

"But why would ye do such a thing?"

"Because ye're cauld and mayhap I dinna wish to see you lose your toes. Now give me your foot," he demanded, as he moved to stoop before her, holding out his hand.

He could clearly see her pride warring with her discomfort. No doubt, it suited her not at all to be told what to do—even when it was for her own good. But at last, she relented. "Which one?"

"The right one."

Untucking the left foot from beneath her gown, she gave it to him, and he nearly laughed at the contrary response. He didn't fool himself into thinking it was for any other reason than because she meant to prove a point—that she was still in charge.

But Keane's smile faded the instant he inspected the soles of her feet. They were filthy to be sure, but even with so much dirt and undercover of night, he could see the open sores that had formed along her heels and along the pads of her toes. It wasn't yet clear how far she'd come, but if he would believe her feet, they said it was far.

Swearing beneath his breath, Keane gently brushed the pads of his fingers along the soles of her feet, trying to remove what dirt he could. Tomorrow, he would see her wash them in the burn. At the moment, it was far more important to see them warmed. He pushed up her skirt to begin binding the wool and froze at the sight of yet another bruise.

Angry and black, it encircled her ankle like a woad bracelet. He studied the mark for an awkward moment, realizing that there was only one way she could have gotten such a bruise. But it was no way for a husband to take his wife—no wonder she'd fled.

Liquid anger shot through his veins, though he said not a word. She was tense, waiting for Keane to remark, but he merely wrapped the wool about her foot and ankle, weaving the wool up, and folding the end above the bruise, taking care not to injure her any further.

And then, once again, he asked for her right foot. This time, she gave it to him without any challenge and he wasted little time in wrapping that foot as well, noting an even darker bruise in nearly the same spot.

Son of a whore.

Keane wanted to ask how she'd received them, but he didn't truly need answers. He knew enough to know that whatever the cause for those bruises, it had everything to do with that dress she was wearing and the bruise on her cheek. If she'd purloined the stones in her flight, well, good for her. By the gods, he would help her find the rest of her stones, and heaven help the fiend who would put a hand to a woman. Keane would break him in two.

"Thank you," she said, once Keane was finished with the task.

Here, in the strange light surrounding them, her face appeared bloodless, making the bruise stand out all the more distinctly. Unable to keep himself from it, Keane reached out to touch the dark spot on her face, but she caught his hand. Their gazes met and locked.

"How di' ye get it?" he asked, tempering his rage.

"More than likely from the fall I took because of you." She shoved his hand away.

There was no way Keane had given her *that* bruise. But he didn't argue with her. She might, in fact, have a few more come morning, but the one on her cheek was already deep blue against her pallid skin. It was at least a day old. Whatever the reason for her lie, she clearly didn't wish to share her troubles with him.

Ye dinna expect a lass to confess herself to a man she does not know.

It was reasonable enough, although Keane couldn't help her much if she would not speak about it. Simply because he didn't know her well enough did not mean he wouldn't kill the bastard who'd dared lay a hand on her—husband or nay. A fierce sense of protectiveness surged through him as he handed the girl his woolen breacan. And then, retrieving his cloak, he rose to his feet. "I'll help ye search for the rest of your stones come morning. Maybe then ye'll be more amenable to telling me where ye're from?"

Her brow furrowed. "Mayhap," she said.

And once again their gazes met and held.

"Or, at least, perhaps ye'll say where it is ye wish me to take ye?"

This time she nodded.

"Will ye at least tell me your name, lass?"

Snowflakes fell upon her lashes, and still she held his gaze, blinking only once. "Lianae," she said, after a long moment.

"Lianae," Keane whispered, repeating the name with the same reverence he'd given Lilidbrugh. "I am Keane," he told her, stopping short of giving her the name of his kin. For the first time in his life, he felt a man between worlds.

I belong nowhere, she'd said. Like her, he was the same. He belonged neither in Dubhtolargg, nor to the man whose livery he wore. So in this sense, they were kindred spirits.

But to Keane's dismay, he spied a telltale gleam in her eyes, and the sight of it managed to further confuse him. She gave him anger when she should have feared him, tears instead of gratitude. Her legs were bruised, her cheek bruised, and the bottoms of her feet were full of sores. Despite her pawky attitude, her silence was hardly the quality of a well-born woman. All the women he'd met at David's court—the ones who'd come dressed as she was—were so full of grievances that Keane had found himself wondering whether there were any women remaining, who were more like his sisters—strong in body and spirit.

"Well, Lianae," he said, "You are free to go. But 'twill be caulder yet afore the night is through, and if it please ye, ye may share my pallet."

Bracing himself for an argument that never came, he added, "To keep warm, ye ken? I have three sisters," he reassured her, as though that fact alone should set her mind at ease.

Once again she nodded, and moisture twinkled in her eyes.

Keane turned away, lest he shame her by remaining any longer and witnessing her tears. She was proud, he sensed. And worse, he suspected his kindness had somehow wounded her. He didn't like to ken what that revealed.

THE INSTANT HE WAS GONE, Lianae swiped away her tears. She was her father's daughter, she reminded herself, and a daughter of Moray should not cry.

As the night grew darker yet, a curious halo blanketed the ruins, but the glow was less the blush of firelight and more a lucent quality, not unlike the illusion of daylight on a snowy landscape. A coat of frost on the moss-covered stones gave the ruins a jewel-like ambience. It was a strange sight, stranger yet for the company she kept.

He knew what her charm stones were. The fact was not lost to Lianae. She took one out of her hem to study the marks.

Her Viking ancestors had used rune stones like these to read fortunes, but each small stone would have held a different rune… unlike these.

Could they be payment to the Other Realm?

Now that their *king* was a man of *faith*, the practice of leaving stones on the eyes of the dead was past, but they had once been used as payment to Sluag, the god of the Other Realm. For those still in the land of the living, the stones drew upon the forces of the Other Realm to heal the sick. And still, for a very few, who lived betwixt this world and the next, the stones were said to be conduits…

Some were fashioned into larger stones, and used as *keek stanes*. But Uhtreda's were not so large. They were the size of little pebbles, each bearing a single mark—two moons and a lightning rod betwixt…

Perhaps they could be used for healing?

In any case, they were now hers and Lianae refused to give them up. Fortunately, no one seemed interested in taking them from her—nor even the least bit in her, if the truth be told. Once the Scots were all tucked into their pallets, she half expected the one called Keane to call her to his bed, but he did not. True to his word, he left her free to come and go as she pleased, but Lianae had no wish to venture out alone, despite the feeling that her brothers might be near.

Mayhap tomorrow.

Heaving a sigh, she got up off the stoop and made another sweep of the area for her stones. Come morning, when they could see a bit clearer, Keane had promised to help her find the rest, but until then… she eyed his pallet longingly.

SHE WAS SEARCHING IN VAIN.

Despite the strange glow they were surrounded by, there was not enough light to conduct a proper search, particularly now with the falling snow.

It was only by chance that Keane had discovered the one beneath his boot, perfectly round and smooth. After seeing the one caught within the folds of her purse, he'd realized what she was searching for. Come morning, the remaining stones would all be buried at least two-feet deep and no one would find them again until spring.

Nevertheless, he'd promised to help her, and help her he would, but in the meantime, he sorely wished she would join him beneath the blankets.

Even from where Keane lay, he could tell that she was shivering beneath her fancy cloak, despite the added benefit of his breacan. And in spite of her threats to leave, she had stayed. By now, he was pretty sure that whatever it was that awaited her *out there*... she feared that far more than she did Keane or his men.

Stubborn lass.

He wished she would relent. Though if there was one thing he'd learned in dealing with his sisters, it was that there was only so far a man could go to assert his will. He'd crossed that line but a few times before his sisters quite rudely put him in his place.

To that effect, Lianae reminded him most of Lael, although there was a softness about her that his sister did not possess. She was more like his brother's wife—prickly, but gentle in her bearing. She appeared every bit a lady in her English finery, and yet she had mettle —a trait that fit quite neatly with the dún Scoti women. Years of living in the Mounth and fending for themselves had given the dún Scoti womenfolk far less complicated tastes, but they were no less capable of leading men about by their noses. Strong women were valued by his kinsmen, and in fact, in days gone by, the line of kingship had come to them, not through their fathers, but through their mothers.

Lianae reminded him of a queen. Like a lodestone, his gaze was drawn to her.

She was seated atop a ruined stoop, warming her hands with the heat of her breath, though her gaze remained riveted upon the campfire. Every once in a while, she would peer over her shoulder at the dark forest behind her, but then she returned to stare longingly at the flames.

Stubborn lass, he thought again.

Full of pride and too headstrong for her own good, she would rather freeze to death than join his men beside the fire. Well, she wasn't going anywhere, he realized. And he'd made it perfectly clear to his men that they should leave her be. Once the girl was cold enough, she would seek his bed, he had no doubt. She didn't strike him as witless or foolish, and on nights like these, both man and beast knew better than to sleep alone. Even the horses were all huddled together beneath the tarp and his men were heaped beneath another, with adjoining pallets that made good use of body heat and blankets. Crowded and a jumble of limbs, Keane would warrant that not a single one of them would complain about feet wandering beneath the blankets tonight. In fact, he was quite certain the most coveted spots to place one's toes were beneath another mon's arse cheeks—not that he wanted anyone near his own.

And yet that was not why he'd taken his pallet so far from the others. His reasons for that were twofold: Now that he would take his place as their leader, it was important to make certain all the men knew their places. Previously, he and Cameron had provided a strong, united front, one that bolstered them whenever they were unsettled. But the second reason, and the one that held most sway, was simply that he would be far more approachable lying separately from his men. For that reason, he'd chosen a spot half hidden from the rest of the pallets, beneath a broken eave, which should afford them a modicum of privacy. No matter that they believed themselves equals, his sisters—all three—had never been very keen on sleeping near the men. Not even Lael, who, far from considering herself Keane's equal and thought herself above most men, would let her guard down enough to sleep comfortably amidst grown men. Only Kellen had ever merited a spot upon her pallet—mostly because Aidan had refused to share his bed with a five-year-old, and somehow, Kellen had taken more to Lael than to any of the rest of his sisters when first he'd arrived in Dubhtolargg. More oft than not, Lael would carve herself a place somewhere alone.

Turning onto his back, Keane placed one hand behind his head to stare up at the starless night, thinking about Lili's son. He would be ten and six by now, but he hadn't seen the boy in five years—not since the day Keane left the vale. Out of everyone, he missed his sister Cailin most of all. For most of their life the two had been inseparable.

The night was calm, but there was a sting in the air that promised colder weather yet. Snow lit upon his lashes, but he didn't particularly care. Back in the vale, he'd spent many a night just like this... and he wondered what his sister Cailin would say if she could spy him now... sleeping in a heap of rubble merely to say he'd slept one day in the cradle of their kin.

He thought of Meara next, the lass he'd once believed he'd loved. But to little avail, he tried to picture her face. It eluded him now, after so long. She was fourteen when she'd died of fever from a contaminated well and she went so fast that Keane scarce had time to blink. One day she was giggling, spying on him at Caoineag's Pool, and the next, she was lying upon a pyre.

"May I?" asked a soft, feminine voice, interrupting his reverie.

Keane blinked, turning to find, not Meara, but Lianae standing a few feet away. There was nothing similar about them. Meara had had dark lovely hair and bright green eyes while Lianae reminded him of a burnished idol. Arms crossed and shivering ferociously, she stared at him longingly—or rather, not at Keane, but at his blanket.

All thoughts of Meara vanished at once.

Smiling, Keane lifted the blanket in welcome.

CHAPTER SEVEN

By morning, the entire world seemed blanketed in white, with a watery sun that teased through heavy, bloated clouds. The ruins were half buried beneath a layer of snow so high that it was difficult to say where the ruins ended and the landscape began.

The surrounding trees were painted with frost, evergreen boughs that sagged with heavy burdens. Every time the wind blew, great gobs of ice shook loose from the trees. The fickle weather was turning yet again, but if they should set out now, in this storm, they'd very likely freeze their bollocks off before midday—something Keane was disinclined to do, particularly now that they were so snuggly and warm. Down in the courtyard, amidst the half tumbled walls, the crew remained sheltered from the wind. Burrowed beneath the covers, with a warm body at his side, he'd slept like a warm, lazy dog, and as yet, most of his men had yet to rise, clearly reluctant to burrow out of their pallets.

Oblivious to the continuing flurries, a red squirrel sat burrowing near his pallet, its rufous tail twitching as it searched for pine nuts beneath the snow. Oddly, it reminded him of Lianae searching for her stones. The squirrel scurried away once Keane adjusted the covers —more's the pity. With an empty stomach, he fancied the little beast roasting on a spit for their breakfast. Alas, but he was far too content to leave his bed, and much too aware of the woman slumbering along beside him…

Lianae.

It was a good name, lovely and strong, much like her.

He might never have guessed for an instant that beneath her fearless facade she'd hid the evidence of abuse.

What kind of man harmed a woman?

If Keane had the chance to face the monster, he would give him cause to rue his actions. It was impossible to know whether he'd taken her against her will, but marks like those meant only one thing… at the very least the bastard had tried.

For his part, Keane intended to reward the girl's trust in him by proving that not all men were rutting beasts…

At the least he was trying.

His lust was difficult to deny, when his cock stood fully erect and throbbing beneath the covers. Despite his best intentions, his morning erection was not a function of his sex.

The scent of Lianae's hair was like a philter—a love potion that spoke to his body in a language that clearly it understood. It had been a long time since he'd craved so desperately to put his old chap to better use…

Oblivious to his struggle for control, Lianae squirmed beneath the covers, moving a little closer to the heat of his body. Keane resisted the urge to reach out and draw her close. She had no inkling what she was doing, he realized, and waking her was the last thing he wished to do. But if she should happen any closer, she would quickly discover that not all his swords were safely sheathed...

He inched backward yet again—for the half dozenth time—reconsidering the wisdom in rising sooner rather than later, if for no other reason than to speak privately with Cameron.

As yet, only Cameron was up and tending the fire—or rather, more accurately, preparing it for their departure. He was pushing snow up and over the dying embers, his shoulders peppered with flakes he didn't bother to shake off. He worked quietly, brooding all the while.

They had yet to speak about what had happened, but Keane wasn't all that concerned. They had been friends too long and if Cameron ever meant to win Cailin's hand, he would never dare challenge Keane—particularly since everything Cameron ever wanted, he wanted solely for one reason: to win Cailin's favor. And he could have her still, if only the man would realize that he already had all he needed to win her favor. His sister didn't care about riches. Nor did she care whether a man was titled. She, like all of his sisters, were simpler in their requirements. They wanted strong, loyal men who would care for them, and not much else. Until Cameron realized as much, Cailin would never have him—never mind Aidan. It was never his laird brother who would make this decision for Cailin. But this was not something Keane could easily explain to a man who was unaccustomed to putting women before him, particularly so long as Cailin remained undecided, because, to a man, Aidan's reluctance to accept Cameron was the one thing that seemed to be saving his pride. Cameron was convinced that was the only reason Cailin had not yet fallen into his arms. But he was wrong. No one told his sisters what to do—whom to marry—and if that were so, Lael and Cat would never have wed outside the vale.

Nay, Cameron still had much to learn.

In truth, Keane was far more reluctant to buck Aidan's authority than any of his sisters had ever been, for he had once been his brother's heir.

Not anymore.

Now, he had... *what?* Not even a sense of purpose, if the truth be known. Aside from listening to Cameron's aspirations and visions of grandeur—the home he'd like to build for Cailin, the children they might raise together—he was jaded and bored with life. Back in the vale, he'd withered in the role he'd been provided, and even this mission had proven mind-numbing, for despite David's fears—that with Henry of England preoccupied in France, the sons of Óengus were scheming to restore the Mormaerdom—all was quiet in the northern territories.

Trying not to think about the woman snuggled beneath his furs, he examined their surroundings. In the cold morning light, Lilidbrugh was a desolate place. No wonder his men were so eager to leave. They should much prefer to be home with their families, where the hearth fires blazed and the auld reekie soup was bubbling in a pot. Like Keane, their hearts were not in this task, no matter what David's promises. Those promises could not fill their bellies at the instant. Nor did they warm the bones, and for his part, Keane wondered what he was doing serving a king he did not trust. The girl lying beside him had given him the only frisson of excitement he'd encountered since beginning his service to the crown.

Ten years ago, David mac Mhaoil Chaluim had stolen his sister Catrìona from her bed in the middle of the night. He took her south, intending to award her to the English as a ward of their court. This was not a man who engendered trust, and yet, these few years past, he had not known the man to be intentionally cruel. He made his decisions, so he claimed, for the good of the realm. This was something Keane might well believe, despite that he disagreed with the methods. Like a game of chess, he moved pieces about his board. But for every decision he made, there were good folk who paid—like his brother.

Aidan's marriage to Lìleas MacLaren could so easy have gone wrong. On pain of losing her firstborn son, Lìli had been sent to murder Aidan in his bed. Had she not fallen in love with Aidan, and had the integrity and fortitude to come forward, all might have gone so differently... Keane would have been laird of their clan.

Thankfully, he was not.

But there was another side to Scotia's king, for when David might have exacted justice over the taking of Keppenach, he had shown Lael and Broc Ceannfhionn infinite mercy—and more. Instead of hanging them as he might have—as they had attempted to do before Jamie Steorling cut them free—he gave Broc a seat at Dunloppe and Lael was commanded to wed the *Butcher,* King David's most trusted commander. These days his sister Lael seemed to have traded her knives for wee bairns, chasing them about, whilst her laird husband continued counseling his king. But Keane had no place in this arrangement. He was a border guard, nothing more. Only now, he feared he craved else...

Lianae stirred beside him and Keane tried not to think of her arse, the shape of which, he now knew intimately, despite the barrier of her gown—and despite the fact that he kept edging backward, for she kept nestling it sweetly against him, and he had no need to touch her to picture the outline of it printed so neatly against his thighs. She wiggled backward, yet again, and Keane swore softly beneath his breath. By the sins of Sluag, he was but a man.

He scooted backwards, away from her, the very instant he felt his cock stir, and he'd kept scooting back again every time she sleepily sought the crook of his thighs.

WITH THE WIND WHISTLING OVERHEAD, Lianae was afeared to come out from the blankets, so she snuggled deeper. Warm and comfy as she was, it was easy to pretend she was still at home with her mother and father, and that her elder brothers had never gone to war. Her dreams this morning were of Lulach—at ten, when Lianae was nine. They were laughing together near the silos, watching kittens chase the hens from their feed, but it was so long ago now that such innocence had been a part of their lives.

Oh, Lulach...

Her heart ached.

Why?

Rather than make the Earl pay for what he'd done to Elspeth, he'd doomed Lianae to the same fate! Her father would be so ashamed, and her minny—couldn't he remember what they'd done to her? Aye, she had died of grief, forsooth, but *they* had driven her to it, taunting her with images of her bonny sons' heads rotting on a field of dead. They'd claimed her sons' heads were put upon pikes, and left to mark the place where MacBeth's murdering heirs had been vanquished at long last.

Didn't Lulach remember?

Why couldn't he remember?

Of course, Lianae had refused to believe their lies. If they'd brought home her father's body on a slag, why wouldn't they have returned her brothers' as well? This, she took as proof that Graeme and Ewen must still be alive. But this was all a nightmare, in truth, and she didn't want to wake now... because that's where the true demons lived, in the broad light of day. Swallowing her grief, Lianae settled herself beneath the covers, and suddenly, she felt a warm hand resting on the curve of her thigh, pushing her gently but firmly forward.

"*Stop*," a male voice said.

His breath was soft and warm as it blew across her nape.

Keane.

It took Lianae a sleepy moment to realize precisely where she lay. And to begin with, the only thing that kept her from flying out from the covers was the bitter cold. It slapped her across the face when she poked out her head. But, then, as soon she remembered who it was who lay beside her, she was quite certain this was precisely where she meant to stay.

It was cold enough out there now to turn flesh to ice. Shivering, Lianae ducked her head beneath the covers and prayed for sun. If it had been near this cold when she'd fled Kinneddar Castle, she might never have left at all—or mayhap frozen to death soon after her escape. *Propriety be damned!* His men might all be still asleep, but Lianae had no doubt they'd already spied her huddled beneath Keane's blankets. Let them say what they would. She had come to him willingly, and the simple fact that he was pushing her away now, left her feeling confused.

Didn't he like her?

It wasn't unheard of that a woman should expect to pay for a man's protection with her body, and Lianae might have been willing to do so if that's what it came down to. *Maybe*. That's how cold she was! The simple fact that she had never been put in such a position was more a testament to the respect her father commanded, even from the grave... but this man had *no* idea who Lianae was, and still he was pushing her away—as though the feel of her somehow repulsed him. That made little sense—not after the way he'd treated her last night.

Shifting beneath the covers, Lianae turned to face her would-be captor, remembering suddenly that he had not taken the least offense to her barb about his biting pillows. "Are ye no' fond of women?" she asked, nonplussed.

HEARING HER QUESTION, Keane nearly choked.

Bloody hell. The scent of her had him so hard at the instant that he daren't allow the girl any closer. For both their sakes, he held her an arm's length away.

Blinking innocently, she stared at him, waiting for his answer—but nay, demanding one, if the truth be known—and Keane marveled that she could ask such a question with the evidence that lay between them.

But, of course, how could she know?

Her brows furrowed prettily. There were no aspersions meant, he realized and the look in her eyes seemed quite sincere. She wished to know if he preferred men, and he had half a mind to lean forward and kiss her senseless as his answer. But there was a certain innocence in her eyes that belied the impudent question.

Swallowing with some difficulty, well aware that his camp was now rising, and that his men were all casting curious glances in their direction, Keane found himself staring helplessly into the girl's *uisge* gold eyes.

Gold, with a ringlet of green, they were the most enchanting pair of eyes Keane had ever seen. She was lovely, and unlike Lilidbrugh, with the morning light, she was twice as beautiful as the night before, with dark golden-red brows that were perfectly arched over almond-shaped eyes. Her skin… reminded Keane of rose petals… soft and unblemished. And those sulky lips… they were the color of ripe rowan berries in fall —albeit slightly chapped for the weather. It made him yearn to soothe them with his tongue. But that bruise on her cheek… it was darker now, and the sight of it successfully cooled his ardor.

She was still waiting, confusion nestled in her lovely eyes, and although Keane realized she didn't mean to, she leaned into the hand he had splayed between them beneath the covers, testing his uncertain barrier.

"Ach, lass, I am quite fond of women," Keane reassured her. And then it was the most difficult thing he'd ever had to say, "Now, please, get out of my bed."

It wasn't simply the cold he knew he would regret.

The lass blinked in surprise, and if the confusion weren't already evident in her eyes, he saw it now tenfold. "You want me to get out?"

Keane nodded a bit awkwardly, half shaking his head, as she continued to lean against the hand he had splayed between them. The curve of her belly teased him mercilessly and he craved naught more than to slide his hand down and explore the delicious cleft between her thighs… and deeper, the soft folds of flesh he wanted to taste as urgently as he did her lips.

Nay, he didn't *want* her to get up, but it was past time for both of them to rise—well past time for his *old chap* to lie down for a rest. Blood simmered through his veins, undermining his resolve...

Now?" she asked, and Keane groaned inwardly. Were it any other moment… had he not a company of soldiers watching… if she hadn't sounded quite so much like an innocent—or mayhap if she weren't gazing at him with that sweet look of gratitude… as though she might wish to repay him for his good will…

And yet, despite all his reservations, he let her ease into his space, craving the feel of her warm, sweet body pressed against his own.

He wanted to kiss her, he did.

More than anything...

And those lips, they seemed to beg for proof of his desire. Ach, god, he wanted her more than any lass he'd ever craved—even more than Meara that first day. By the stone, he could warm an entire village with the heat emanating from his loins.

She moved closer yet, leaning her face into his, and Keane cursed, if only to himself, finding his resolve weakened. He tried to will himself to speak—to warn her to get up—now, before he lost his head... but she puckered her sweet mouth just a bit, and he growled deep in his throat.

Just one kiss?

There was little chance he would simply take her here and now, surrounded by all his greedy-eyed men, and yet if the lass wanted him to kiss her... who was he to deny her?

Keane reached out to touch her cheek...

And this time, Lianae didn't push him away.

IT WAS in that instant Lianae realized what she must do.

The answer to all her prayers came to her as she stared into Keane's bold green eyes... It wasn't as though she would trap him into wedding her... The king would never allow it, for this man was but a lowly border guard, with a handsome face and a kindly disposition. And yet he was far more like the man she had envisioned losing her virginity to—nothing like the Earl. And the more she considered it, the more she realized it was the right thing to do...

She wasn't wholly unwise to the ways of the world.

Virginity was only a boon if one wished to wed a king, and even then it wasn't all it was said to be. Her mother had certainly never complained a day in her life.

Kissing this man, embracing him to her bosom… it was *not* the worst thing that could happen to her by far, for then, if they should happen to catch her, she could tell the auld lecher Earl she was ruined, that another man had claimed her long before him. His prickly English pride would never allow him to accept another man's leftovers, and he would repudiate her before kith and kin—most assuredly before his king. And then mayhap she would be free to wed no one at all.

He wanted to kiss her.

She recognized the desire in his eyes.

And suddenly, she wanted to kiss him too… and it wasn't all a ruse.

But she had never kissed a man before.

Not even the sound of men rising from their pallets could dissuade her now, for then she would have all the witnesses she would need to prove she spoke the truth.

And anyway, they were mostly sheltered from prying eyes, half hidden behind a mound of snow where once had been a crumbling wall. Lianae couldn't see anyone so she surmised they probably couldn't see her either—not entirely.

Curling her toes, she reached out to boldly press her lips against Keane's mouth, inhaling sharply at the scent of his male skin—horse and man and *something else*… something she had never scented before now. Cocooned as they were, he smelled oddly like pollen, like that sweet, heady aroma that flared her nostrils every spring. But this was the essence of *him*, a tantalizing aroma that sent her pulses skittering and her heart beating like a hapless prisoner against her ribs.

"Ach, lass," he said, and followed the protest with a low, confused groan.

Emboldened by his reaction—by her will to be free of the Earl—Lianae arched into his embrace, reaching down to pull his hand out from between them, wanting to feel him lean into her, his body heavy and full with ardor. She had never had a chance to ask her sister how it should feel, but this is how she'd always imagined it.

And that was all the encouragement he seemed to need. His arms enfolded her, and Lianae pressed herself more fully against him, marveling at what she encountered. Ach, but nay, the man was very, *very* fond of women—and particularly fond of her, she realized. Words alone would not serve her now, and so she said naught. Instead, she moved closer, into Keane's space, pressing her body more fully against him.

With a guttural sound, his hand swept the length of Lianae's body, stopping to cup the curve of her bottom and pulling her hungrily against his arousal. Lianae cried out softly, her body convulsing in secret places. His lips softened and his tongue found her own, unexpectedly foraging into her mouth. Dazed by the gesture, and intoxicated by the taste of him, Lianae lay for a moment, until he slackened his embrace—as though he meant to stop. And before he could pull away, she shoved her tongue between his lips, mimicking his actions, and moaning softly as he let her come inside to explore...

"Ach... nay, lass," he said, but he didn't stop. His hands continued to explore Lianae's curves, dancing over her thigh. Too lost in the moment to care precisely what it was that was happening, Lianae reveled in the feel of his strong hands exploring her flesh. Even despite that she was a virgin, she knew very well that she wasn't behaving like one, but right now, she didn't care overmuch. It was for a good cause, she assured herself, and the simple fact that she was enjoying it so immensely was a wonderful surprise.

He shifted his weight so that he straddled her beneath the covers, and Lianae's heartbeat quickened as she peered up at him, meeting his gaze. With a tiny knowing smile, she nudged him gently at his loins… urging him to continue.

"You're a wee siren," he whispered. "A kelpie for sure…"

Beauteous faeries who seduced men to ride and then plunged them into the raging sea.

"Dinna stop," Lianae whispered against his mouth. "Dinna stop."

He enfolded her once more, and Lianae marveled at the strength of him, the feel of his hard body, and very much unlike that time with the Earl, she did not pray for someone to save her… and yet someone did. The instant he bent to kiss her again, someone cursed roundly, thoroughly breaking the spell.

"Ach… I am so sorry, lass," he said, thrusting his long fingers into the hair at the back of her head and tugging her gently away. He held her down so she couldn't follow.

And that was that; he was up and out of the covers faster than Lianae could blink.

Her would-be savior was gone.

CHAPTER EIGHT

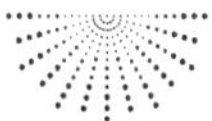

The blare of a shepherd's horn heralded their approach.

Straightening in the saddle, Kellen dún Scoti rode side by side with his new bride—he on a winter-white mare, and she on a Barbary black.

Riding ahead, along with his captain, Kellen's father picked up the pace, eager to be home. So was Kellen, although he was overanxious about what his mother might say about the lovely woman riding at his side.

The past few weeks had proven a wonderful adventure, and he had come home a brand new man, but he cast a nervous glance at his bonny new wife and felt far less grown than he would have liked.

Would his mother welcome Constance with open arms? Would she be angered over the present circumstances? Would she acknowledge that, at sixteen, he was a man grown and allow him to establish his own home?

Or would she embarrass him before his MacKinnon wife?

Either way, Kellen realized that his mother was bound to be disappointed, if for nothing else, for not having been present for his nuptials. But ultimately, he hoped she would see it as a boon, for by his marriage to Constance, they now held blood ties to the MacKinnon laird, a man who was well respected throughout the north. These were turbulent times, and it would behoove them all to bind themselves together.

Painted white beneath a great blue sky, the hillside meandered into a valley that was protected on three sides by corries and on the fourth by a beautiful loch. Down in the valley below, encircled by bare-limbed rowan trees, sat row upon row of stone cottages—one of them soon to be his own. Today, the vale appeared much the same as it did when he'd first arrived at the tender age of five, but during the summer those same trees would all bloom, and in the fall they'd be filled with bright red berries that would hold fast to their boughs until frost. Even now the last stubborn fruits were layered in frost, shimmering like jewels beneath the waning sun.

He grinned, for the look on his wife's face was worth the wait and she smiled beauteously as the small cavalcade approached the village, and one by one, his people filed out of their houses to welcome them home.

Out on the loch stood an enormous structure with a cone-shaped roof. This was the crannóg he'd spoken to his wife about, where he and his family kept their beds. While at Chreagach Mhor, she had been fascinated by Kellen's stories and he couldn't wait to show her the crannóg firsthand, although his father had already promised him a cottage of his own. After all, it wasn't fitting for a man to bed his wife under another man's roof—or so his father had said. It was far more meet for Kellen to make himself a home all of his own—so long as his mother agreed.

"'Tis lovely as ye said," Constance avowed, and the sweet sound of her voice filled Kellen with joy.

"Not more lovely than you," he countered.

How far he had come since Keppenach, eh?

At Keppenach he'd been just a wee lad, all alone, without any friends, and no siblings. His room had been cold and his bed as hard as stones. If they'd stayed there any longer, he might have been dead by his uncle's hands. Neither he nor his gentle mother had ever had any love from Rogan MacLaren, but Kellen rarely thought about that odious man anymore. His real father had died when he was but a tot, and Aidan was the only father Kellen had ever known. While Stuart MacLaren had been a goodly man, Kellen was far more a dún Scoti than he had ever been a MacLaren, despite that he did not share his step-father's blood. Through his years, he'd come to understand that familial bonds were not forged by blood, but by mutual respect and love. "Ye will love my sister and my aunts," he reassured Constance.

"If they are anything like Cat, I know I will," she happily agreed. "And ye may have yoursel' another sister soon," she suggested, referring to his mother's new babe. "What think you of that, Husband?" she asked with a smile.

Like a sapling that had been shown the sun, Kellen sat a bit straighter in the saddle at hearing her endearment. "I hope it will be a boy," he confessed. It would be good to have a wee lad to replace him, for his father' sake. No matter how well his step-father loved him, he realized that it plagued Aidan quite a lot to lack an heir of his blood. They had a legacy to continue, after all, and Kellen did not bear the Guardians' blood. He said naught for a moment, trying to picture his mother with a wee bairn. It was a strange thing to think about—particularly if he and Constance were breeding as well, though he supposed his mother was not so old as she liked to believe.

How would that work? he wondered. His son or

daughter might be a niece to his infant sister. Confusing, though it was no more confusing than to think of his step-sister Sorcha as his aunt, as well—a fact that was *not* known except by a chosen few. Since Kellen shared none of their blood, his mother had been quick to reveal this truth so that he might never think of Sorcha untowardly. As yet Sorcha still did not know, and Kellen was sworn to secrecy. But Dubhtolargg was full of secrets—not the least of which included the Stone that had been stolen from Scone and now lay hidden in their ben.

"And your aunt Lael wed the demon butcher?"

Kellen swung about in his saddle, peering over his shoulder to see who else might have overheard. He lowered his voice as he turned to his wife, placing a finger to his lips. "Shhh," he said. "I wadna use that name about here. Lael wadna like it verra much."

"Oh." Constance replied. "Will she be here as well?"

"Nay," Kellen said, though he wished it were otherwise. His eldest aunt was by far his favorite aunt of all. Lael had embraced him first, protecting him with her life that wintry night he'd arrived in the vale. In fact, he sorely regretted having told Constance about the Butcher at all, for how many times had his mother and father both cautioned him to carry no tales of the vale. It was for this reason Kellen had yet to tell her about the Stone from Scone. He'd lived here many, many years before he'd ever learned about the Destiny Stone himself—and not before he was old enough to comprehend its value. And it was the first thing his father had pulled him aside to warn him about, even before he'd taken his vows...

The secrets of the vale remained in the vale, he'd said in his firmest voice.

"His name is Jaime," he corrected her.

Constance nodded obediently, although her words

were not quite so conforming. "Dinna fash yoursel', husband. I will not speak the Butcher's name again."

Husband.

She'd said it again, and Kellen felt the tell-tale heat rise into his cheeks. "Verra good," he said, puffing up his chest. "He saved my aunt from the gallows," he informed Constance. "That's how they met. He cut her down from the gibbet, took one look into her eyes and fell in love—at least that's what my uncle claims." Constance blinked prettily, her long blond hair blowing softly in the cool breeze, and Kellen could scarce believe his good fortune. "A bit like you and me," he explained "I knew I loved you from the instant I looked into your lovely blue eyes."

Constance blushed and smiled. "You have such a way with words and such exciting tales to tell. Nothing ever happens much in Chreagach Mhor."

Kellen lifted a brow. "What about FitzSimon?" he asked her, referring to the ordeal they'd only just left behind. Her cousin Malcom had saved his stepmother from certain death at the hands of a brother she'd not even realized she'd had. In the process, Malcom slew his own grandfather. Kellen heard tell now that Malcom might inherit a castle in Northumbria that was three times the size of Keppenach. Whether he did so or not would be a matter for kings to decide. Nevertheless, Kellen was content enough with his own lot. His tiny cottage in Dubhtolargg was worth a thousand castles anywhere else and he couldn't wait to make a home with his lovely new bride. But he could see that Constance was still worrying her thumb, nibbling it thoughtfully—a habit that reminded him very much of his aunt Sorcha.

"Do you think your mother will like me, Kellen?"

Kellen wanted so much to tell her yes. His sister and aunts would embrace her easily. But his mother…

well, that was another matter entirely. Despite that she had rarely ever taken a dislike to anyone, she had long expressed other ideas for the course of Kellen's life. She might not wish to be thwarted, and she could very well blame Constance for the way events had unfolded.

But this was the truth: Kellen never touched Constance untowardly, not until they were properly wed. They had merely sought a bit of privacy up in the stables so they could kiss awhile. Not once had he put his hand up her skirt, nor did he place his palm across her breast... not until their wedding night. In fact, the very thought of it still made his cheeks burn, and he hated that fact for he was supposed to be a man.

They were near enough now that he could spy his mother emerging from the crannóg, unmistakable with her belly and her wobble and the pit of his stomach heaved, even as she waved and hurried down the long pier to greet them.

"Dinna worry, Constance. She will love you as I do," he said, and prayed to God it would be true. Whatever the case, they would know it all too soon, for awaiting them below was the moment of truth.

THE RATIONS WERE GONE.

Upon receiving the news, Keane's mood went from optimistic to ominous—not unlike the weather. As the morning proceeded, the hint of sun that had teased them at first light vanished as completely as the contents of their satchels. The surrounding bluffs no longer shielded them from a bitter wind. The trees thrashed in protest, shivering away loads of snow. If there had been prints left in the snow following the theft, they no longer remained. Wind lifted and shifted the drifts, making it impossible to say whether anyone stole in or out of their camp.

Quite convenient, Keane thought.

Donal and Wee Alick both stood, scratching their big heads, icicles hanging from the hairs of their nostrils, whilst the rest of his men all argued heatedly amongst themselves, producing far too much body heat in their arguments to grow icicles themselves.

"*You* were the last to handle the rations, Brude. *You* were the first to rise!"

"Not me! It was Cameron. I only came to take a bite. We had plenty left after two nights of grouse," Brude explained. "My belly craved a biscuit after all that grease."

"Aye, well, if ye dinna drink your own piss oot o' the burn, mayhap your stomach wadna need any settling, eh?"

"Let's see what comes out o' his arsehole this morn, then we'll ken how much a bite he took. My belly is achin' too an ye dinna see me stealing food."

"Wee clipe!"

"It was the damned grouse—Alick, lazy bugger—probably found it dead."

"Nay! I dinna!"

Brude turned on them now. "How would any o' ye whoremongers know what I was doing, lest ye were sitting here watching every single move I make like beady-eyed hawks—and why would ye do so lest ye meant to steal a bite for yourselves?"

"It was the faeries," interjected auld Teasag, his tone distressed. The man reminded Keane quite a lot of auld Fergus, back in the vale. "A penance for poaching upon their lands—so be the aching bellies. Mine isna well either."

"What penance? This isna Holy Church, *eejit*. We're no Sassenachs!"

"Aye, it *is* like Holy Church," argued Teasag. "This place—" He waved a hand to indicate the whole of Lilidbrugh— "is no longer in the realms of men."

Murdock made a face. "Ach, ye dolt! What faerie would want aught to do with a pile of broke stones? Shut up about it already, ere I break your bones!"

"Aye, we're tired o' listening to ye, *Tea Sack*."

Through all this, Cameron remained silent, occupying himself by folding the small tarp they'd used to shelter the horses from the weather, preparing for their imminent departure.

"Shut your gobs," Keane commanded them at last—before anyone should happen to brandish a knife. The snow was wet. No need to turn it red, although Keane certainly understood the inclination. At the moment, aside from having blue balls, he was cold and angry that these bunch of dafties would argue like auld biddies.

They'd begun their campaign with rations enough for ten days. After six in the saddle and quite a few supplemented meals, they should have had more than enough remaining for a week or more. With a bit of luck, Keane could have seen their bellies filled for a good sennight or more. But now *everything* was gone, as though some faerie had indeed waved a hand at their satchels and everything comestible had vanished.

With fourteen men, one woman, and no biscuits, no salted pork, no cheese and no liquids, except for a few flasks of ale, it went without saying that remaining to explore Lilidbrugh was completely out of the question.

By the same token, taking the girl back to whomever she'd fled from was also not on Keane's list of destinations—even if it so happened that she'd come from allies who would welcome them with a feast and buckets full of ale—not unless he meant to start a war.

"Empty your flasks," he commanded his men. "Fill

them with snow." It was better than water from the burn, considering everyone's upset stomachs and considering what he knew about the dangers of drinking contaminated water.

"Ach, Keane! The ale's the one thing keeping my bollocks from freezing in this bitter weather," Teasag complained.

"Empty your flasks," Keane demanded again. And though his tone might appear harsh, he, more than anyone, knew how quickly sickness could take them.

His command was followed by a profusion of curses, though he didn't linger to see that they obeyed. He simply expected them to do so. He didn't care if they chugged down the ale in a single gulp. At least then it would keep them warm—for a while—and there was little to no chance of drunkenness in this sobering weather. Most folks drank little water by choice, but the ale would dehydrate them quicker and he wanted everyone to have good, clean water at the ready, no matter how much they protested.

They should all be pleased enough to be on their way, but the change of plans did not suit Keane very much. He'd been counting on a leisurely morning to speak to Cameron, and then to gain his bearings, before helping Lianae find her lost stones, and better determining what to do with her. As it was, everything was in a muddle.

But the one thing he wasn't confused about was this: He would kill the bastard who'd dared lay a hand on her—not simply because his mood was foul. And not because of what had happened between them this morning. But Keane felt fiercely protective over her. She'd looked at him with such a look of gratitude upon waking—such veneration—if Donal hadn't distracted him, he might have completely lost himself in her arms. Only now, with his head a bit clearer, he realized what she was trying to do—thank him for coming to her aide.

The very idea made him sick to his gut. He would *never* have a woman that way.

Despite the number of lassies who'd rubbed their arses against his lap, the last woman he lay with was Meara. He did not partake when his men all went whoring. He much preferred a wank all to himself, far too aware of the consequences he would face, if his seed were to plant itself where he would not wed. To this day, Meara was the only woman he'd ever contemplated wedding, and the gods saw fit to keep that from happening.

Someone sabotaged them.

Who?

No one had been overly pleased over the prospect of making camp at Lilidbrugh, but no one—save Cameron—had opened his mouth to voice a complaint. By the same token, no one had any clue that he'd wished to remain, so hurrying their departure couldn't possibly be the reason behind the theft. Keane was half tempted to empty all their saddlebags, just to be certain the thief wasn't one among them, but if he did such a thing, without proof, there was no turning back from such an accusation. It would put their half-militant band of Scots out of their gourds. Already, they were edgy and ready to disband, partly because, until now, there had been no clear leader. This was something Keane intended to change.

His next thought was for Cameron, who seemed to have spent the entire night awake and brooding, if his look of fatigue was any indication. However, he was more than certain Cameron would never do such a thing. Even if they had no friendship between them at all, in a single word, Keane knew precisely what would keep him from sabotage: Cailin.

Which left Keane with three more possibilities, none of which were pleasing.

It could have been another one of his men, hoping to divert them from their destination, though if this was the case, that man would suffer right alongside them before he could fill his belly again. And it would be easy enough to catch someone if he kept sneaking away for a piss and a chew.

It could also be that their thief might be whomever was out there searching for Lianae, but then, why hadn't they made themselves known? Why come into a camp, steal food and naught else, then leave behind the very person they hoped to find?

Unless they hadn't realized Lianae was there, and simply needed supplies? But if they had followed her trail so far, why abandon any camp they encountered without learning something more than they already knew before they'd arrived?

Unless they knew she was here and were outnumbered and meant to dwindle their numbers—and in such case, why not take the horses as well as the food?

Nay. None of these scenarios made any sense, and the possibilities were endless.

The most reasonable explanation was that it was the men they'd been tracking before stumbling upon the ruins. If this were the case, mayhap it was not a matter of men stealing into their camp, but someone stealing out, and since all heads were presently accounted for, it could be they did, indeed, have a spy, after all—someone who'd snuck away in the middle of the night whilst they'd slept to rendezvous with the scouts, and then returned and slid himself back into his bed, hoping no one would be the wiser. But why take the rations? To give them supplies?

One thing was certain: The contents of their saddlebags didn't disappear by *magik*—no matter what Teasag claimed.

Whatever the reason for their rations' disappearance, they could no longer linger. They must go now and make use of whatever daylight hours they had remaining—which also meant that they didn't have the luxury of time to stick around and dig in the snow to locate coldstones. Keane loathed to disappoint the lass, but there was nothing to be done for it. He allowed Lianae to search while she could, rallying his men and readying the horses, never telling her that he intended to cut her time short, but she already knew.

She was on her knees, shoveling around heaps of snow and he cursed beneath his breath as he thought of her meal last night—and his own empty stomach—wondering how long she could make it in the saddle. Already, his belly was grumbling and with the storm, it was a waste of time to try to hunt. Even the squirrel he'd spied this morn was wise enough to find shelter. Tomorrow might be the soonest they could hunt a proper meal. He pulled Cameron aside, issuing orders privately, so as not to muddle things further between them. Loyal or not, Cameron would have his pride.

"When you have the occasion, check Murdock's and Brude' satchels. One or both have something to lose once we reach Dunràth." Both were under suspicion for treason, though as yet there was no proof.

"Should we press on?"

"Dunràth is but a day's ride at most. The entire point was to dawdle along the way, to lure out the spy, so nay. Rather I am thinking Dunloppe, where we can resupply."

"The men will suspect, since they have no knowledge of our mission. Why not Ailgin or Nairn—or even Keppenach? All these are closer and Jaime would see to our needs without question."

So would Broc, although Cameron clearly did not wish to involve his cousin. It just so happened that Dunloppe belonged to Broc Ceannfhionn, who ruled the fortress in the MacEanraig name. He followed David by oath, but not by blood. If Keane should feel the need to defy David over the girl, he wanted to be in the most neutral place. Pondering that fact, Keane looked over his shoulder at Lianae, who was still crawling about upon her hands and knees, rifling through drifts of snow. Her gown was now damp and her hair lashed about her face. Unmindful of the snow that pelted her in the pate, she continued to search.

He dared not go to Keppenach… not yet.

Jaime Steorling was far more loyal to David, and Keane didn't want to place his sister in a position to defy her husband.

"Dunloppe is the better choice," he maintained.

Cameron gave a nod, his jaw taut, and Keane knew he understood instinctively why he had chosen Dunloppe. For a moment, he appeared as though he wished to argue the point, and then he shook his head and walked away.

Keane understood the position he would be placing Broc in, but until he knew for certain what Lianae was running from, he didn't intend to place the girl at further risk. It couldn't be helped. Nor did he intend to simply hand her over to David. Alas, the last place he could take her was the safest place he could go: to the vale. Despite that his brother had never refused him aught, Keane knew very well that Aidan would refuse him this—although what *this* was, he wasn't entirely sure. In the end, all that would matter to Aidan was that Keane had brought conflict to his precious vale.

He gave Lianae until the final moments to search for her stones, and then Keane went to fetch her. "It's time to go," he said.

With the wind rising, it was nearly impossible to say whether she'd heard him or not, but she remained on her knees, tunneling desperately through the snow.

"Lianae," he said, louder this time. "The snow is much too thick, lass; you'll never find your stones."

When she wouldn't look up, Keane reached out to touch her arm. She shrugged him away. Refusing to be denied, Keane gripped her about the arm, gently drawing her to her feet. "It's time to go," he said again, more firmly.

Her eyes were full of unshed tears. "You promised!"

"I know I did, lass, and I had every intention of helping, but now it's time to go."

"Nay!" she shouted, shrugging away. "You go—I dinna have to!"

Only a madwoman would think to stay in this raging weather, without food and without shelter. Cailleach herself would have had naught to do with the place. The best thing they could do now would be to press on and find shelter elsewhere. It would be colder yet come nightfall, so Keane tilted the girl a sympathetic look, lifting a hand to her face, brushing a thumb against the bruise on her cheek. "Do ye truly mean to stay? I would not see you come to harm, Lianae."

He couldn't make her go—not without force—but he wasn't entirely certain he could walk away. If she forced him to decide one way or another, he would send the men away rather than force her where she would not go. But that would breed a whole new set of problems for them all. Fortunately, her anger seemed to melt away at Keane's touch. She lifted her hand to his. "Ye dinna ken," she said, her eyes beseeching him. "I *need* those stones."

"Why?"

"Because."

She guarded her mysteries as well as Dubhtolargg,

but Keane was no stranger to secrets. He could see them in her eyes, undecipherable as they were. "Are they worth your life, Lianae? What of the men who are after ye? Would ye have them find you here... *alone*?"

More than aught, Keane wanted to help her find her damned stones. In terms of gold, they were worth more than his horse, but this was not the time. The storm was worsening and they had one more mouth to feed and no rations to sustain them. As it was, Dunloppe was within two day's reach.

"We will come back," he said, and meant it. "I swear."

"We?"

"We," he affirmed with a nod. "Ye have my word, Lianae." And with that promise, she gave him a nod and then her hand.

CHAPTER NINE

We.

The way he'd said the word was strange to Lianae's ears.

Whilst her father and mother still lived, there had been a sense of *we,* but that *we* had been different somehow. Her father had been a leader of men, a lesser *Ri, a minor king,* and her mother, a woman who'd cared for his brood. That *we* was never the sum of two.

She contemplated this fact as she rode with Keane in the saddle. She rode behind him, his body shielding her from the worst of the storm. In keeping to the woodlands, they avoided the wind, but it also shielded them from whatever bit of sun there was to be had. Cold and wet, shivering, Lianae leaned against his back for warmth.

But she would not fool herself.

Wherever it was they were going, she was a heartbeat away from being returned to the Earl—like so much chattel. There were few enough of her people remaining and fewer yet who would be willing to risk the Scot's king's wrath. And yet staying in Lilidbrugh was not in her best interest either, whether or not Keane kept his promise to retrieve her charm stones.

After a mild beginning, winter was a raging boar. Every minute grew colder than the last. The simple flurries that had graced the sky yesterday evening had become cutting sheets of ice, bombarding them from a black and blue sky. They couldn't gather the camp quickly enough, and in a short time they were mounted and on the way.

Through it all, Lianae might as well have been a specter, for it was as though she were invisible to everyone, but Keane. None of the other men ever dared to look at her, much less talk to her or treat her unkindly, and she had a feeling she knew why.

Keane.

They feared him.

It was impossible to see aught past the length of one's hand, but she knew there were fourteen men in all. She spied only six—the one called Cameron, who every so oft cast Lianae dubious glances, and five others. These handful of men remained nearest to Keane, riding in a pack. The others lagged behind, forming yet another. And even surrounded by trees, the wind blew so furiously that Lianae had little choice but to put her arms about Keane's chest, tucking her cloak beneath her arms to keep it from billowing in the wind.

This morning's embrace had been so vastly different and the memory of it continued to warm her cheeks albeit nothing else. Fortunately, if he thought less of her for the liberties she had taken, he didn't say so, nor did he behave as though Lianae had offended him. If aught, he seemed even more solicitous, reaching back now and again to steady her in the saddle and to pull her legs close. Lianae didn't bother trying to speak to him, not even to thank him. Despite their proximity, he wouldn't have heard her anyway. Like an angry banshee, she heard only the wind shrieking past the trees.

Cold wind rushed up her skirts, and she tried to adjust them now and again so that they wrapped more firmly about her legs—as much to hide her bruises from prying eyes as to keep her legs warm. But no matter how many times she made the adjustment, her skirt billowed out with the wind, whipping furiously. And with every furlong they rode, she felt the loss of her stones more acutely. More than a few times she'd wanted to check to see that the remaining stones were still safe in her hem, but it was all she could do to stay warm in the saddle. Thankfully, Keane had allowed her keep his thick woolen breacan and her greatest solace was that she had his thick wool still wrapped about her feet. Savage or nay, the man was a godsend after all.

It was early afternoon before the winds began to ease and the sky turned some color besides rude grey. Finally, a hint of sun peeked out from between somber clouds and through the pine trees. After a while, a small grey hare raced before them, and Lianae's stomach complained loudly. "We'll stop soon," he said, patting her on the leg.

Realizing that he'd very likely heard her belly grumble, Lianae's cheeks burned. "Thank you," she said, and was grateful for his care. He had already done more for her than most men might do under the same circumstances. As yet, he'd not even asked her but once what she was doing so far from home. And truthfully, at the moment, she regretted having repaid his kindness with naught but rudeness when he'd inquired about her dress. "If you must know, I was to wed," she confessed belatedly.

He was quiet a long moment, and Lianae waited for him to speak, prepared to tell him anything he wished to know—apart from revealing who she was. It was the least she might do to make up for her rudeness and repay him for his kindness.

"Somehow, I dinna imagine ye a dutiful wife."

Lianae smiled, for she sensed 'twas not said as an insult. In fact, there seemed to be a note of admiration in his voice. "You flatter me, I believe."

In truth, she had never envisioned herself wed to some fat, greasy lord. It was always Elspeth who was meant to spend a dowry. Lianae had been more than content to tend her father's farm, and Óengus too seemed perfectly pleased to allow her to stay. Her mother had been the one who'd had other notions, for she'd longed for a passel of grandchildren. Because her sons hadn't seem overly inclined to give them to her, she'd hoped both Elspeth and Lianae would wed and soon.

"Is that why you fled? Because ye dinna wish to wed?"

"Nay." Lianae would have done so simply to please her mother. But up until a few days ago, she had never realized how cruel men could be. Fortunately, her mother had not lived to see Elspeth's sightless eyes, her bruised neck and blue lips.

Keane made no more inquiries, and Lianae didn't elaborate. Enough words had been spoken for now, and it eased her to know he would not pry. She rested her cheek against his back, stealing his warmth and allowing the steady beat of his heart to lull her back to sleep.

When she awoke after a while, she couldn't be certain how long she'd slept or how long they'd been in the saddle, only that her tummy was growling all the louder and that her lashes were frosting together. But the wind was now gone, and she could hear the crunch of hooves marching endlessly through the snow. This was something that amused her: In the stories her grandmother often told—of times long past—she'd spoken of Vikings marauders stealing quietly through the snow. In Lianae's experience, there was naught very quiet about snow. The sound was more a loud crunch, and just now, with fourteen horses and fifty-six legs, the din was relentless. But, alas, not louder than her wrathful stomach.

He patted her yet again. "Ye're awake?"

Lianae nodded sleepily. "But I wish I were not."

"Why lass?"

Swallowing with some difficulty, Lianae clung to his cloak lest she topple from the horse, weary from lack of food and sleep. Her stomach hurt, and everyone else's seemed equally as uncomfortable as hers, all except Keane's. "'Tis my belly," she said, despite that she suspected what ailed the men was something other than hunger.

"I am sorry, lass," he said. "'Tis the grouse, I suspect. We'll find something to settle your belly, I promise."

Lianae smiled, for he sounded like her mother, despite that he looked like a murdering savage. Not even her brothers had ever coddled her so, and she found herself wishing his men had not interrupted them this morning. The taste of his lips stayed with her and she didn't have to try to remember that tantalizing scent. She needed only but inhale a breath...

What would it be like to spend the rest of her days with a man like Keane?

Far better than with the Earl, that much was certain. Lianae had the sense that Keane would be quick to protect the people and things he valued most, unafraid to stand up to men like William fitz Duncan. *Unlike her brother Lulach.* And he was handsome, as well, even without any finery and garbed as he was in rudimentary clothes—like some warrior of old.

In fact, he reminded her a bit of the Viking warriors her grammy had gone on about, except that he was darker in countenance, not golden haired—more like the Painted Ones who'd once inhabited these Highlands before. They were gone now, although Lianae sensed they were still around, like the men and women of Moray, hiding in plain sight.

Of course, it was better for the people of Moray to hide. There weren't enough of them now to stand against the usurpers. But the next thing one knew, the Moraymen would all be gone, and if any remained—like Lulach—they would keep their fancy clothes and attend their fancy chapels, and raise their sons and daughters to be good little Sassenachs. This was the destiny she envisioned... unless she could find Ewen and Graeme and they could restore the Mormaerdom. She liked to imagine them as hundreds strong now... waiting for the chance to rise up and retake what belonged her people.

As soon as Lianae had the chance, she would retrieve those charm stones and find a way to reach other brothers. There might be enough coin left over that she could donate to their cause.

"How many did you recover?" Keane asked, as though he'd read her mind.

"Five," Lianae replied.

"How many did you have before?"

"Twelve."

She felt more than saw him nod and once again she rested her chin on the small of his back. "You know what they are?"

"I do," he confessed.

"Ha' ye ever seen any before now?"

"I have."

"Ach, do ye speak more than two words at a time?"

"I do," Keane said again, and once again, she sensed rather than saw him smile. It was there, in the tone of his voice. The muscles of his chest seemed to relax beneath her hands.

Lianae laughed softly, wondering why he'd been so

reluctant to take what she'd offered him this morn. Did he have a wife already? That possibility both pleased and frustrated her at once, for she had never known a man to be so loyal to his woman—and this must be a good thing, though now that she had set her sights on gaining Keane's protection, she needed his heart to be free. "So, then... if you're so fond o' women, ye must be wed?"

KEANE'S LIPS curved over the arrogantly phrased question and the unmasked curiosity in her voice. She said it rather like a statement, as though there could be no other cause for his shooing her out of his bed. And aye, he knew intuitively that's what her question was all about: *that kiss.* "I am not," he replied.

He felt her sigh—a long, hot breath against the small of his back. He felt it penetrate the layers of his garb. "Well, there we have three words," she said, and Keane couldn't quite suppress his mirth.

His shoulders shook with laughter. "Nay, lass," he said, to be clearer. "I am no' wed."

Perhaps it was his imagination, but she seemed to scoot a wee bit closer after his admission and, despite the relenting weather, that fact pleased him more than he could say.

"And you are certain you're no pillow biter?"

Once again, Keane stifled his laughter, clearing his throat. "Quite certain."

"I see we're back to two words. Does it anger you for me to ask?"

"Why should it anger me? If you're curious, how else will ye know if ye dinna ask?"

She sighed again, leaning her sweet cheek against his back, and Keane inhaled a deep, heady breath, enjoying the feel of her. "That's what I used to tell my da," she said. "When he complained I asked too many questions."

"Used to?" Keane peered over his shoulder, glimpsing the top of her pale red curls.

"Aye."

"Is he no longer with us?"

"Aye."

"And your minny?"

"Dead."

"Ach now, Lianae, do ye speak more than one word at a time?"

She laughed quickly, and the sound was like music to Keane's ears.

"Ha'e ye anyone left?"

Her lean arms encircled his chest—a gesture that felt not unlike a hug, and the sensation gave Keane a strange lump in his throat. But he sensed her answer before she spoke again, and it filled him with sadness.

What must it be like to be truly alone?

He'd often thought of himself as alone, but the truth of the matter was that Keane had kinfolk who loved him and who would welcome him home no matter the circumstances.

"No," she said after a long moment.

"No brothers, no sisters?"

"I *had* three brothers, one sister."

She didn't offer up any more information and it took Keane a long moment to vanquish the instinct not to pry.

"I've been told my brothers and my sire all fell at Stracathro in Forfarshire, and my mother—well, she died three years past."

"And your sister?"

"Murdered."

Keane didn't anticipate that answer, and sensing they were venturing into painful territory, he refrained from making jokes about her return to one-word answers. And yet she seemed in the mood to talk, and so he asked the one question he wished to know. "Tell me, lass... who were you running from?"

Her entire body shuddered, and her fingers unlocked about his chest, her hands falling away, though she didn't answer and Keane frowned.

"If ye dinna tell me, ye'll leave me with no choice but to hand you over to the king."

Her tone was flippant now. "And is that what you do with all the strange women you encounter?"

"Of course not."

"Why then would ye turn me over to *your* king."

There was naught simple about the girl, Keane decided. And, in fact, she might be the most complicated woman he'd ever met—his sisters included. As for the barb—although it wasn't meant to be one, he took offense at her reference to *his* king. David mac Maíl Choluim was not his king.

And then there was this: There were some who as yet did not welcome David's rule—particularly in Moray—but more and more every day the choice was no longer their own. David mac Maíl Choluim had won himself Northhampton and Huntingdon, as well as most of the lowlands. Now, after the victory at Stracathro in Forfarshire, he ruled Moray as well as much of the Highlands. After all these years, he could rightly call himself the High King of the Scots and Chief of Chiefs. Whether Lianae had intended to or not, she had revealed much to him with her simple question, and now more than before he was glad he'd chosen Dunloppe as their immediate destination. And still he pressed her. "*My* king?"

He heard the resentment in her tone. "Well, he is, is he not?"

"David mac Maíl Choluim *is* the rightful king of

Scotia," he told her. It was true, whether they liked it or not. "He *is* your king as well." He waited to see if she would take offense over that.

But she said naught, nor did she return to her current resting position and Keane felt the separation acutely. It was a strange feeling, considering that he had known the lass less than a day. But now his curiosity was piqued: Who was she that she would not accept David mac Maíl Choluim as her rightful king?

She was dressed like an Englishwoman—or at least a Scot under the Scot's king's banner. But she'd called herself a maid of Moray… not *de Moray,* in the Norman fashion as was *de rigueur* these days. At first hearing the small distinction might not mean overmuch, for only a highborn woman would intentionally style herself *de Moray*. As a commoner, she might easily say she was a maid of Moray and yet… as a highborn, to use Norman distinction—or not—was quite telling. With the death of Óengus of Moray, William fitz Duncan had attempted to adopt the title of Mormaer, but the people revolted, despite that Fitz Duncan was a Morayman by blood. His father was the King, deposed by MacBeth. By all rights, the throne of Scotia could have been his for the taking, and yet he'd aligned him with David instead—a move that had made him wildly unpopular in the North and led to a revolt, five years past—a battle Keane had refused to enter, for he considered the men of Moray to be his kindred far more so than any of the tribes of Scotia.

Keane was a man of few words, as his men could attest, but he was also quite keenly aware that silence spoke volumes. They rode in silence now, whilst he contemplated the subtlety of words… those spoken and those unspoken as well.

CHAPTER TEN

It was not Aidan's way to rush straight to the *uisge*, but Lìli understood why he did so today. She had a mighty yen for it herself.

He was not pleased.

She was not pleased.

"She's but a child," Lìli argued.

"Her name is Constance, Lìli, and they are nearly the same age."

Her mood soured even more. Rarely did her husband ever speak her name, not like *that*. She was most often his *sweetling*—never Lìli with that horribly impatient tone.

They had returned from Chreagach Mhor, with a surprise en tow. Her husband and son were home in one piece—thank God—but her son Kellen had brought along with him a wife.

A wife!

To Lìli's way of thought, this was taking charity a bit too far. They'd gone merely to carry supplies to an allied clan, and she had supported this rare show of solidarity in her husband, but *this* was not what she had anticipated when she'd agreed he should leave the vale so close to the birth of their new bairn. "That is not the point," Lìli argued, as Aidan poured himself a dram.

Already, her son had been deprived his birthright with the enfeoffment of Keppenach to Jaime Steorling —not that she begrudged Jaime the keep. Her son would not have been old enough to accept his patrimony for many, many years, and in the meantime, the demesne would have remained unsecured or fallen to ruin. But she'd had modest hopes for Kellen's future, and now they were all dashed. Someday, her father would die, and as yet Padruig had begot himself no heirs. It seemed that God had cursed him for his evil ways, and made him barren as a brick. Because of this, Kellen should have married well enough to put him in a position to inherit what Lìli could not. Her father might loathe her still—he might even count Lìli amongst his greatest enemies for what he had considered a betrayal—but she was still a child of his blood. She was a Caimbeul whether he liked it or not.

But of course, she was content here in Dubhtolargg. It wasn't that. It was merely that a man without a demesne was ever destined to serve others, and even where there was no greed, or ambition, it undermined the relationship even so. Much as she loathed the truth of this fact, she saw the way it had separated Aidan and Keane—brothers who had once been inseparable. A boy could not become a man until he left his father's house and someday Kellen must make his own way, whether Aidan agreed or not.

At any rate, Dubhtolargg was no longer the safe haven it once was. Slowly but surely the world was encroaching upon them—more surely than only a few weeks before, for here, now, was yet another mouth to feed.

But a new bride?

Did Aidan truly mean to gift them Lael's cottage?

Outside the protection of the crannóg? Already Cailin had insisted upon her own home. Next it would be Ria and then the babe, and then she and Aidan would inhabit the crannóg all alone. It was far too cavernous for just two people!

Aidan lifted his tankard to his lips, quaffing the *uisge* down, his body tense. Lìli felt the tension as well—in her belly, wherein she ought not feel it right now. They rarely ever argued. That she must needst greet her husband with harsh words, especially now when she was so grateful to see him, upset her more than he could know.

Out in the hall, her son sat cooing over his sweet new bride. She was lovely, in truth, but the thought of Kellen bearing bairns of his own—well, he was only a boy!

"Why di' ye not say nay, Aidan?"

His stark green eyes begged her to understand. "The evidence was indisputable, Lìli, particularly since Kellen admitted to the deed wi' his own two lips. Would ye have me begin a feud with the MacKinnons?"

"Well, nay," Lìli confessed. "Though ye should ha—"

"I should have what? What choice did I have, my love?" Once again, his gaze begged her to understand, and Lìli's shoulders fell despondently. Tears pricked at her eyes. She moved backwards and sat on the bed, feeling weak in the knees as she tried to make sense of all she'd heard. Her son was found in the arms of a girl —both cuddled together in a loft atop the MacKinnon's stable. Hair mussed, clothes full of bits of hay. They'd been left all alone to fondle each other, and who knew what more!

But who had been watching them all the while? No one, this much was clear! And yet… it was true… he was not a wee bairn to be coddled all the time. She must confess at least this much. "What if she is already pregnant?" Lìli worried.

Her husband tilted her a sympathetic look, appealing to Lìli's sense of fair-mindedness. "Then we will have a new grandson afore long." His beautiful, full lips turned up at one corner, as though to wrest a smile from hers.

Feeling cantankerous, Lìli's hand went to her belly. "Ach, Aidan! We will have a child and a grandchild both nearly the same age."

Aidan shrugged. "Surely we will not be the first?"

Defeated by her husband's sense of reason—and the soft lilt of his gentle words—Lìli lay back upon the bed, with one hand splayed upon her belly, surrendering to the facts. "But he is not ready to be a father," she whined.

Her husband's tone was calm and reassuring. "Kellen is a fine lad. He'll make a good husband and a verra good da." And then he reminded her, "He is only two years older than I was when I became laird of this clan."

Lìli considered that truth as well. On that day when her father betrayed the dún Scoti clan, Aidan took up his sword beside his father as a youth of ten and four, and then after his father was slain, he became chief. So, aye, two years younger than Kellen. It was a sad, sad story—one her husband might never have forgiven her for, and yet he had.

Unbidden, Lìli pictured her sire looming over Aidan's father's body, his long grey beard splattered with blood. Padruig Caimbeul had gone to Dubhtolargg under the pretense of friendship, supping at their table and partaking of their ale and then altogether, he and his warriors had risen up in the midst of the festivities and slaughtered half the dún Scoti clansmen whilst their noses were deep in their cups. It was the gravest of transgressions amongst Highlanders—to shed innocent blood under another mon's roof when one was invited in friendship, and for that alone, her father would rot in hell.

And to imagine... all this her father had done without any knowledge about the stone hidden here in the vale. They had come simply to appease their monstrous pride—to say they had driven the heir of Black Tolargg to his knees. They'd defiled Aidan's mother, left her with a babe in her belly. And that babe was Sorcha, although Sorcha did not realize the truth of her patrimony as yet. Lìli had been sworn to secrecy—as was the rest of the clan—until the day Aidan determined it best to reveal this news. Alas, insofar as transgressions went, Lìli was hardly in a position to hurl any stones.

Reading her so well, and sensing the turn of her thoughts, her husband came and sat beside her on the bed, caressing her thigh.

Lìli smiled, despite her quarrel with him, for she knew him so well. Whenever he touched her belly, he was content to be a father. When he avoided that round, unavoidable, lump that was her belly, he was in the mood for something else...

He continued to caress her thigh. "Will you forgive me?" he asked. "I have missed ye so, my *sweetling*."

Lìli inhaled a breath. She was not an old woman, and despite that she had two children and another on the way, she refused to behave like an old woman. In response to his sweet words, she spread her legs a bit—an invitation, if he should like to take it. She was still too vexed to confess it, but she would welcome Aidan's peace offering.

Her husband chuckled. "I take it you're pleased to see me, despite our son's indiscretions?"

Of course, she was pleased to see him—so pleased,

that her nipples tightened beneath her gown, aching to be set free. Pouting still, Lìli turned her head. "I am pleased," she said, and then spread her legs a little wider. "I suppose he is a man, after all, and men will do what they are led to do."

The wicked gleam that returned to her husband's bright green eyes nearly stole her breath away. "And what are men led to do?"

"Things they ought not," she answered coyly.

"Like this?" He snuck a long finger up the hem of her gown and Lìli's breath caught on a gasp. There he teased her inner thigh. "Should I not do this?"

As an answer, Lìli spread her legs a little wider, reaching down to pull up her gown, but slowly, teasingly, enjoying the feel of the soft wool sliding up the length of her skin.

Aidan chuckled darkly, and stood, looking down on her on their bed.

Lìli had been feeling quite frisky, cleaning everything within sight. The room was cozy with a fire she'd had waiting now for days. Even after all these years, she felt little doves fly inside her breast at the sight of her husband undressing so purposefully before her. He was not a man who shied away from pleasures of the flesh.

At six and thirty, Aidan was still darkly handsome, his hair as black as raven's wings. His green eyes boldly inspected her, ravaging her body without ever touching her. And yet she felt his gaze as surely as she would his big, strong hands.

As he looked down upon her, he took himself into his hands, teasing her. "Is this what you want, Lìli?"

He stood bare skinned now, his body tinted copper by the firelight and he began to stroke the length of his shaft, smiling wickedly as his thumb caressed the glossy tip.

Gooseflesh erupted over Lìli's flesh, and she licked

her lips gone dry, but she knew something more than she once did about pleasing her lover and she smiled back, nodding only once.

That was all it took.

Her husband fell to one knee… intending to kiss her until she became wet. He loved the taste of her, or so he'd said. But she was already wet, didn't he realize? From the instant she'd spied that gleam in his eye and the first naughty turn of his familiar lips. Arching into his soft mouth, she reveled in the heat of his tongue…

Aye, this was a fine way to end an argument… a fine way to greet her husband… and, even if she didn't crave him deep inside her—which she did—she would have let him take her if only for the simple fact that she wanted this babe born.

Right now.

"Make love to me, Husband," she demanded.

Ever dutiful, and never inclined to disobey… Aidan hooked his arms beneath her knees and pulled her to the edge of the bed, wasting little time in giving her his warm, thick flesh. Lìli felt him slide inside and melted into the bed.

I am his master and he is the master of me.

So it was, and so it should be.

CHAPTER ELEVEN

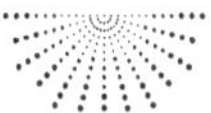

Dunloppe was another two day's ride southwest, near the borderlands.

But if Cameron was angered over the destination and turn of events, he didn't say so, nor did he give any appearance of undermining Keane's authority. He remained steadfast, quieter than usual, but otherwise not much changed. Considering that Keane was battling the weather, he was grateful not to have to wage war with his friend, or his men.

By late afternoon, the mesnie was weary and ready to make camp. Keane recognized the signs of their exhaustion in the slumping of their shoulders. And although like Cameron, no one spoke a word in complaint, they were forced to make quite a few unforeseen stops along the way. But this fact was ever telling: whatever proclivity these men once had toward whining, it was thoroughly quashed. Keane wasn't sure that was entirely a good sign, though at least they no longer had the propensity to test the leadership. And yet it would behoove him to see to their needs, because if there was one thing he'd learned: unhappy men were all too eager to leave. While stopping early for the day was hardly optimal, no good would come of pressing on.

Like the men, Lianae too endured without complaint. She rode behind him companionably, her mood far less contentious than yestereve.

They found a spot near a grove of whitebeam trees. With the mild winter, they'd had a late bloom and the boughs still held their clusters of bright red fruit. Like rowan berries, whitebeam was generally harvested after the first frost, once they'd had a chance to properly blet. He suspected they would be good and soft by now, and perhaps even sweet. The bletted berries would make a soothing tea to soothe their aching bellies. But he was perplexed as to why they were all ill, when Keane was not. If the supplies had not been stolen he might not be so quick to cry foul play, though as it was, it gave him reason to suspect. Could someone have meant to poison them? Or mayhap it was simply the grouse, which he'd had none of because he'd given his share to Lianae. Now his belly was grumbling louder than Taranis. A red blur raced across the snow, darting into a nearby thicket. A red fox was after a meal, and so too was Keane. If he waited much longer, he was liable to consume his own limbs. He gave a sign to the men, and found a good spot to tether the horses. And then he helped Lianae dismount before taking Cameron aside. "I've a taste for something more than grouse," he said.

Automatically, Cameron's gaze slid to Lianae and then back, clearly mistaking his meaning.

"Food," Keane snapped, and Cameron smirked. Little amused by the direction of his friend's thoughts, he commanded, "Take Murdoch and Brude, see what ye can find to eat."

Cameron peered over his shoulder at Brude. "Why them?"

"Because they are better archers than you, and because we're better off not letting them out of our sight," Keane explained, and then he challenged his old friend with a winning smile. "I'll take the lass. Let's see who comes back with the better feast."

Cameron lifted both brows. "Three men to your one? Di' your minny e'er teach ye modesty, my friend?"

Even as long as they'd known each other, Cameron probably didn't realize that Keane's mother was dead by the time he was two, his father before he was one. Aside from his brother, who'd had his hands full with the rule of the clan, and Una, who'd spoken mostly with the butt of her staff, no one ever told him aught. Keane fished his bow and his arrow out of its fittings and slid the quiver onto his back, ignoring the barb, returning yet another. "Think you can bring back something other than grouse? Judging by the number of times we stopped today, the last one nearly killed us."

"Save for ye?"

"Aye, well, I gave mine to the lass." He flicked a glance toward Lianae to find her petting Beithir, and he felt a warm glow in his breast.

"She looks well enough to me?"

"I dinna give her much." Yet it made Keane wonder... He cast another glance at Murdoch, who now seemed perfectly hale. And unlike the others, he was the only one, aside from Keane and Lianae, who'd not needed to stop and seek his privacy along the way, despite the fact that he'd complained about a bellyache. Lianae, he understood, for she'd barely had enough to eat, but Murdoch was the one who'd hunted for their supper last eve. He and Alick had jointly prepared the food. Murdoch would have had first dibs at his share of the meat. And he was the one who'd been caught rifling through supplies this morning—as though he were still hungry. But if he'd stolen their provisions, he would also have known that none remained. Perhaps the two events were not connected?

"What's the winning prize?"

Keane grinned. It wasn't going to be the command of the men. That particular prize was already won, and now there was far too much at stake. "The loser will give up half rations to the winners. I vow I would eat a cow this night," he said.

Cameron lifted a brow. "Does that include the girl's share?"

"Nay," Keane replied and his tone brooked no argument. Remembering the way Lianae had devoured her meal last eve, he was certain she needed all the sustenance she could get. If it came down to it, he'd give her his share yet again, though he had little doubt over the outcome of his wager, even with the odds stacked against him. Not a one of these men—not even Cameron—had his skill with the bow. For the most part, they were all more adept with their swords.

Cameron assessed him, his look discerning, though Keane didn't much care what conclusions he came to. He intended to look after Lianae, come what may, for she was the entire reason he'd risen to this task in the first place.

"Vera well," Cameron relented. "We have a bargain." And he smiled as he turned away, marching over to Brude and then to Murdoch, rallying both men to his cause. Keane watched all three disappear into the woods, laughing as they went, and then made his way over to Teasag.

"See to the horses and start a fire. Send Wee Alick to gather firewood, then tell Donal I said to boil a bit of water." Whitebeam could be bitter, but they would thank him profusely once the tea was brewed. At the moment, he was more than grateful for his brother's wife's knowledge of simples. Lìli had taught him much these ten years past.

Once he was finished ordering the men, he found Lianae seated upon a rock, her legs crossed and her feet up out of the wet snow. He could scarce blame her. Glenna's wool was weather tight, but it was not leather, and hardly meant to be used for shoes.

"How are your feet?" he asked.

Her golden eyes were wide, her pupils dark. "Better," she said softly.

"Well enough to walk?"

She nodded, and Keane took her by the hand.

"Where are we going?"

"To hunt for supper."

She was lovely in this winter light. Her golden-red curls were beautifully mussed and her pale blue gown gave her face an ethereal pallor, like a milk-skinned faerie. "What shall we hunt?" she asked, hobbling along beside him.

"Hare, if we're lucky," he said.

"And if we're not?"

He smiled a little crookedly. "Grouse."

She smiled back. "Grouse is good," she said.

He supposed that right about now, everything sounded good to the lass, but they'd probably steer clear of the grouse.

Unaccustomed to walking with women—particularly one who was injured—Keane's steps were too long and his gait too quick, so he let go of her hand and stopped to give her a rest, making a pretense of inspecting the string of his bow. He peered down at her feet—at the unraveling cloth—and frowned. Hooking his bow over his shoulder, he swept her up into his arms. "But first we have something else to attend."

Squawking in surprise, Lianae wrapped her hands

about Keane's neck. That too made him frown, although not because he didn't like the feel of her warm, sweet fingers at his nape...

His sisters were all entirely self-sufficient. He wasn't accustomed to thinking about the discomfort of others, and he wondered how much he'd already overlooked. Clearly, Lianae wasn't spoiled, but he must make an effort to anticipate her needs—although why he should feel inclined to do so for a woman he barely knew and would likely never see again once he found her a safe haven, he didn't particularly know. Ever since yesterday, it was a growing need, and it was a longing he was wholly unaccustomed to.

As they neared the whitebeam trees, replete with their bright red fruit all topped with tiny white hoods, she marveled aloud. "How lovely!"

Grunting his agreement, Keane put her down beneath a snow-laden branch to gain his bearings, and to search for the brook. She had yet to tell him any of the troubles she'd endured, but he suspected she'd been through quite an ordeal, and still she marveled over simple berries.

Inspecting a low-lying branch, she placed her hand gingerly beneath the crimson fruit, and the look on her face was full of wonder. "I take it ye have been here before?"

"Once."

"When?"

"On the way north."

"Oh," she said and plucked the frozen bunch from the branch. Afterward, she stood inspecting the berries, squishing one between her fingers and lifting a finger to her lovely mouth to taste the juice. The small gesture made his cock twitch and that simple fact annoyed him beyond measure.

Remembering the way to the burn, he lifted her up

once again without a word of warning and carried her down. There, he settled her next to a large boulder then slid his bow from his shoulder and set it down beside her.

"I am *not* an invalid," she complained.

Confused by his own actions, Keane didn't immediately respond.

Indeed, she was not. She had come miles on her own without shoes, cutting her feet along the way. It shouldn't be much of a surprise that she hadn't yet griped. But he couldn't seem to stop thinking about her —or anything else, aside from the taste of her lips.

She had kissed him so unexpectedly this morn, arousing his hunger, and it had taken him a long, intoxicating moment to realize what she would do, and then something snapped inside him. He wanted to taste her body with a fierceness he had never known—the same way she craved the taste of those berries. But the truth was, not all whitebeam berries were sweet, and still some part of him craved to know what he would get with Lianae.

Would she be bitter in the end?

Would he crave her only to be denied?

Keane was not the sort of man to sew his seed with abandon. He wanted to bed her, aye, but he wanted to keep her as well—and that was unreasonable. She was not a dog to be leashed and, besides, he had no home to provide her.

Which only led him to wonder what the devil he was doing taking her to Dunloppe. What was Broc supposed to do with the lass? Was he merely hoping that the further they traveled together the more time he could give himself to figure it all out? Did he think he would find a way to convince her to stay with him, even despite that he had nothing to his name? She was a woman of substance, he was certain, and he was a border guard, with naught but a bunch of men to his name. The more he thought about it all, the less clearly he could think, and so he ought not be thinking at all.

Stooping to test the water's temperature, Keane peered up at Lianae and swallowed the lump that appeared in his throat. The look of innocence she gave him felled him more swiftly than any seduction ever could. Finding it difficult to speak, he waved a hand at the boulder where he'd lain down his bow. "Sit," he demanded, more harshly than he'd intended.

For an instant, he thought she would protest, but she lifted a golden brow and limped to the boulder without a word. She sat down. "*Tha thu a' dèanamh cus odharmanachaidh,*" she said, without much heat and a bit of a smirk.

Keane reached out to snag her right foot, without bothering to ask, irritated with his own lack of wits. "Clearly, you speak the old tongue."

"Of course—and ye must as well?"

"Aye."

She sounded coy. "Well, what did I say?"

Keane continued unwrapping the wool around her foot. "You said I was officious."

She laughed. "And ye are."

Keane shrugged, despite that his lips maintained a hint of a smile—until he saw the bottom of her foot in the broad light of day. It wasn't infected yet, though it was filthy, and the wounds were filled with debris. He marveled that she hadn't complained even once, not even with the bitter cold. His own feet were drier than hers, wrapped in boot leather, and his toes were half numb.

He jerked her foot down a bit more roughly than he'd intended to, furious with himself for not asking after her comfort long before now. Splashing cold water over her foot, he washed it as best as he could, massaging it carefully to be certain the blood was flowing well. He worked quickly, plucking out the tiny rocks he encountered, and then shook out the wool and rewrapped her foot, doing the same again with her left foot, vowing to see them both wrapped more thoroughly once they returned to camp. Glenna's wool was tightly woven, weather tight and warm, but it was still permeable and there was only so much of his breacan he could rent, without leaving her with little to warm the rest of her body. But he could dry her bindings near the fire and rewrap the foot again once the cloth was toasty and warm. Later, he would find her a pair of shoes. He didn't give a bloody damn what his men thought as he catered to the lass. Let one of them speak out of turn.

It didn't occur to him to wonder why he believed she would be with him long enough to supply her with shoes... he felt connected to the lass in a way he had never quite experienced before. In fact, come to think of it, this was the first time in his life he had ever taken responsibility for anyone besides himself—at least insomuch that he knew he must be the one to care for her, above all others, and even above himself.

It was a long, long moment before he realized that the copse had grown quiet, all but for the tinkling of the brook. Her hand rested upon the boulder, half holding her branch of frozen berries. If she should happen to twitch her fingers, they would drop onto the snow. Keane peered up at her with a longing so great he could scarce defy it.

She had a glimmer of tears in her eyes and she swallowed once before trying to speak. "'Tis been overlong since anyone looked after me this way, Keane. Thank you."

Keane did know what to say. His throat felt suddenly too thick to speak. It only seemed like the right and natural thing to do, but when she put it that way, it made him feel as though he'd somehow overstepped his bounds… or taken on responsibility he ought not. "'Tis no more than I would do for any lass," he reassured her.

"I see," she replied, and the glassy look in her eyes vanished. She lifted up her berries, inspecting them closer with a look of disappointment in her amber eyes.

They could hear men chattering in the near distance, but here, the air was so still and thick Keane could cut it with a blade. "Those are whitebeams."

"Yes, I know," she said tightly, and Keane welcomed the icier tone, for he knew far better how to deal with her anger than he did her gratitude.

In fact, Lianae didn't know.

She had never seen such bright red berries so full and bletted during the ides of winter. There were many such berries she recognized, but not this one.

It wasn't his all-knowing attitude that perturbed her —or his officious demeanor. Rather, it was the notion that he did not particularly feel drawn to her… as she was to him.

Not since her family had been wrested from her so rudely had Lianae known such a gentle hand. Truth to tell, there was something about Keane that made her wish for things she ought not want—and yet she barely knew this man.

It was too easy to forget.

"They make a good tea to settle the belly," he said matter of factly, dropping her bound foot, as though she were a child who'd needed help to dress.

Lianae was a woman grown, and yet he did not seem to notice this fact, and it annoyed her immensely. She was hardly the beauty Elspeth had been, but she wasn't an ogre either. Some men thought her pretty, and some even said so.

Gruaidh may not be able to bear your children, nor is she quite so... pleasing.

Neither is your sister once she opens her mouth.

Lianae frowned, remembering William fitz Duncan's words. "Do you think me ugly?" she asked, before she could think to stop herself. She had never learned how to be any other way, but direct—not even when it was clearly in her benefit to keep her mouth shut. She should have learned that lesson from her dealings with the Earl, and yet... she *must* know.

Both Keane's brows shot up, and his eyes nearly crossed. It might have been a comical sight, if Lianae hadn't been waiting so breathlessly for his answer. "No," he said after a moment, composing himself. "How do your feet feel?"

"Lovely," she replied. *Not nearly so battered as her ego.*

Wrathfully, Lianae squished a berry between her thumbs, and then tossed the detritus away rather petulantly, thinking herself a silly little fool for considering such things as *feelings*, when only yesterday she had escaped a fate worse than death.

She plucked another berry and lifted it to her mouth to test it with her tongue. "Are they bitter?" she asked, sounding bitter herself.

Keane rose from his knees. "Sometimes."

"This one is sweet," she said, sliding the berry over her tongue.

"Is it?"

"Aye."

He wrapped his hand about her wrist and gently tugged her up. "There's a much better way to eat them," he said.

Lianae dared to look Keane in the eyes. They were so green... as green as a new leaf in spring, and the black of his pupils were inordinately large—as deep and dark as Lilidbrugh's well. If she leaned just a bit, she might fall deep inside and be irrevocably lost.

Plucking the entire bunch of berries from her hand, Keane pinched off a tiny piece of fruit, biting it gently, as though to test it for himself, never leaving her gaze. "Sweet," he agreed, and then his lips turned up slightly at one corner.

Something about the look in his eyes gave Lianae a little start. Her heart kicked against her ribs as he leaned toward her, so slowly, staring intently into her eyes, as though she were a rabbit and he were a wolf, willing her to stay and be his prey.

She would do it, she realized.

He but needed to ask.

And then he pulled her close, offering Lianae the berry with his mouth, pressing her close until she parted her lips to receive the fruit. Once she did so, he pushed the juice and the berry deep into her mouth.

For a long moment, Lianae forgot to breathe.

His soft, warm tongue explored the depths of her mouth with barely restrained hunger, brushing softly across her trembling lips and then sliding across the ridge of her teeth. The sensation gave her a strange little quiver. Warmth filled her breast and slid… *lower.*

Never in her life had she felt such a heady, silvery warmth. It flowed into her most private regions like warm honey. The berry melted into the depths of her mouth, and after a moment, he pulled away, and looked her straight in the eyes.

"Lianae," he whispered.

"Aye?"

"Did that seem to ye like a mon who thinks ye ugly?"

For a long, long moment, the world fell into a hush

as the sound of her own blood rushed through her ears. Her heart pounded furiously.

A short distance away, she could hear the sound of laughter, the sound traveling from their camp. He gave her a playful wink. "Now let's get some dinner," he suggested.

CHAPTER TWELVE

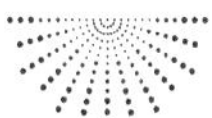

Keane brought back the biggest haul—two hares, one grouse, and to be certain no one had any doubt who'd won the contest, he added a squirrel to the pile of meat to be prepared.

The grouse could not be helped, for it seemed to dance along before him, as though to tempt him. Even when he turned his back on the creature, it circled about, fluttering its wings and undermining his resolve —not unlike Lianae.

He tried his best to ignore the promise of her lips, the taste of her mouth, but in the end, he realized he was weak. His stomach grumbled, reminding him of its emptiness, and he reared back his bow, let loose the arrow, and in the end, the grouse lay skewered for the taking. And yet, despite his hunger for actual food, all he could think about was the taste of Lianae's mouth.

She was a distraction to be sure.

He'd asked her to pick and carry back a hem full of berries. Whilst Wee Alick and Donal skinned, gutted and cooked the spoils of their hunt, Keane brewed a bit of tea.

Like the rowan berries, whitebeam could have an adverse effect if too many were eaten fresh, but once the seeds were plucked and the bletted fruit was boiled, the bitters produced would quickly settle the stomach. A wee bit would do them, and with a good night's rest, by the morrow they would all be rested and ready to travel.

As Keane prepared the tea, his gaze reverted to Lianae more often than it should have. Together they'd made a fine team. She was not at all like his sister, Cailin, who competed with him shoulder to shoulder for each and every kill. Nay, Lianae had served him well as his eyes and ears. "Look!" she would say. "A hare!" And then she would watch whilst Keane found the beast in his sights, and clapped exuberantly when the animal was won. He must confess he liked having her at his side, and he found himself driven to keep her safe. But bedamned if kissing her again hadn't been a heinous mistake, for now he could think of little else. Taking a chug of the whitebeam tea only made him hard. She sat beside him now, laughing softly whilst the men all sang a bawdy song, sharing from a single flask of bitter tea. Turn by turn, they hoarded the warm tin, rolling it greedily between their fists.

The moon was high tonight, the stars all visible within a mostly clear sky. With a wee bit of luck, they would be spared any more inclement weather and sometime on the day thereafter they would arrive at Dunloppe. By then, Keane might better determine what to do with the lass.

"And what's it ye say the whitebeam is good for?" Brude asked.

"Stopping up your arse," replied Murdoch with a bark of laughter.

The men all laughed and Keane chuckled low, casting another glance at Lianae to find her blushing fiercely.

She leaned close. "Mayhap I need a moment *alone*..."

Even under the moonlight, Keane could see that her cheeks were bright—as bright as the berries had been—and he caught her meaning at once. He had to force himself not to go along with her, not really wanting her out of his sight. "Dinna go far," he cautioned.

"I can take care of myself," she said, rising and smoothing down her skirts. She smiled at Keane—a devastating smile—and turned on her heels, then hobbled away, her gait much improved.

REPLETE, and needing no more tea, Lianae rose from her spot beside Keane. Pulling her cloak together—first the breacan he'd given her and had never taken back, and then her cloak—she ambled away from the easy, companionable chatter of men.

Making her way quickly away from the glow of the camp fire, she felt giddy, even without the aid of spirits and deep down, she realized it must be *that kiss*—that remarkable moment by the brook, when Keane touched his lips to her own. He had a way about him that made her melt into his arms, and even now, her legs felt like pudding beneath her as she searched about for a secluded place to minister to her needs.

Forsooth, when she considered where she'd been only yesterday, the gods had surely blessed her. Of all the men she might have happened upon in her flight, she had somehow found *him*. Keane was a good man, she decided. Fair-minded. Strong and capable and ready to do his duty. Humble enough—but just enough. Although no one would ever accuse the man of lacking confidence. He exuded it from every pore of his being, and still there was little arrogant about him. He was born to lead, and she watched his every gesture with a sense of wonder. He did not shout his men down, nor did he toss them about with threats. He spoke firmly, issuing commands without a backward glance to see that any were obeyed. And then in the same breath, he showed kindness, caring for them as a mother might. Lianae supposed she understood why, for it made one feel as though he valued them. And even she felt as though she belonged with him—as though she had known him for years—as though he were her devoted guardian.

It was a strange feeling.

Although she realized she shouldn't dwell on him overmuch, it couldn't be helped when the first thing he'd done upon returning to camp—even before preparing food or boiling their tea—was unwrap Lianae's foot and set her bindings to dry near the fire.

Despite that the wool was weather-tight, it grew damp whenever she walked in them too long, and he'd promised to find her a good pair of shoes the instant he could. Once the bindings were dry, Lianae had insisted upon wrapping her feet herself. Not even her mother had coddled her quite so much!

And despite all that she was feeling, she had begun to consider that maybe she should slip away at the first opportunity, but she lacked the desire to go. Cold as they were, hungry as they'd been, there suddenly seemed no safer place to be than with Keane. But that made no sense. She didn't know the man.

Would he treat her so kindly if he realized who she was?

Not a one of his men seemed even remotely curious over discovering aught about her. Either they had decided a woman in their company was of little import, or it truly didn't matter to them from whence Lianae had come. Alas, she believed it was the former. And likely they believed she was a runaway, nothing more, nothing less. Judging by the dress she wore, they would easily have mistaken her for an English sympathizer—like King David and all his minions.

Now she considered her options. It was all well and good to pretend for awhile, but there would come a time when she must leave, no matter how *safe* Keane made her feel. She *must* find her missing brothers, and if it was the last thing she ever did, she was going to make William fitz Duncan pay for what he'd done to Elspeth. Now that Lianae was no longer in fitz Duncan's grasp, vengeance would be hers to give and it would be so very sweet. No matter how much she enjoyed Keane's company, that was not something he would agree to do for her—that much she knew for truth. However, kind he might be, he was still loyal to David mac Mhaoil Chaluim. And David was William's fitz Duncan's king. Thus Keane was her enemy, whether she liked that truth or nay.

One didn't crave to kiss one's enemy.

But yet she did.

And more.

In fact, if Lianae didn't leave soon, she might find herself thinking with her heart and not her head. For the love of Cailleach! She was already thinking with her heart, though once she found her brothers, Ewen and Graeme, they would know exactly what to do. She had so much to tell them both—about their sister and Lulach's betrayal.

As for Keane, she owed him naught, she reminded herself. Naught more than kindness. Despite that she longed to give him the truth—or at least as much of the truth as she could bear to give without endangering her cause—she could afford to say nothing at all.

But maybe she could tell him she was searching for her brothers, without revealing who they were. She must also learn his destination, so she could make plans to leave before the chance had passed. And yet despite the fact that Keane wasn't a part of her future—she didn't dare amuse herself with that notion—there was much she wished to learn about him, so much she wished to share.

But not *this*!

The instant her necessaries were completed—thankfully—she heard someone approach through the brush, and she hurried to repair herself, thinking it must be Keane. "I am fine!" she shouted.

"Ho, what have we here?" a male voice asked.

It wasn't Keane.

Startled, Lianae focused her gaze on a dark figure that came ever nearer, footsteps tramping noisily through the snow. But there wasn't just one, there were three shadows approaching, their silhouettes black against a pale, moonlit sky.

"Looky here," the man said. "It's a wee lassie."

"But can she can piss and wield a dagger all while brushing her pretty haid?"

Hushed male laughter followed the impertinent question.

Lianae's heartbeat faltered. None of the voices were even remotely familiar. She tamped down a lump of fear that rose in her throat as three men now stood between her and her destination.

"She has something far deadlier than a dagger."

Keane!

Lianae had never been more grateful to hear the sound of a man's voice. She bolted toward her two-time savior, relieved unto death that none of the strangers attempted to stop her.

"Aye?" asked the newcomer. "And what might that be? A bonny smile?" He didn't sound overly concerned over Keane's arrival and one of his men sniggered.

"*Me*," Keane said, and there was an unmistakable threat in his voice.

"Is that so?"

"Aye," Keane said, stepping in front of Lianae, and

for the first time in her adult life, Lianae hid behind a man. Only belatedly did she realize that these men also wore the king's livery.

"Dinna mind these laggards," the youngest of the three said. He came closer to show his face. "We come as friends... with a bit o' news."

CHAPTER THIRTEEN

King Henry of England was dead, felled, not by a broadsword, but by a lump of eels. Rumors were circulating that he'd been poisoned, and he'd left no clear heir.

At one point, Henry had supported his Empress daughter, but Matilda had since roused the rebels against him, and so the instant Henry was pronounced dead, the king's nephew, Stephen of Blois, rushed to England to seize his throne whilst Matilda remained in Anjou, supporting rebels against her dead father. These were not the actions of a beloved daughter and the people of England bore the Empress little love. Unfortunately for King David's niece, they gave Stephen a king's welcome, embracing him as the new sovereign lord. Stephen was crowned on the twenty-second day of December; and the matter was settled. But perhaps not entirely...

The three messengers had been sent by David mac Mhaoil Chaluim. They settled themselves before the fire, partaking of the evening's meal—a fact no one saw fit to complain about, because they'd brought along with *bit o' news* a bit o' bread and ale—gritty ale and stale bread, though on a cold night like this, even dirty ale was a far more welcome than tea. At hearing the news, even Keane had a taste for a wee dram tonight.

The youngest of the three messengers had broken the news. Keane recognized him from Keppenach, where he served Jaime. The other two served the king directly. Peering at Lianae—wondering how this should change his plans—he cut away at an arrow fletch, trimming it whilst he listened to the report. Lianae sat beside him, leaning against his shoulder—a fact that may have pleased him were it not for the simple fact that the discussion at hand brought with it an undeniable note of dread. A wolf howled in the distance, the sound mournful and prophetic.

"Matilda claims she'll nae kneel to Stephen," Luc said, while the elder messenger stuffed a chunk of meat into his gob and then followed it with half a loaf of stale bread.

"What d' ye suppose it'll mean for Scotland?" Murdoch asked.

"He's her uncle, ye ken," he elder messenger said, speaking of David. "So he rallies his liegemen, even now."

By virtue of his marriage, David mac Mhaoil Chaluim would no doubt claim all of Northumbria, though Stephen of Blois was bound to oppose him. Keane brushed a thumb across the sharp blade of his knife, directing his question to Luc. "Where is he now?"

"Keppenach for the moment. He awaits the MacKinnon's response to a call for arms."

"MacKinnon?" Cameron interjected. He slid Keane a glance.

The messenger nodded. "They sent cartloads of grain and men enough to see Chreagach Mhor rebuilt —I saw them off myself. All he asks in return is for MacKinnon's alliance once the time arrives."

A few weeks ago Chreagach Mhor had burned to

the ground—storehouses, silos, supplies, all lost. Keane knew this secondhand, because Aidan never bothered to send him word. At the moment, his brother was not his greatest fan.

Peering down at his feet, Cameron offered, "MacKinnon has rarely chosen sides." But the fact that he did not reveal his kinship left Keane curious.

The quiet messenger spoke up now, struggling around mouthfuls of food. "Word is… he will now… his wife is heir to Aldergh, in the disputed lands… her father has died."

The disputed lands were in essence the entirety of Northumbria—land that had been mostly enfeoffed to David, albeit with Henry as his lord. It was an arrangement that suited both kings, only because the two were thick as thieves. This was not the case with Stephen of Blois, and David would waste little time in fortifying his claims. So long as MacKinnon swore fealty to David, giving Aldergh to him should suit David well. However, should Ian choose to do so, he would clearly be taking Matilda's side. It was a gamble to be sure, for there was none to say Stephen would remain seated upon England's throne.

Cameron tilted the man a look. "An' so ye say FitzSimon is dead?"

The same messenger nodded, his lips shining with grease. "According to Broc Ceannfhionn. I hear tell the man was slain by MacKinnon's brat—that boy who was held by FitzSimon some years past."

"Malcom?"

"Aye, that's the one." The messenger swiped at his mouth with a dirty sleeve. "Guess he's no longer a wee one."

The flames cast a feverish hue on the faces surrounding the fire. Outside the glow of the campfire, the night had long turned black.

"Imagine that," the elder messenger said. "The boy put thirty inches of good steel into his granpappy's belly and he gets tae keep the spoils. I'd say 'twas vengeance well done."

For a moment, the camp went silent, each man considering this fact. Justice, it seemed, was as fickle as the Highland weather. After a moment, Cameron asked, "So, then… David plans to approve the claim to Aldergh?"

"Something like that." It was Luc who now replied. The other two sat, staring across the fire at Keane, devouring their meals whilst they assessed Lianae.

"Willie here—" The elder man waved a hand at his silent companion— "overheard him say he planned to send troops to Carlisle within the week."

"We'll go to war," Cameron said.

"Aye, well, war is what 'twill be."

"War is what it always be."

Every man nodded to that truth, their looks solemn and full of uncertainty. Between them, the burning fire sizzled and sputtered.

His mood soured, Keane returned to his fletching.

Lianae placed a hand about his arm, squeezing gently. He wished he knew precisely what to say to allay her fears, for the thought of Scotia again at war—a battle never-ending—could hardly set any man or woman at ease. It had been less than five years since they'd laid down their arms.

And yet… with David pre-occupied in Northumbria, he would have little enough to say about the fate of the woman sitting beside him. With a bit of luck, and a bit more time, mayhap he could see to her himself…

He could then return her to Lilidbrugh to retrieve her stones, and he could help her determine where best to go from there—not back to her *husband,* this much was certain. Though in his dreams, mayhap the vale?

In the meantime, David would expect them to return to Keppenach—not Dunloppe. And now there were more important things to consider: How might Scotia's war affect the vale? Would David force Aidan to finally take a side? And if so, what would his brother do?

Keane knew Aidan well enough to predict he would never agree to do battle to further David's cause—particularly not down in the borderlands. And once again, he would defy Scotia's king, and how would this go? For Aidan? For Lael?

Everyone would be forced to choose a side.

Including Keane.

As for Lianae... not for the first time, Keane found himself wondering: Who were her people? Where did they fit in this battle David planned to wage? And clearly, he wasn't the only one who was wondering...

"What about you, lass? What's your sad tale?" the elder messenger asked. He was staring at Lianae.

Picking at the underside of her fingernail, Lianae slid Keane a nervous glance. "I have no story," she claimed.

THE MAN SCREWED HIS FACE. "No story? *Everyone* has a story."

Lianae shook her head.

King David's soldier considered Lianae a long moment, before sweeping his gaze over the rest of the men as though to gauge their expressions as well. And now everyone was staring at her as he turned to address her once more, squinting his blue eyes at her. "So, then, how di' ye come to find yourself... here... amidst these wretches?"

Lianae blinked. "Me?"

"Aye, lass," he said a bit impatiently, his tone a little

more condescending. "I ken how the rest of these dolts all came tae be here." He waved a hand to indicate the lot of them. "They were sent by decree of the king. 'Tis why we came searching, after all. But what about ye?"

"I..."

Lianae peered from one man to another, uncertain how to continue. Fear paralyzed her tongue. The only one thing she knew for certain was that she could not afford to reveal aught to these men about whence she had come. At the moment, they were content enough to loathe the English, though if she revealed who she was, she was certain they would return to hating her people all at once. She looked toward Keane for salvation, praying silently that he would intervene, silence their conversation once and for all. But he did not. Like the others, he too seemed to be waiting for an explanation, and Lianae inhaled a shaky breath and decided to appease them with a half-truth. "I am... searching for my brothers."

The elder messenger lifted both his brows. "Your brothers?"

Lianae nodded, averting her gaze almost as once, her heart beating a little faster.

"An' ye happened upon these wastrels... where?"

"Lilidbrugh," Lianae replied, swallowing. There was no true reason for anyone to be near Lilidbrugh... unless they were leaving a changeling for the faeries... *or hiding.*

The one called Luc eyed Keane with a lifted brow. "That auld pile of rocks?" He returned his gaze to Lianae and she nodded uncomfortably, once again averting her gaze. A heavy silence followed her declaration and Lianae could feel the tension mounting in the air.

The elder messenger persisted. "Where might be these brothers o' yours, lass? Er' they friend o' the faeries perchance?" The men all laughed a little awkwardly. "I believe that's all what be hanging 'round those parts."

Most of the men quieted at once, waiting to hear what Lianae had to say.

Keane watched her as well, his curious green eyes catching a glint of moonlight.

The sound of their horses nickering softly outside the warmth of the fire was the only sound to breach the silence. "I dunno," Lianae confessed. "I ha'e not seen them in… a while…"

"Is that so?" the elder man asked. "An' ye say ye ha'e two?"

"Two brothers?"

"I'm nae talkin' 'bout faeries, lass."

The men all snickered yet again.

"And what be their names?"

For a moment, Lianae's throat felt too thick to speak. She searched all their faces, reassuring herself that she did not know these men and neither could they possibly know her. And how many men shared the same name? "Graeme and Ewen," she replied at last.

The eldest of the three messengers nodded slowly. "And so Keane here…" He slid a chin in Keane's direction. "He agreed to help ye find your brothers?"

Nodding uncertainly, Lianae looked belatedly to Keane. He lifted a brow, although he did not refute her, and his friend Cameron cast them both a narrow-eyed glance.

"I see," the man said, and after a painfully long moment, he nodded and then went back to mauling his piece of bread.

Lianae had little more to say, so she sat, picking at the imagined grime beneath her nails. After the hunt, she'd washed her hands thoroughly down by the burn, and they were perfectly clean, but she didn't know what else to do with them whilst so many pairs of eyes were trained upon her now.

The camp went silent after that, bored, it seemed, with Lianae's thin, unimaginative tale. Admittedly, it wasn't nearly as intriguing as the death of a king and the *politiks* therein.

After a while, the fire began to wane, and Cameron was the first to rise, excusing himself, he claimed, to go searching for more wood to keep the fire going through the night.

Murdoch rose as well. "I'll go wi' ye," he said, and grumbled again about his belly. The two of them whispered together as they went, and then Murdoch suddenly sprinted ahead, into a thicket.

"Well, now, that was a welcome feast," the elder messenger said, as he watched the two men disappear. "We had nae idea ye'd be so near. We thought for sure ye'd be at Dunràth by now."

"Tis good fortune," Keane said, leaving it at that. He continued to trim his fletching. After another considerable moment, the man hoisted himself up, brushing himself off. The rest of the men took it as their cue to go make their pallets for evening and maybe see to their mounts. Only Lianae and Keane remained seated before the fire.

Already, Keane had beside him a small pile of grouse feathers that he planned to use, or so he'd claimed. Lianae searched for something to say. She might tell him more now—about her brothers and the Earl—if only he would ask. She sorely needed an ally, she realized, but she still was afraid. He was, after all, King David's man…

He watched her out of the corner of one eye.

"My brothers always used hawk feathers," she remarked, uncomfortable with silence.

"That works well enough if ye plan to put your arrows on a shelf."

Lianae heard a note of something in his tone—scorn perhaps—and took offense. "My brother said most feathers are too easily frazzled."

"And which brother was that?"

"Graeme."

Keane smiled tightly and nodded. He said, "An archer must use what he must, else he's an archer only for sport."

Lianae narrowed her eyes, prepared to take offense in her brother's behalf. He could not know her brothers and had no idea of what he was speaking about. Neither of her brothers were fat rich men, who'd used their bows only for sport. Nay, they were brave men of Moray, who'd lived to serve their people.

"My father *never* used grouse," Lianae assured him, even despite that she didn't know it to be true. But her father would have known best, for he was a great man. Too bad she couldn't say so, and so she held her tongue, wanting desperately to say that her menfolk were not milk toast—unlike a king who licked English boots.

"Ach, lass... but ye dinna even ken what grouse was until yesterday."

Lianae grit her teeth and clenched her fists within her lap. That was neither here nor there, and his questioning tone annoyed her. Still, she sensed there was something more behind his needling and he wanted her to say something more.

Well, let him pry all he wished! She wasn't about to tell him aught more than she already had. Clearly, she was wrong to want to confide in him.

Whatever warmth she had felt for him fled now, Lianae rose from her place beside him, and eyed his waiting pallet. He'd made it beneath the low-lying branch of an ash tree, just in case it should begin to snow again. Alas, despite the fact that he had angered her, she realized his bed was still the safest place to sleep. "Well… g'nite," she said.

He smiled up at her, an enigmatic smile that didn't quite reach his eyes. "I'll be along behind ye soon," he said. "Sleep well, *maid of Moray*."

Sleep well yourself! Lianae longed to say, but in truth, she suspected none of them would sleep a wink tonight after drinking all that tea. Without bothering to tell him where she was going, Lianae headed down to the burn, rebuking herself for warming to any man under David's rule. Keane was her enemy—had always been her enemy—and simply because he didn't realize it yet, didn't make it not true.

KEANE WATCHED HER GO, knowing instinctively where she was off to. He didn't like it overmuch, though he couldn't follow her every time she left to do the necessary and he couldn't prevent her from going. All he cared about was that no one followed her down to the burn, and so he resigned himself to wait for her return, watching his men come and go.

Lianae didn't strike him as a liar, but she wasn't telling the truth—at least not all of it. There was far more to her story than what she would allow. But then he had already surmised as much, long before now. The question was: What was she hiding that was more injurious than stolen charm stones—which, by the by, she'd left behind, albeit reluctantly?

He had half a day to discover what it was, for Keppenach was no more than a half-day's ride. In fact, they might have made it there tonight without the stop, except that he hadn't intended to go there at all. But now, with or without him, these men would return to Keppenach to report to the king, and if Keane did not arrive along with them, he would find himself in David's ill graces… or worse.

Contemplating the lass's secrets, he waited for Lianae to re-emerge from the thicket, resting easier when he spied her pale hair beneath the moonlight, and then he gathered up the materials for his fletching and put them all away. He watched her climb into his bed, and something deep in his gut thrilled at the sight. Once she was abed, he checked on his men one more time before making his own way to his pallet and climbing within. Lianae was already asleep. Lying beside her, he dared to pull her into his arms, embracing her protectively. "Who are ye, maid of Moray?" he whispered at her back.

She didn't answer, and Keane unexpectedly found his lips pressed against the back of her head. He gave her a chaste kiss, but her only response was her smooth, even breath.

CHAPTER FOURTEEN

His question made Lianae's heart ache.

But not more than his kiss.

Every time he offered his lips, it stirred some new part of her; and this time, it was her heart. He reached out, drawing Lianae firmly against his chest and then lowered his arm so that it encircled her waist and she held her breath, afraid that he might discover she was wide awake. For a long, long moment, her heart refused to calm, and Lianae feared the pounding would betray her. After a moment, he buried his face into the back of her hair. Inhaling deeply of her scent, he then exhaled with a throaty sigh that made goose bumps arise upon her flesh. It was a lover's embrace—unlike anything Lianae had ever known.

No man had ever held her so tenderly.

She had the most overwhelming desire to turn in his arms, to kiss him once more... But fear kept her still. After another moment, she heard Keane's smooth easy breathing, and knew he slept.

Ach, it was time to go!

Whatever had she been thinking when she'd come along? Men like Keane had little to give, and she was in no position to take. She was a woman without a home, nor even a country, and he was a king's sworn man.

His is your enemy, she tried to convince herself, but it didn't' feel right. And yet, her plan to seduce him seemed suddenly all the more preposterous. Soon they would depart for Keppenach, and Lianae could not join them for Keppenach was the last place she should go—especially with the king in residence. Never in her life had she felt so confused.

Stay, go, she was lost either way she turned.

And what did she even know of Keane, in truth?

He was more a mystery than she. He wore the king's livery, yet she sensed he had no interest in the king's *politiks*. He tested her at every turn, and then he showed her kindness. He called her a liar with his tone and then he kissed her sweetly upon the head. Who was this man who dressed himself in wolves' clothing, but appeared to be as gentle as a sheep?

Shivering, she burrowed deeper beneath the covers, acknowledging that there was little about his looks that reminded her of soft wooly sheep. For all she knew, he might be her executioner! Now, before it was too late, she must find a way to leave…

Tonight.

Acutely aware of the comings and goings of the men —all suffering the same malady—Lianae tossed and turned, waiting for her chance to steal away. She was not ill as they were, and she had no idea what had befallen them, but she had used their excuse to steal away time and again, some part of her instinct urging her to get away.

Now, more than ever, she must find her brothers.

❧

AT FIRST LIGHT, Keane immediately came aware of two

things: One, it was snowing yet again, and two, Lianae was gone. At first, he supposed she must have gone down to the burn, as she had once or twice during the night.

He'd slept heavily—far more so than he had expected to and lifted his head, raking a hand through the back of his scalp, squinting against the rude mist. There was no wind this morning, but the snow was falling so thickly that it was difficult to see aught past his own pallet. Were it not for the ash bough overhead, he might have been covered in snow. His heavy cloak lay atop the blankets, abandoned.

Accustomed to winters in the Mounth, Keane was no stranger to sleeping in the snow. Back in the vale, at least once every sennight—spring, summer, fall and winter—he'd taken a watch on the hill. They all did so, and even Aidan would now and again, although his brother endured them far less often now that he had Lìli in his bed.

Rising from the pallet and making his rounds, he nudged a few of his men awake while waiting for Lianae to return, ready to be on their way. And then he realized the king's messengers were gone as well—not a one remained. Keane took another look about.

Neither were Cameron or Murdoch in their beds.

How long since Lianae had been gone?

His heart clenching with sudden fear, he bolted toward the burn.

❧

FOR HIS COUSIN Broc's sake, Cameron had intended to take Lianae to David himself.

He waited for her down by the burn.

Too oft in his life he'd made the wrong decision, but never again would he place his kinsmen at risk—not for Keane, who was, by far, his closest friend. And not for Cailin, whose affections were as fickle as the weather. One day she kissed him as though the morrow might ne'er come, the next, she scarce could bear to look at him.

Lovely, infuriating lass.

Someday, he hoped to make her his wife.

But not today.

Today, he was following three men whose intentions were becoming perfectly clear.

All three together had ambushed Lianae down by the burn. As Cameron had meant to do himself, they followed her down, and took her per force. From there, it was easy to steal away without rousing the camp. Covering her mouth, they'd bound her arms, arresting her like a prisoner of war.

And well she might be.

There was nothing he could say without giving himself away. These men were not brigands. They were the king's men, sworn to David as Cameron was. If he raised arms against them, and Lianae were, in fact, a spy, he'd mark them all as traitors—particularly now that Keane had publicly admitted to helping her search for her missing brothers.

What the hell was the man thinking?

Keane had never been a greedy man, and it had never occurred to Cameron that he might desire aught more than he already had. In this way, he'd done Keane a disfavor by assuming he would stand aside and allow Cameron command of their men. The dún Scoti lived simply, traveled with little, and seemed uninterested in aught of value—insomuch as Cameron could tell. With Jaime's support, Keane's sister had attempted to raise him where she could, but Keane would sooner gut a bear to wear its hide as dress himself with Sassenach gold.

And now he suddenly wished to lead?

Because of her.

But as much as it had galled him, he well understood the inclination, for he suffered the same malady of the heart, and Keane had as much right to lead as Cameron did.

But despite his own thwarted plans to take Lianae to the king, Cameron was loyal to Keane. They had been friends now too long to play the man false. He simply hadn't been willing to put his cousin at risk by allowing Keane to harbor the girl at Dunloppe, nor did he believe Keane was thinking all that clearly. He would save the fool from himself.

Conflicted although he was, Cameron persevered through the worsening weather, tracking the messengers along their journey south.

At least this way he wouldn't be forced to make a difficult decision.

It was snowing thickly enough now that their hoof prints would be buried beneath a goodly amount of snow. The further they traveled south, the more he realized he couldn't turn back, despite that he wanted to warn his good friend.

Trusting Keane to go to Keppenach first, he continued to follow. No matter what his original intentions, Dunloppe was no longer an option, although he didn't like to think what Keane would feel once he awoke to find Lianae gone. And worse, soon thereafter, he would realize Cameron had left as well and he worried Keane would believe he'd been betrayed. He sorely regretted now not having taken him aside to tell him what he knew…

Lianae of Moray was a daughter of Óengus.

Cameron had surmised as much back in Lilidbrugh, though he hadn't been certain until she'd spoken her brothers' names aloud. He'd recognized them only because Murdoch named them as the rebels being held at Dunràth—a fact not even Cameron and Keane had been told. They'd been told only what David wished for them to know—that men were being held and that someone who rode amongst them was suspected of spying. Murdoch was that spy, for he'd known precisely who it was that awaited them at Dunràth.

To make matters worse, Cameron also discovered a small vial of *dwale* in Murdoch's satchel, which might well be responsible for all their aching bellies. The poison had been used once by MacBeth's soldiers to fell an entire army, and in the wake of King Henry's death, it could be a wide-reaching plot to remove those who would oppose Stephen's rule. Of course, Cameron had no proof, but he knew in his gut Murdoch was up to no good. He'd been a rat once himself, so he could easily smell one. To test his theory, he gave Murdoch a small portion with his meal, and within moments, the man had gone sprinting into the woods. The only question now, was why the *dwale*?

Had he meant to poison the entire crew? If Murdoch should happen to murder the entire company, and had men at the ready to trade clothes, he might easily gain entrance to Dunràth under the king's banner to free Óengus's sons.

Was Lianae a spy as well?

Was Keane?

In his heart, Cameron prayed it wasn't so, though if not, it was a rather unfortunate coincidence that Lianae had happened upon Lilidbrugh when she did and that Keane had been so hell-bent upon seeing the pile of rubbish for himself. And then, there was this: Keane took to the lass rather quickly. All in all, the entire ordeal left Cameron with a bad feeling in his gut that he'd rather not explore. He only prayed Keane would prove innocent of any wrongdoing, although the truth would soon be known…

Keppenach's walls rose up before him like an immense grey specter, looming up from the snow. With little wind, the king's lion rampant banners hung limply from staffs on the ramparts, the bright golds and reds scarcely visible through a thick flurry of white.

Ahead of him, one of the messengers called to the watchman on wall, and after a moment the heavy portcullis rose. The gates groaned with their burden as they opened and Cameron sat mounted in his saddle, wondering where to go from here…

Follow inside?

Or go back to warn Keane?

He had only seconds left to decide.

If he went in, he might plead their case to the king, though if he did… Keane would unknowingly walk into treachery. And if Keane were guilty? Where did that leave Cameron?

Either way, they were at the king's mercy.

With a creak and a groan, the chains began to tighten…

SOUTH HAD NEVER BEEN the dún Scoti's favored direction to ride.

Trudging through thick drifts of snow, Keane's mood remained sour. His men spoke not a word, but every last one had accompanied him, save for Murdoch. For all he knew, Murdoch might well be with Cameron.

Sullen bastard.

Despite Cameron's obvious dissent, this was the last thing Keane would ever have expected from him. A smack to the jaw, perhaps, or a brawl in the snow, but to steal Lianae away? He realized the king's men had been suspicious of her, and he could well comprehend their actions. If he'd been in a different position himself, Keane might have done precisely the same thing. But the one thing that spurred his ire more than aught else, and made his temper blacker than he could e'er recall, was the simple fact that Cameron had forsaken him. Some part of him understood why, but it galled him just the same.

Only briefly had he contemplated riding north. He didn't believe Lianae would return that way. Deep in his gut, he sensed she was running—not searching for her missing brothers, despite what she'd claimed. There was no mistaking the bruises on her face and on her legs. She was running, or she would never have left so unprepared. And were she inclined to go back, she would have done so whilst they'd remained at Lilidbrugh, where she clearly knew the way home.

If there was a single bright note to the occasion, it was this: His men followed him without question, despite that they too must sense what was to come.

It wasn't long before they reached their destination.

The gates of Keppenach opened at once. Keane hesitated but a moment before spurring his mount through the gates. The very instant they entered the courtyard, the gates were closed at once. And despite that his brother by law was laird of this keep, the king's men at arms spilled into the courtyard, marching toward Keane and his company of men. He spied his sister's countenance in a tower window, and he knew the situation was dire. Even from this distance, he could see the worry in her face.

They were surrounded.

"Stand down," he commanded his men, for despite the livery they wore, not all were loyal to David. He knew that as well as anyone. Raising his hands in the air, Keane slid out of his saddle and his men all followed suit.

The laird of Keppenach appeared on the doorstep of the keep, arms crossed his expression foreboding. He was followed by David mac Mhaoil Chaluim.

"Keane dún Scoti!" the marshal announced, the very instant Keane's feet touched the ground. "By command of David mac Maíl Choluim, Prince of the Cumbrians, Earl of Northhampton and Huntingdon, the *Righ Art*, the High King of the Scots and Chief of Chiefs, heir of Kenneth MacAilpín, we must place you under arrest. Lay down your arms!"

Keane's eyes met Jaime's, and Jaime gave him a nod, as he plucked his sword from his scabbard, and tossed it down on the ground. He pulled the dirk from his boot as well and cast it down. And then the knife at his belt followed. He flung it before him. It clattered noisily across the stone courtyard.

"I am disarmed," he announced, and all at once, the king's men rushed forward. Binding his arms behind his back, they dragged Keane out of the courtyard.

CHAPTER FIFTEEN

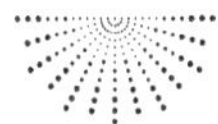

Lael blew into the gaols like a wrathful wind, her long, pale blue skirts sweeping the length of the crude dirt floor. "Keane! What ha'e ye done?"

Despite that he had not seen her now in more than a year, her face was unchanged. At thirty-two, after having borne four children—one nine, one eight and two wee ones under the age of four—Lael still looked like a lassie herself. The last time he saw her she was still pregnant with bairn number four, and he had yet to meet the youngest of her brood.

He leaned back against the prison wall. "I thought for sure my return to Keppenach would see me cozied in your new keep, with a brazier burning at my bedside. Instead, you toss me into your brig." He smiled wryly, though his sister didn't appear the least amused.

Her hands seized the prison bars. "Would that you had ne'er laid eyes upon this scabrous piece of my home," she lamented. "Ach, Keane! I ha'e no love for these gaols."

Keane shrugged, uncertain what to say.

"At least ye are no' in chains," his sister said, pointing at the wall beside him, where a pair of ancient, rusted irons with sharp-edged cuffs were bolted into the stone wall. By the looks of them, they would rot a man's arm off. "Broc was held here once."

There were few who'd not heard that tale. Troubadours sang of it still. Ten years past, his sister Lael had ridden out from Dubhtolargg, beside Broc Ceannfhionn, intending to take Keppenach. Instead, they'd found their heads in a noose. At the very last moment, the Demon Butcher rode through Keppenach's gates, like a devil in black. Jaime cut her down from the gibbet, then promptly wed her. Unfortunately, Cameron's cousin hadn't had quite the same reception, despite his good fortune in the end. "Here, in this cell?"

Lael nodded. "Aye," she said, and then she turned to face him with tears glistening in her stark green eyes. "Tell me what happened, Keane."

"Haven't they already said?"

Despite her glittering eyes, Lael tilted him an impatient look—that same impertinence he knew and loved so well. "Ach, now, would I be down here askin' if I knew? Nay, Keane. They've ensconced themselves in Jamie's solar to discuss the matter—away from prying ears."

"Yours included?"

"You are my brother, after all."

Keane attempted to laugh, but the sound came out bitter. "A lot of sway that won me at your gates."

Lael's face fell. She gripped the bars with both hands. "Dinna make light of this, Keane. This is a *serious* matter, and ye dinna catch the king in a forgiving mood."

"Is he ever?"

Lael gave him another impatient look, clearly in a less jovial mood than even Keane—which was saying quite a lot. "Aye," she said quickly. "I have come to know the man and he is not the villain I once feared."

"So says the woman who once cuffed him in the face?"

His sister's cheeks blossomed with color. But she was being sincere, he realized, and she was defending the man whom she'd once sworn to kill—the very man who'd stolen their sister Catrìona from her bed in the middle of the night and then carried her south to barter in marriage to a fat, greasy-haired English earl. "So now ye tell me ye've a fondness for the *eejit?*"

"Shhhh!" Lael demanded, turning her head to be certain the guards did not overhear. "Dinna say such things! 'Tis no time for jests, brother."

"Apparently not. It appears to me ye lost your good humor, right along with your desire for vengeance."

"Aye, well, at least I do not wear his livery and then break his faith with every other word!"

Leave it to his sister not to mince words. Keane said naught in response, for it was the truth she spoke, and despite that he was innocent of whatever charges he had been accused of, he was indeed being a hypocrite, for he'd accepted a post he was loyal to in action, but not in spirit. He served a king he did not believe in.

Lael released the prison bars, crossing her arms, stepping back to survey his cell. "If they dinna release ye soon, I will send blankets and food."

Keane nodded a bit more soberly, realizing his sister was tormented. He didn't wish to give her any more grief.

She pointed to the cell beside him. "Even after all these years, I canna come here and *not* think of *her*. This is where they found *her*, ye ken."

Aveline of Teviotdale.

Even without her speaking the name, Keane knew instinctively that it was who Lael was referring to. Aveline had been Rogan MacLaren's mistress, sent to spy upon Lìli in Dubhtolargg. Though instead of counting her good fortune to be away from Rogan, the lass begged Aidan to return her to Keppenach to bear Rogan's babe. And then she'd vanished, just as simply as that. Apparently Rogan buried her alive. When they discovered her body, her mouth had been stuffed with a wad of cloth, her hands were gnarled, her fingers bent to claws, as though she'd taken her last breath while attempting to scratch her way out of the casket she'd been buried in. There were claw marks along the ceiling of her tomb, bloodstains marking the splintered wood and splinters beneath her black nails.

Lael pulled her cloak together against the damp chill of the gaols. "They locked me in the cell with her. I found her only by chance, digging to pass the time."

Rogan MacLaren was long dead, but the stories of his terror lived on. Keane could still spy the agony of it writ upon Lael's face. "Rogan was a bastard," he said.

"Tell me about it," she agreed. "And while you're at it, tell me ye dinna know that *she* was a daughter of Moray."

Keane's gaze must have registered his shock.

"You did not know?" his sister asked breathlessly, clearly relieved to discover it was so. She exhaled a long breath and her shoulders rested, a bit more relaxed.

"Lianae?"

Lael nodded. "'Tis true," she said. "She confessed as much before the king, and I heard it with my own two ears."

"A daughter of Óengus?" Keane said, just to be sure he did not misunderstand.

Lael nodded. "The very one."

Closing his eyes and leaning his forehead against the bars, Keane processed the new information. For a long, long moment, he didn't know how to respond. He thought about the bruises on Lianae's legs, and realized what it meant: The man she would have been promised to would be a man of consequence... the Earl of Moray came to mind—a rightful claimant to the throne. Despite that fitz Duncan should have inherited the crown as King Duncan's eldest son, he took a bribe instead, settling for the title of Mormaer. The man's temper was renown. He was a cruel bastard on the field, to be sure. Clearly, he was in his bedroom as well. It was said he, himself, had felled Óengus of Moray on the field during the battle at Stracathro in Forfarshire...

Fitz Duncan killed Lianae's father.

Had they already spoken their vows?

The pit of Keane's stomach turned at the thought.

His sister accurately read his expression. "Ye dinna mess around, brother dear," she said, and then she laughed softly as she shook her head.

Squeezing his eyes shut, Keane knocked his head once against the cold, hard steel. "What else di' ye hear?"

"Not much," his sister confessed. "Even despite that I kept my gob shut—for once—they tossed me out."

"Jaime?"

"Nay." She shook her head. "It was David. But I, for one, have never seen him so furious, and Jaime daren't defy him over this. Nor would I."

Lael shivered yet again, and this time Keane understood it was probably not from the cold. The look in her eyes was full of agony and for the first time since his arrest, he fully realized the severity of his position.

This was not a simple matter. Not only had he abetted a woman who would flee her given duty—by the king's writ—it was Lianae's brothers who had been suspected of rousing the rebels. It was their men his mesnie had been sent to ferret out from the northern woodlands.

While Lael was once held here and somehow escaped the gallows, she was not proof against Keane meeting the same fate. With the kingdom so much at odds, it would be an easy enough decision for the king to make to simply wipe this frustration off his plate. He had more than enough to deal with in Northumbria, and Keane had never once made his loyalties known. If he were David, he would wish to eliminate *all* trials in the north before traveling south. Cailleach only knew, where the man stood now—with most of Scotia under his rule—not even Aidan would be a threat. And now—only now—did he understand the true folly in never choosing sides. "What do ye think he will do?"

"It all depends."

"On what?"

"On what *she* says to him now." She eyed Keane meaningfully. "They brought Lianae into the solar as they ushered me out."

❧

"Una! Una! The babe is come!"

Realizing time was of the essence, Constance shouted at the top of her lungs, tripping over her own two feet as she stumbled up the stone-littered hill. There was just enough snow on the ground that she couldn't see the smaller stones and she didn't know precisely where to go. Alas, but everyone else was far too busy, boiling water and preparing for the birth of the laird's new child.

Someday, she and Kellen would be expectin' their own.

The very thought renewed her pace—past the guards on the hillside. Like stone effigies, they seemed completely oblivious to the falling snow, and she marveled that they could remain, night and day, guarding the vale, come what may. She had never witnessed such steadfast loyalty as she did in these men, not even with her uncle Iain, who claimed a blood lineage to Kenneth MacAilpín!

Forsooth, but it was cold, despite that the sun was shining brightly. Still, Constance was pleased to help with this small task and she wished desperately to prove herself useful. It was a wonderful feeling to belong somewhere, at long last.

Although Chreagach Mhor was the only home she had ever known, and she knew well that her kinfolk loved her, she had never had a true sense of belonging living in Chreagach Mhor, particularly after her cousin Broc left. Thereafter, she had lived mostly alone, in a small cottage, cooking for no one. Her brother Cameron was never around for long, and even when he came to visit, he was most often distracted by one thing or another. Constance had always been an afterthought, a forgotten child.

But *now*, now she was a wife—duly wed—and she intended to be the very best wife Kellen could ever hope for. If Constance would have her way, her sweet husband would want for naught and he would never have cause to regret the moment he took her as his bride. That night, up in the loft, he had been such a sweet, sweet soul. He had only kissed her all night long. But in the morning, faced with Iain's wrath, he'd stood up for Constance and offered to wed her, then and there, even despite that her virginity was still intact. Later, once the vows were spoken, they had discovered the pleasures of the flesh together. Smiling, she patted her flat belly now beneath her cloak and prayed she would find herself growing a wee bairn very, very soon.

Life was good today!

Picking up her pace, Constance thought of the house Aidan and Lìli had gifted them with—a small but well-kept hut—and she vowed to fill it with all the love in her heart. She would cook and clean as a good wife must do, and she would mend all her husband's clothes. Already, she had them neatly piled into a coffer, with those that still needed mending sitting on top. She would learn to make soup that was never bitter to the tongue, and she looked forward to the day when she could sew for her wee bairns as well. Praying Lìli's babe would only wait until she could retrieve the midwife, she called for Una again.

It was curious the old woman would live in a cave on the hill, but certainly not unheard of. Constance once knew a woman back in Chreagach Mhor who'd lived in a cave in the faerie woods with her da until the day she'd wed. Seana was her name. Her *uisge* was both a scourge and a blessing to men, depending on the time of day one dared to ask. And yet as soon as Seana had been given a choice, she abandoned that cave in the blink of an eye. To Constance's way of thought, there was little reason to live in a cave, but to each his own.

She found the opening easily enough and passed through, noting the crates that were filled to brimming with supplies. Curious as she was to their contents, she was in far too much of a hurry today to stop and explore. She found the ladder Sorcha spoke of, went down quickly, but to her dismay, she found Una's grotto empty.

Mist rose from an opening beneath the old woman's table. Puzzled, but too excited about the babe to consider where the hole might lead, Constance hopped down from the ladder, and went to see what she could see. She peered down the hole, and found another ladder made of rope. "Una?" she called hesitantly.

A frisson of something like fear raced down her spine. For a moment, she considered going back, but Lìli needed the auld woman, and Constance would not fail her new mother by law. She was well aware that

Lìli did not wholly approve of their marriage, and so she must prove herself worthy here today.

Clearly, there would not be a rope here if it was dangerous. What a ninny she was being. For the good of her marriage, for the betterment of her relationship with Kellen's mother, she climbed down into the darkness below.

"Una?"

Still, there was no response, though now she heard something odd—a strange rumbling, like the sound of a hungry belly. Shining through the darkness, she spied a bit of virescent light coming through a crack in the wall, a fissure through which she might squeeze through. Making her way quickly over, she pushed her way through to the other side.

There, in a cavernous room, lit by a strange pale light, the old woman lay upon the ground, next to an altar bearing a very large stone. Horrified because Una looked as though she might be dead, Constance ran to her. Her skin was a little blue, and her white hair stood straight on end as though she'd rubbed a palm across the entirety of her head and made the strands rise up. Her lips were blue as well—darker yet—and the one eye that was not covered by a patch, remained closed.

"Una?" she called softly, shaking the old woman gently by the shoulder. Her body was still warm, as though she were merely sleeping.

Despite the mist that had coalesced outside the room and up into Una's grotto, inside this chamber the air was perfectly clear and still, filled with a strange energy that seemed to hum. It made Constance feel as though bugs were loose and crawling across her scalp and that her teeth were rattling in her skull.

Blinking with confusion, she peered up at the dark smooth rock upon the altar. There were holes on the sides where handles must have once been, but clearly, this wasn't an object meant to tote about. On one side, it bore a plaque, and sensing it was an important discovery, the babe was forgotten for an instant as Constance reached out to touch the stone, brushing her fingers over the worn, etched letters. Her brother Cameron had taught her to read and so she knew precisely what it said. She spoke the words aloud:

Unless the fates be faulty grown
And prophet's voice be vain
Where'er is found this sacred stone
The blood of Alba reigns.

The old woman screeched like a banshee, opening her eyes, and bounding up from the floor. Constance screamed.

With a terrible cacophonous shout, Una raised her staff high and brought it crashing down on the chamber floor. There was a boom and a crack and the room erupted with blinding, white light.

CHAPTER SIXTEEN

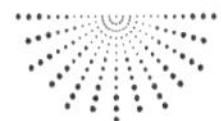

Dirty ocher light filled the chamber, fueled by fat tallow candles and a short, husky brazier smoldering beside the king's chair.

But no sooner were the words out of Lianae's mouth when she regretted them at once. If possible, they made her feel dirtier yet than the hateful gown she still wore—even dirtier than the warm, stale smoke that thickened about her nostrils.

May God forgive her; she would *never* return to the Earl.

The mood in the room grew more somber yet. All five men present stared at her across the table, none with any measure of charity, despite the atrocity she'd only just confessed.

With narrowed eyes, King David sat in his chair, tapping his fingers on the wooden arm, considering her allegation. "And you have proof?" His expression was sober, his long, lean face stern and his complexion nearly as rufous as his beard.

Until now, they had fed her, and mostly treated her well, but Lianae was wise enough to know that despite these small courtesies, her fate would be decided here today with a flick of that long finger the king was using to abuse his chair. He could very easily send her back to the Earl—and why should he care what happened to her from there? Why should he give a damn that her sister had died at William fitz Duncan's hands? *His ally, in truth.* And yet, there was something in the depths of the king's gaze that gave Lianae hope—some inkling of compassion.

"Lianae... have you proof?" the king persisted.

It just so happened she did. The bruises William gave her had been so dark and injurious that they had left her with twin bands of his rage. That he did not finish what he'd started had been a mere matter of minutes and her brother's infuriating sense of diplomacy—for this alone she could thank him for, no more.

And yet, she was not implicating the Earl here today.

If she were defiled, fitz Duncan would never take her back. His pride was too great to allow it, whether or not she was a princess of Moray.

She had been horribly afraid the king would consider it the right of a betrothed to taste what would be his. Theirs was a precarious alliance betwixt two men who would both be king, and she feared David would need a better reason to keep her from William fitz Duncan's bed, and what better way to do so than to claim she was defiled by another man?

And it *should* have been true.

She had shared Keane's bed every night since finding him at Lilidbrugh. It should have been easy enough for anyone to believe—that a man like Keane—so big, so strong—could take it upon himself to plant his seed inside her.

But Lianae had been so desperate to escape her own fate that she had never stopped to suppose what it would mean for Keane. Guiltily, she met Cameron's gaze. He would know her claims weren't entirely true, though unless she meant to prove herself a liar, her words could not be undone. For better or worse, she must press her case.

Wanting to weep now, Lianae slowly pushed her chair away from the table and stood. Her tears were real. She didn't have to pretend. Her grief was genuine and the taste on her lips was bitter—a sour blend of guilt for the honor of a man she had just impugned as much as for the memory of what she had endured at the Earl's hands. Fear left a fouler taste in her mouth and an even uglier taint upon her heart.

Reminding herself that a woman must do what she could to survive, she cast a glance at the other occupants of the room, her gaze returning to the king's. She bent to pull up the hem of her gown, showing the king the bruises that encircled her ankles, angry dark rings that were still visible even days later.

"Keane did this?" the laird of Keppenach asked. His gaze snapped to meet Luc's and then to Cameron MacKinnon. His tone was clearly disbelieving, leaving Lianae to wonder how well Keane knew this man. Aside from the king and Luc and Cameron, she had little inkling who any of these people were. But she felt a sudden rush of fear, for the look in Jaime Steorling's eyes was none too pleased, and his ire seemed directed at Lianae. Still, she nodded, quite certain that it was her only choice.

If she did not mistake the sound, the King growled. Startled, Lianae took a step backward and an instant of true fear squeezed at her heart.

If the king would not believe she was defiled, he might send her back to Fitz Duncan. "I-I am… late," she hurried to say.

Another lie.

They were piling up now faster than Lianae could remember them. And still she pressed her case. For emphasis, she moved a hand to her belly, watching the king's eyes as they fell upon her once more, also moving to her belly. Neither did the laird of Keppenach miss her gesture and he shared a look with his king, arching his devil's brow.

The king turned now to Cameron MacKinnon now, asking for his counsel, rather than the laird of Keppenach's or Lianae's. "You have spent the past five years in close quarters with the man, the past few months without fail. Is Keane dún Scoti capable of such a thing?"

Lianae could see the muscles in Cameron's jaw working. There was no telling what he would say. She knew the two men were at odds, but she also sensed his disapproval of her claims.

"The mon I know would ne'er abuse a woman," Cameron said, his expression sober. He shook his head, belying Lianae's claims. And he shot Lianae another look of contempt.

Lianae nearly cowed over the hateful glance. Confused, disheartened, she wanted nothing more than to throw herself over the table and beg for forgiveness—for lying about his friend most of all—but if she didn't do this, she might well find herself dead. Like her sister Elspeth.

The king's gaze reverted to Lianae. He gave her a pointed glance. "I have him down in the gaols," he apprised her, his dark eyes piercing.

Panic rose up in Lianae's breast.

Keane?

He was here?

Now?

"I could have his head for this," the king continued.

"Ach, nay!" Lianae exclaimed. She shook her head desperately. "Please, nay!" she begged. "It was not his fault, Your Grace!" And she fell at once to her knees.

David slapped his palm down upon the table,

making a terrible clatter. "*Not his fault?*" he roared. "How can ye say such a thing in the very same breath ye would impugn him?"

Hot tears pricked at Lianae's eyes. *By the gods, this was going terribly, terribly awry.* She'd never meant to bring Keane to harm.

"He followed to be certain you would be safe," the laird of Keppenach said. "That hardly seems the actions of a man who would do as you would have us believe."

Lianae shook her head, her throat too thick to speak. Tears welled in her eyes.

"He now awaits the king's justice."

Justice?

There was no justice in this world! Else her father would still be alive. She had to force the words past the knot in her throat. "He treated me with kindness, Your Grace," she confessed.

"And yet he forced himself upon ye?"

Lianae shook her head yet again.

The king turned his dark, uncanny gaze on Cameron now. "Did they share the same pallet as she claims?"

Cameron nodded, but reluctantly.

"And yet ye dinna believe he abused her?"

Cameron shook his head with far more certainty, and Lianae was both relieved and horrified at once. Keane was innocent, but it proved her a liar.

"Rise now, lass," the king commanded, his voice like thunder.

Wide eyed and fearful, Lianae immediately did as she was bade, rising from her knees.

The laird of Keppenach spoke again. "Do you ken what I would do to a man who forced himself upon my wife?"

Swallowing with some difficulty, Lianae shook her head yet again.

The laird of Keppenach's fury was apparent in every muscle in his body, including those now twitching at his neck. "I would take his head, sever it cleanly from his body, and then shove his cock between his lips. Then I would place his head upon a pike, as a feast for the crows."

He let her think on that image a moment, horrifying as it was. Lianae couldn't bear it. Sweat pooled between her breasts, despite the time of year. Inside this room, she felt stifled and suffocated.

After a moment, the king interjected. "Isn't this what you might expect, Lianae?"

Half nodding, half shaking her head, Lianae was terrified by the fate both she and Keane might now face—all her fault. Either way, it was a travesty. If the king sent her back to William, it would be her end. If he believed her, then Keane would hang—or worse. She thought about his head upon a pike and... and it made her physically ill. She covered her mouth and tried not to gag.

The king fixed her with a narrow eyed glare. "Lianae of Moray, what would *you* have me do with Keane dún Scoti?"

She did not hear, at first, the name he'd called him. It completely escaped her in her moment of terror.

Accord him honors.

Reward him with riches.

Keane did not deserve his head on a pike!

Tears slipped down Lianae's cheeks. Her face grew hot. "Your Grace, 'tis the truth, he dinna force me," she confessed. "I laid with him willingly."

At least it was partially true.

She had shared his pallet, after all—come to him willingly.

King David eyed the laird of Keppenach once more and then returned his gaze to Lianae. "If I should send in my physician to... *tend* ye... he would agree that you are no longer... a virgin?"

Lianae's cheeks heated, but she managed a nod—despite the lie.

"And you say you lay with him willingly?"

She felt as though she would swoon. "Aye, Your Grace."

The king turned to Cameron. "And what of this, MacKinnon. Is this true?"

"That she carries Keane's babe? How am I to know this, Your Grace?"

Lianae's heart tripped painfully as she inspected her thumb—raw now after two days of nervous picking—unable to face the contempt in Cameron's gaze. He was bound to loathe her by now, and he, above all the rest, would know her for what she was—a liar.

For a long while, Cameron seemed reluctant to reply, but then he did, and he nodded at last. "Aye, they slept together, but I never saw them do aught more than kiss."

Lianae's gaze snapped to meet his, surprised by the admission.

More tears brimmed in her eyes at the memory of the sweet kisses she had shared with Keane—tender moments that she would never trade for aught in the world. And Cameron had clearly witnessed at least one of them. *The one they'd shared in the pallet on the first morning she'd awoken beside him? Or the one down by the burn when she'd very nearly offered him her virginity? The chaste kiss on the back of her head where he stole her heart?* They were all proof of Keane's good character and will, for despite that she had placed herself boldly in his arms, every time he had pushed her away...

Keane was the first man she had ever known who'd made her heart trip—who treated her so familiarly and yet so gently, without a trace of lechery.

Is this how she should repay him?

The silence in the room was deafening. The king's fingers returned to abusing the wooden arm of his chair. The sound of his fingers beating the wood grew in intensity until it matched the quickening beat of Lianae's heart.

Would they hang a man for such as she'd claimed?

Just to be clear, and just to be certain they would not harm Keane, Lianae cleared her throat and said, "I *wanted* to lie with him."

And this much was wholly true.

With every fiber of her being.

"What of your intended?" David asked, feeling the need to remind her. "William fitz Duncan."

Lianae's heart squeezed painfully at the mention of the Earl's name. Fear paralyzed her tongue. Her eyes alone must have spoken loudly enough, because the king sighed and swept a hand across the table in disgust. "Very well." He nodded to the guard who'd brought her into the room. "Escort the Lady Lianae to her chambers."

Lianae wasn't a *lady*; she was a princess, but she didn't feel like one at the moment. She felt lower than low—a scourge on the face of the earth. *A liar. A coward.*

It had merely been her intent to render herself unmarriageable and in the process, she had impugned a good man's character.

She desperately wanted to make amends, but self-preservation held her tongue as the servant escorted her out from the solar. In the hall, Lianae shrugged free of the man's grasp and peered back into the room indecisively.

Speak now or forever hold your tongue, Lianae.

Keane is innocent! She wanted to shout.

But she did no such thing. She merely stood, as unbidden, an image accosted her—of Keane down in the gaols, awaiting his end. In her mind, she saw him marched out from his cell, taken to the gibbet and then hanged, and everything would be her fault.

She opened her mouth to speak the truth—no matter what may come—but the solar door slammed shut, and before she could speak another word, the guard dragged Lianae away.

CHAPTER SEVENTEEN

The babe's jet-black hair was slick and shiny against his tiny head. Like the fire in the brazier, he sputtered a bit and gave a throaty wail. Sorcha held him high in her hands, lifting the child with awe. "We have a boy!" she announced.

Exhausted, her sister by law laid down her sweat-dampened head, smiling at the sound of her newborn son. Judging by the bawl he made, his lungs were good.

It was the first child Sorcha had ever helped bring into the world, and the feeling was stupendous. At last—at long last—Aidan had himself a boy—a son—an heir of his own blood to carry on the guardian's way. Although Kellen was a splendid young man, he did not bear the blood of the Guardians in his veins. But this child did!

"What will be his name?"

"Alasdair," Lìli said, her voice barely above a whisper, now that her labor was done.

Sorcha smiled. "Defender of men… a verra good choice," she agreed and gave Lìli a wink. "Now shall we deliver his father from torment?"

"No need," Aidan said, stepping in through the bedroom door, with a grin bigger than any Sorcha had ever seen before. "I warrant everyone heard that wail unto Edinburgh itself!"

Indeed, who had not, with a howl like his? By now, even Una and Constance should have heard the delightful sound as they hurried down the mount. Lìli simply couldn't wait, though she tried. The child had been overly insistent about making his entrance into the world, and Sorcha had been there to see it through.

"A son!" Lìli exclaimed, weary though she was.

The look on her husband's face was one of surprise as he met his wife's violet eyes. He had said he would be pleased with another girl, but if the look on his face was any indication, her brother was overjoyed. "Truly?" Sorcha thought he sounded like he might actually weep.

Her face flushed with her exhaustion, Lìli nodded happily.

"Come see," Sorcha bade her brother. She had the babe in her arms and she laid him down beside his mother, pulling the blankets atop them both and tucking them in to keep them warm. His tiny little fists opened and closed and his arms punched at the air like a wee warrior, ready to conquer the world.

In a few short strides, Aidan was at his wife's side, falling to his knees at their bedside and Sorcha stepped out of the way to allow his brother to comfort his wife and to adore his new babe.

But Lìli held her hand, keeping Sorcha close. Her smile was so full of love. "You did well," she said, lifting her hand to Sorcha's arm.

Sorcha wiped her bloody hands on her skirts. "No thanks to Una," she quipped, though she laughed. "Although now I may tell her she's outgrown her usefulness." She winked and laughed good-naturedly, despite that she worried now. "I wonder what is keeping her," she said aloud, thinking about their conversation the day before. Una had been odd, giving away precious items. Nor had she come down to sup the night before, nor even to greet Aidan upon his return.

Lìli smiled, as though reading her thoughts. "I dinna put it past her to have lingered simply to show you your worth. Dinna underestimate your part in this, dear friend. Your nephew is as stubborn as his Da and for a while he dinna wish to come."

Aidan peered down at his wife, caressing her cheek with the back of his hand. "Why would he?" He grinned a lecherous grin. "Would that I could spend all my days in your flower as well."

Lìli's face flushed, the color heightening in her cheeks, and Sorcha laughed, accustomed by now to her brother's passions where his lovely wife was concerned. Aidan was like a drunkard, in truth. That he'd taken time to ride south to the aid of the MacKinnons had been a complete surprise to all, considering that he'd had to leave his wife. And yet Sorcha noticed, by the by, that he'd returned the instant he could. And after all, Una was right, he'd brought back another mouth to feed, and it took him all night long, but Lìli did indeed go into labor upon her husband's return.

"Thank you, Sorcha. 'Tis a good thing you were up to the task," Aidan said, peering over his shoulder at her. "Una's auld legs seem to fail her more and more. It takes her a sennight to make her way down the—"

All at once, there was a terrible rumble. It began slowly, building to a crescendo. And then without warning the sound was deafening enough to make Alasdair scream. It was a noise unlike any they had ever heard in the vale. The crannóg shook fiercely. Outside, snow slid from the rooftop, dumping into the loch, the sound like a terrible explosion. The floor shook beneath them.

Aidan and Lìli shared a horrified glance and then

her brother bounded up from her bedside and flew out of the room, out of the crannóg, and onto the long pier, where Ria and the rest of the household had congregated to watch.

Ash, not snow, rained down from the sky. A plume of smoke rose up from the mount, creating an enormous cloud like a mushroom. Sorcha's first thought was for Una, but immediately thereafter for the young lass who'd gone up to fetch her.

"Constance!" Kellen bellowed, and then her nephew bolted down the pier, shouting frantically after his wife.

❧

THEY CAME to retrieve Keane after long hours down in the cells.

The smell of damp earth and images of Aveline's rotting corpse had begun to fray his nerves. The sun was already making its descent, the castle's crenellations casting shadow teeth upon the courtyard.

Lael swatted the dirt from her brother's cloak, fretting as she tried to keep the pace. "Dinna lose your temper, Keane," she demanded of him. "And dinna be rude. Remember, he is *not* the same man who once stole our Cat."

"He is precisely the same man," Keane argued, unwilling to wipe the king's sins from existence merely because he'd managed to rally most of Scotia to his side.

Lael swiped something from his back, smacking him hard, and if he didn't know better, he might think she was smacking him for his argument. "Ach! Ye sound like Aidan! David has proven to be a fair and wise mon, and indeed, were he no', he'd never ha'e managed to win over so many hearts."

"Clearly, he has won yours?" Keane lifted a brow, casting his sister a dubious glance without breaking his stride. If they meant to hang him, he refused to crawl.

Lael had the good sense to hesitate before speaking. "Aye, well… now I see him through my husband's eyes. And, aye, he *is* the king of Scotia, by right or by might—and ye must trust him as I do."

Ignoring the men who kept pace alongside them, and the grunts of displeasure when he stopped to take his sister by the hand, he folded Lael's long fingers into his own. No longer were they so callused from practicing her blades. The feel of her hand was far different than it was the last time Keane held it. She had been the bigger one then, his eldest sister leaving a lanky youth to ride for Keppenach, defying their laird brother to do what she felt she must. He pressed his lips to her knuckles, loving her for her fierce, loyal spirit, but the years had softened her overmuch. Tears glistened in her eyes.

"I am nae longer a child, Lael. If I should lose my temper, I will accept the consequences, but dinna fash yourself' o'er it. I've nae death wish, I assure ye."

His words were meager consolation, if the worried look in her eyes was any indication. But she did not press Keane again. She nodded, accepting what he'd said.

The guards tugged him by the sleeve, once again leading him through the courtyard, but they did so respectfully for his sister's sake. This was her demesne, after all, by right of her laird husband. Still Lael cast them all a warning glance and Keane couldn't help but hide a smile. His sister was a force of nature. He envied Jaime not at all. If the truth be known, Lael was the very reason he'd never pursued a wife, for if they were all as stubborn, independent and willful as she was, he would die of stress before his time.

They entered the great hall, much changed from the days when Rogan MacLaren had served here as laird—much changed from merely a year ago. Now, the keep was larger, and far more modest. Additionally, they'd built a second keep to accommodate the influx of castle folk. Like his father before him, Jaime Steorling was a renowned warrior, with skills the nobles all coveted for their sons. These days, he accepted many young charges, and his sister had adapted well to her role of chatelaine, giving every man and woman she passed a welcoming smile. But today, Keane could tell that each smile was a bit of a trial. She was worried, he knew.

All along the walls, her hall was filled with tapestries—none of them quite to Keane's taste. They were far too pious in nature, and he wondered if that were more for David rather than for Jaime or Lael. Scotia's king spent a fair amount of time at Keppenach, which was probably one of the reasons Keane naturally stayed away.

They escorted him past the hall, past the dais where he knew Jaime entertained his tribunals. They marched him up the tower steps, to more private quarters—into Jaime's solar, where Keane had been many a time before—but never escorted by guards. The guards all fell away before the door, and only Lael remained by his side as the solar door opened.

Inside, David mac Maíl Chaluim was seated in a chair near the brazier, half turned away from the table. With a long face, Jaime stood to greet him, smiling rather tightly. He came about the table, though he did not clap Keane on the back as usual. He took his wife by the arm and escorted her out of the room whilst David bade Keane to sit.

For a moment, Keane stood, unmoving, pride interfering with his common sense. The fire in the brazier trembled with the draft from the open door. It was a good long moment before he finally bothered to acknowledge Cameron, who was seated at the table, and then when he did so, it was with a nod, his jaw taut and teeth clenched.

Aside from the three men, no one else was present in the solar, but there were a number of half-empty tankards abandoned before vacant chairs, which led Keane to believe there had previously been people seated there, clearly discussing Keane's fate. The simple fact that they'd not even allowed the maids to enter to clear away the dishes spoke volumes in itself. Behind him, Jaime closed the door on his wife and Keane watched his brother by law edge his way back around the table and seat himself in his chair.

"Sit down," David said, more firmly now.

Despite the sober expressions, it was a casual setting. Keane hoped that meant something. And yet, something grave was amiss here, or he'd never have found himself trapped behind bars. Following Lael's advice, Keane held his tongue, as much as it pained him.

"Today we have heard serious allegations against you, Keane dún Scoti."

Keane's teeth grated at hearing the bastardization of his name. He turned a baleful look toward Cameron, surmising that whatever allegations the king had heard, they must have come from him. But instead of looking away, Cameron held his gaze.

"Tell me how you plea," asked the king.

Keane's tone was full of contempt although he tried to mask it. "It would help to know what I am charged with."

Something in the king's expression softened. "And ye dinna ken?"

Keane felt himself growing impatient. "If I did, I am quite sure I would not have asked, *Your Grace*."

The king hid a smirk. "I always liked you as a lad, Keane dún Scoti. You are more like your sister than your brother," he said. "Fair enough."

Keane refrained from any response at all, because he could not return the compliment. He didn't suffer liars well—nor did he appreciate the king's continued use of the dún Scoti name.

David waved a hand dismissively. "Let us dispense with the trivialities," he said.

Keane blinked, uncowed.

"You have been accused of defiling a princess of Moray."

It was the last thing Keane expected to hear. "Lianae?"

"Indeed.... *Lianae.*"

"And does this accusation come from *Lianae's* own two lips—" He turned to Cameron. "Or is this the word of ambitious climbers?"

"It was Lianae," Jaime interjected soberly, sensing Keane's unspoken accusation of Cameron MacKinnon. "Cameron stood by you with every word he uttered, Keane. He is not your enemy here today."

Only now did Cameron look away, his expression clearly wounded.

"Who is my enemy?"

"Not I," Jaime said.

The king merely smiled and Keane inhaled a breath. He shook his head, trying to comprehend. "It was Lianae who said this?"

"Indeed," the king said, and continued to tap his long, lean fingers on the arm of his chair. "Of course, none of us were inclined to believe it, and after some time she did rescind her claim. And yet," the king continued, his gaze studying Keane. "She did also confess the two of you lay together willingly and this poses a problem."

For a moment, Keane remained dumbstruck, uncertain what to say. Close on the heels of a sense of relief that he might not face the gibbet, after all, was the simple realization that Lianae had lied. He'd never once touched any part of her save her lips, and her hands and feet, and aside from the kiss itself, none of it had afforded him much pleasure. He had merely meant to help, and instead, he stood here, facing an inquiry from the king...

"The problem, you see, is that she was promised to de Moray."

I am but a simple maid of Moray, she had said.

Keane felt the truth impact him like a blow to his gut. Although Lianae clearly hadn't been lying about *that,* damn her to hell for choosing her words so carefully Keane never suspected her relation to the man.

And yet... why hadn't he, dressed as she was?

All the signs had been there, and yet he had chosen to believe she was a woman still within his reach. He had kissed her as though she could be his. He clenched and unclenched the fist he held at his side.

"And then... there is the matter of those bruises..."

Clearly, David wished to see what Keane would say about that, and when he said nothing at all, the man continued.

"I fear I know how she received the marks, and despite that I dinna wish to anger the man—for the sake of peace, ye ken, not because I fear him as a rival—I canna in good faith return the lass to Moray."

It was another moment before Keane opened his mouth to speak, but the king held up a hand to silence him.

"You did lay with her, after all."

It wasn't a question.

Neither Jaime nor Cameron spoke to defend him, and Keane realized they all believed it—that he had bedded the lass, in front of gods and men alike. The notion infuriated him, and yet he held his tongue.

"You have a choice now," the king said.

Keane's jaw tightened with his anger. "What choice is that?"

"Wed the lass."

Silence fell upon the room. Keane shot Jaime a beleaguered glance. "You would see me wed a liar?" he asked.

"Now that you have bed her, is she no longer pleasing to you?" David interjected, clearly annoyed.

Pleasing? Pleasing! That was not in question here. Even now, seated in Jaime's solar, faced with a scourge upon his honor, his cock stirred at the memory of their kiss… the scent of her hair. But whether she pleased him was not the point!

David slapped a palm atop the table. "But not all is lost, you'll ken. I have a proposal," he suggested. And when Keane did not immediately speak, he continued, "Wed the lass, confess yourself as the father of her child, and I will give you Dunràth in payment."

Lianae carried a babe?

"Dunràth?"

The king gave him an affirmative nod.

Giving him Dunràth would only heighten the potential conflict with de Moray. "Moray is still a place of unrest," Keane argued. "Ye dinna realize, but despite de Moray's oath, ye are but a spider's breath away from losing what ye have gained to the Mormaer."

"Which is precisely why I would give you a seat in Moray."

"What about the sons of Óengus?"

Lianae's brothers.

The ones she'd been searching for.

"I cannot concern myself with the sons of Óengus when there are matters of greater import at hand."

David threw up his hands. "Have you not heard the news of Henry's death?"

Keane nodded.

"He was more than my friend, and far more than my sister's husband. He was an ally. It is by his leave that we have maintained the peace in Northumbria. But here, you see, is my dilemma: I ride for Carlisle soon, and I would not leave the North solely in de Moray's hands—not when I know he still craves to seat himself upon the stone at Scone. Do ye ken?" he asked.

Stunned by the unexpected offer, Keane met Jaime's gaze.

"Steorling has assured me you are a man of honor, Keane dún Scoti, and I have come to love your sister well. So... I can hang ye here, today, *now*. Or I can lift you up and grant ye Dunràth and you can swear me an oath of fealty as your rightful king—as your brother should have done years ago."

The room remained silent.

Keane had spent the whole of his life denying the dún Scoti name. And here, today, the king would have him join his ranks, and name himself a Scot. On pain of death, Aidan would have denied him. But it would serve no one for Keane to hang for this offense, and least of all Lianae.

"Only think of it," David added. "You are, after all, a man whose blood bears the soul of Scotia... your bride would be a daughter of kings."

David mac Maíl Chaluim continued to stare, watching Keane's reaction, though Keane merely sat, mouth agape, contemplating the offer—contemplating Lianae all the more, if the truth be known. She had accused him wrongly, but beneath his outrage, he sensed her underlying desperation.

Had the Earl given her those twin bracelets? Had he violated her already? Planted his seed in her belly? He felt both furious for Lianae's sake—and for himself. Never in his life had he experienced such a rage of conflicting emotions.

He thought of Lianae's sweet face on the morning he'd awoken next to her, the innocence with which she had embraced him, and his vision darkened with ire.

Close on the heels of these confusing images, he imagined her face as she'd stood right here, in this very room... and *lied. To the king of Scotland. To Jaime.* Keane's gaze fell upon his brother by law. *By virtue of this fact... she had lied to his sister as well.* Did Lael know that Lianae had accused him of getting her with a babe? Did these men not realize it was impossible to ken such a thing in only two days? If the girl was pregnant, it wasn't by Keane. He shot Cameron a glance. "Do my men all remain under my command?"

The king's dark eyes glinted. "All save Murdoch, who will hang for his treason. And I will provide you one hundred more to safeguard your seat in Moray."

It was a generous offer—one that likely had as much to do with safeguarding the king's interest in Dunràth Castle, but that was nothing less than to be expected.

Keane thought about Lilidbrugh, and the demise of his kinfolk, the prophecy Una had shared with them as children—the last words she'd said to him before leaving Dubhtolargg: *I ken ye'll know what to do when the time arrives...*

Keane spoke before he could stop himself. "I will wed the girl," he said. "And I will take Dunràth Castle, but I want Lilidbrugh as well."

"Lilidbrugh?"

There was an echo about the room. "Lilidbrugh!"

The king screwed his face. "God's teeth! That wretched pile of stones?"

"Aye," Keane said resolutely, his gaze meeting the

king's, his jaw taut with conviction. And once again, silence ensued, as the king considered his counter offer.

"Your fealty for Lilidbrugh?" he said after a thoughtful moment.

"*And* Dunràth," Keane insisted. And merely so no one could mistake him, he said with deadly earnest. "My oath of fealty for Lilidbrugh and Dunràth, and I will wed Lianae of Moray and claim her child as my own."

"And will you give me a *true* oath of fealty... despite what your brother might say?"

"I am my own man," Keane assured him.

David mac Maíl Chaluim smiled, like a cat who'd waited very patiently for his meal to come to play. "Then the deal is done," he agreed with a fierce note of satisfaction. "Now," he said, magnanimously, "let us prepare a feast in celebration!"

CHAPTER EIGHTEEN

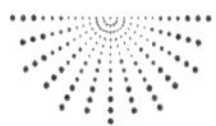

On the altar behind the dais, a sea of candles danced, their celebratory glow lending the front of the chapel a golden light. But no lutes played this day, no violas, no voices rang with cheer. It was a somber occasion.

Lianae stood next to Keane before the king's prelate, begging her knees to cease knocking beneath her new gown. For the first time in days, she felt clean. She'd scarce been able to wait to rip off that other gown—the one belonging to Elspeth. It had offended her every second she had worn it, despite that it was more lavish than the one she now wore.

This gown was simply made, but made of blue and gold sendal, with gold trim about the neckline and sleeves and a girdle made of gold. The cloak was velvet, trimmed with minerva and Lianae wore it thrown back, clasped at her throat with a golden broach. Her battered and bruised feet were swaddled in pale blue silk.

Standing at her side, dressed in dark blue and gold, Keane looked more a prince than a simple warrior. His shining black hair was clasped at the back, as were his hands, as though he meant to keep them from strangling Lianae where she stood.

The priest cleared his throat. "Who comes forth to be wed today?"

It was the king who replied. "Keane dún Scoti and Lianae of Moray."

"And who gives the bride to be wed?"

"I do," said the king.

Lianae swallowed her grief, for she had hoped it would be her father's right—and if not her father's, mayhap her brothers. Behind them, the congregation remained silent, so silent she could hear the drip, drip of melting snow outside upon the eave.

"Do any oppose these two be wed?"

Keane cleared his throat although he did not speak, and Lianae held her breath as she watched the candles shiver in their sconces.

No one else spoke a word, but she had visions of the Earl bursting in through the chapel doors. Or mayhap Keane's sister tearfully beseeching the King on her knees. None of these things came to pass, however. The room remained painfully silent, waiting for the priest to continue.

"Enough," the king bellowed impatiently. "There will be none who oppose this union."

And the prelate cleared his throat. "Very well," he relented. "Will you, Keane dún Scoti, newly appointed laird to Dunràth, have this woman to be thy wedded wife, to live together after God's ordinance in the holy estate of matrimony? Wilt thou love her, comfort, honor and keep her, in sickness and in health; and forsaking all others, keep thyself only unto her, so long as ye both shall live?"

The priest was looking straight at Keane and when Keane didn't immediately respond, he asked, "Will you?"

Her betrothed's reply was curt. "Aye," he said.

The priest settled a far less nervous smile upon Lianae. "Very well now, Lianae of Moray, wilt thou have this man to be thy wedded husband, to live together after God's ordinance in the holy estate of matrimony? Wilt thou obey and serve him, love, honor and keep him in sickness and in health; and, forsaking all others, keep thyself *only* unto your laird husband?"

It seemed to Lianae that the priest accused her with his question. "I will," she replied.

"Louder, child, so all may hear!"

"I *will*," she repeated, enunciating the words more distinctly.

The priest smirked at her, avoiding Keane's gaze. "Very well, then may God, who is merciful and just, bless this union and make you fruitful that you may bring forth sons and daughters to praise his name."

"So be it," Lianae said, when Keane remained silent.

"So be it," Keane said tightly.

Lianae turned to face her new husband, vowing never to give him cause to rue this day. She would be a good wife to him, bear his bairns and she would cherish him until the day she died. She begged him to understand, pleaded with her eyes.

Forgive me, Keane.

The priest held up a small reliquary, asking them both to place a hand atop the sacred relic to consecrate their vows. Lianae did so, and was acutely aware of the weight of Keane's hand as he placed it atop hers.

"As this man and woman have now sworn afore God and the bones of St. Peter, henceforth they will be known as man and wife. Amen."

"Amen," said the king very quickly.

"Amen," said all those gathered in the chapel.

"Amen," whispered Lianae.

Only one man did not voice the final benediction: The man standing at her side.

But it was done, and it was far more than she had dared to hope for, when all she'd ever wanted was to be spared a life from the tyranny of William fitz Duncan.

Her husband clearly did not share her joy. He stood beside her, his expression grim, and he could barely look at her, despite the lovely attire his sister had dressed her in.

WHAT MORE FITTING UNION?

A prince of the forgotten Pechts and a daughter of the conquered Moray. Her people, like Keane's, were the last of their kind, and for this alone, he might have welcomed her into his bed… into his home… and, aye, even into his heart. But some part of him longed to walk away, even now—the prideful part of himself that would be wounded by her lies.

"You may exchange the kiss of peace with your bride," the priest allowed.

His bride.

His beautiful, treacherous, lying, conniving bride.

Kiss of peace?

How could there ever be peace now betwixt them?

Lianae met his gaze boldly, standing as tall as she could. Even despite that she wasn't particularly small, she rose only as tall as Keane's shoulders. Her golden-red hair was braided like two silken cords and her eyes glistened like polished amber. She made the loveliest of brides—far lovelier than he might have imagined—but this too was beside the point.

Her cheeks blossomed with color and she bit nervously at her lower lip, swelling it with her blood. And despite Keane's fury, their bodies seemed naturally drawn together.

They were so close now that Keane could feel the heat emanating from her mouth. The scent of her dizzied his senses, and still he refrained... hovering near.

Only this morning he might have given anything to kiss her just once more, and if he merely did so now, he would walk away with Lilidbrugh, Dunràth, a seat on the king's council and a lovely new bride.

But he hesitated, wanting more...

He wanted what Aidan had—what Lael had discovered. He wanted what Cameron only longed for, and until this instant, Keane hadn't realized he did too.

Lianae stood waiting, anxiously nipping at her lip and finally, resentfully, he pulled her close. She swallowed visibly and he held her more firmly yet, wanting her to comprehend what it meant to be forced. It would serve her right after all the lies she'd told. But he could not force her. Nor did she test him. She melted into his embrace and grew pliant, and only then did Keane bend to cover her mouth with his own.

Sweet and heady, that was her taste.

She promised him heaven and yet she'd already sent him to hell.

Keane's body tensed, and for one ungodly moment, he forgot entirely where it was they stood. Once again, they were standing in the snow-covered woods, her hands clinging to his waist. The taste of whitebeam filled his mouth and he stifled a groan lest it slip like juice betwixt her lips. His loins tightened at the feel of her so near and he longed to deny his own desire—until such time as Lianae could look him in the eyes and speak the words he longed to hear...

"Ahem," the priest said, clearing his throat.

The kiss was bittersweet, and it took much of his willpower, but Keane peeled himself away, inevitably leaving a piece of him as he did so.

The priest's eyes shifted from Keane to Lianae, and then he declared, "What God has joined let no man put asunder."

No man... or woman...

But she already had...

Needing succor, Keane sought his sister's gaze. In Lael's familiar eyes, filled with equal measures of hope and regret, he found what he needed to see, love without condition and freely given. Until he spied that in his wife's eyes, he would harden his heart. A kiss might have sealed his fate, but it would never rob him of his hope.

❧

For all that they were much too pious, Jaime was pleased with the tapestries Lael ordered for the great hall. The thick material easily muffled the sound of idle chatter and the deep reds and golds, coupled with the new chandeliers, managed to give the room warmth and cheer, neither of which the wedded couple managed to exude.

Somehow, his wife had managed to rouse the entire household to prepare a feast fit for a king. She'd served Jaime's favorite—a dessert called *blancmanger* that she'd introduced to him at their own wedding. And along with the *blancmanger,* she'd served currant cakes, pheasant, *brawn en peuerade,* a delicious pork in wine sauce, *connynges in grauey*—rabbit in broth—and *dauce egre,* a wonderful fish cooked in a sweet and sour onion sauce. There was plenty of warm bread, sweet cheese, mead and ale. The only one thing there wasn't enough of was laughter. The evening was entirely too sober. Despite twinkling candles, music and a smattering of *uisge,* the great hall had all the good cheer of a funeral. In fact, he'd attended hangings that were far more joyful than this. The entire affair reminded him all-too-much of another wedding some years past—his own.

Lianae stood dutifully beside her new husband, her expression sullen and full of—in Jaime's estimation—what appeared to be regret.

For Keane's part, he looked like a man who'd been led to the gibbet rather than to an altar. His smiles were few and far between, and most were directed at Lael, in order to reassure her. Betimes he envied their close-knit sibling relationship. Even all these years later, he and Kenna scarcely knew each other, despite that she lived beneath his very roof. In fact, she was closer to Lael than she was to him.

All day long Kenna had been brooding, and now it appeared she had eschewed the celebration entirely. He was searching the crowd to see if he could find her, when his wife came tugging at his sleeve. She looped her arm about Jaime's, drawing him close. "Do you think they will be alright?" she asked.

He followed her gaze to the dais, noting the couple's general discord. "I do not know. In truth, have never seen him quite so..."

Wooden. Stoic. Quietly seething.

"Unyielding?"

Over the past five years, Jaime had come to know the man well. Thanks to Keane, Jaime had been able to join the battle at Stracathro in Forfarshire with some more peace of mind whilst he'd remained here at Keppenach along with Lael. He knew it had cost Keane his brother's affections, and the two rarely spoke anymore. For that alone, he felt an obligation to see to his wellbeing.

Lael sighed loudly, her fingers tightening about his forearm. "I would be furious, in truth, had I not spent a few moments with the girl when I took her the gown. She was reticent, and yet every other word was, 'will

Keane like this?' 'Will Keane like that?' To my way of thought 'tis a lot of fretting over a man she'd only meant to impugn."

Jaime considered that a moment, remembering the wild look in the girl's eyes in the solar. "'Tis my opinion she was merely trying to save herself."

"Save herself?" Lael peered up at him, her lovely brows lifting. "From what, perchance?"

"Aye, well, that would be the question." He stared down at his wife, knowing the answer to the question he would ask, despite his need to hear a little white lie, "Did you carry on that way before our nuptials?"

"Like Lianae?" Lael laughed and then shot him sideways glance. "Nay, husband!"

"So, then, ye dinna wish to please me, not at all?"

His wife tilted him a coy smile. "I dinna care to remind ye, husband. I would have greatly preferred to pluck out your eyes."

Jaime's shoulders shook a bit with laughter, realizing that she likely spoke the truth. That night so long ago, there had been naught between them but lust, and mostly on his part. His beautiful wife would have preferred to gut him from head to toe—and she might well have, given her skill with the blades. Even after all these years, she far surpassed most of his men and had shown little desire to put away her sharp little toys. Even now, despite that she was far more adept at concealing them, he knew she secreted one beneath her dress, strapped to her ankle in a soft pocket of fine silk—a gift from Jaime on their fifth year together, the day he'd left her to do battle in the north. Alas, his eldest daughter had taken up her torch. God help any man who dared to cross the Ste-orling women.

"Where are the children?" he asked.

"Here and there," Lael replied, waving a hand dismissively, no doubt as much an accomplice to their foolery as were his errant daughters.

They had four—four clever little sirens, who would all someday lure hapless men to their doom—as surely as their lady mother had done to him. But be damned if he didn't love his life. His gaze returned to the newly wedded couple, considering what his wife had said.

He had a good feeling about Óengus's last living daughter, and it was a good thing, because elsewise, given Keane's demeanor, Jaime doubted he could have supported the king in his decision to force them into matrimony—which by the by, confused him a bit...

William fitz Duncan was a clear and present rival for Scotia's throne. By the letter of the law, he would have had a greater claim than even David. That David mac Maíl Chaluim would have given Óengus's daughter to fitz Duncan in the first place was a risk to be sure and Keane had spoken the truth. As much unrest as there remained in Moray, fitz Duncan could easily claim the greater right to the throne by virtue of his own birthright, strengthened by the royal blood of his Moray bride. The one thing David had in his favor was that the people did not like fitz Duncan. But, on the other hand, they adored the sons and daughters of MacBeth. So give Lianae a man of might—like Keane—someone people were naturally drawn to follow. Give her someone who also brought to the union the blood of much revered kings—again, Keane, despite that the dún Scoti abstained from Scotia's politiks. Add to this the fact that Keane was also Pecht—no matter that his kinsmen no longer referred to themselves this way. He, together with Lianae, could wage a battle for the North... and win. And given that they held a man within their dungeon at Dunràth a man who might see it done... well, he did not understand what David was up to... and yet he knew his king well enough to know that he did not take chances. Whatever was unfolding was well within David's command. Alas, Jaime was sworn to keep this secret from his lovely wife, and God's truth, these were the moments when he most loathed his position. But his brooding thoughts went unnoticed by his wife.

Up on the dais, Lianae seldom took her eyes off Keane. Whatever he did, she did. When he smiled, so too did she, despite that Keane seemed completely oblivious to this effort. Jaime cast a knowing glance at his wife. "Would that you were always so biddable as she."

Lael returned his smile, her brilliant green gaze twinkling by the candlelight, and the gleam in her eyes made him wish they were alone. "Ye wadna like me verra much, I think."

They shared a meaningful look, and a private smile. "Quite right, love."

Husband and wife returned their gazes to the newly wedded couple, watching Lianae as she watched her husband brood.

"Those are not the actions of a woman who holds a man in contempt, wouldn't ye say?"

"And yet… she spoke such terrible lies about my brother. It will bode them ill. Keane hasn't a mean bone in his body, though he does not have a particularly open, or forgiving way once he has been crossed."

"Aye, well, I've a good feeling, nonetheless," Jaime confessed.

"Aye?" There was hope in her voice.

"Di' ye not see *that kiss?*"

"Who could have missed *that kiss?*"

"Aye, well… that," he reassured his lovely wife, "Is not the mark of a man who would loathe his bride. I'll vow every witness thereof has been hornier than a two-peckered dog all night long."

"Even you?"

Jaime grinned lasciviously. "Especially me, wife."

The entire evening was a lie.

A sham.

A ruse.

A bitter pill to swallow.

The more Keane thought about it, the angrier he became.

"Bed her!" came the cries. "Bed her!" The insistent shouts grew louder, infinitely louder, into to a deafening roar, until the voices nearly shook the rafters.

"Bleed her!"

"Bed her!"

The energy in the hall was palpable, and the more people drank, the more they fueled their own base desires. Despite that he struggled to keep his wits about him, Keane was not immune to it. Ever since that kiss, his nerves had been on edge, ready to shatter with merely a word from his mendacious wife. But all the while she remained silent, sullen and looking like an exquisite little martyr, standing dutifully by his side. He could scarce even look at her now, but he felt her presence like a sharp blade turning in his side.

Once the crowd began to gather around them, pressing ever closer, he gave in, sweeping up his beautiful, treacherous wife into his arms. He carried her out of the hall before the throng could see fit to follow. Squealing with surprise, Lianae clasped her hands about his neck, holding tight as he bore her across the dais, straight to the tower steps. He didn't bother to look back. He trusted Jaime to stop the guests before marching up the stairs. Ribald jests shot up the stairwell when it became clear the guests would not be allowed to follow in order to witness the bedding—or the bleeding, for that matter. *Distasteful affair.* It wasn't his people's custom and perchance it might be hers, but he wasn't about to admit witnesses for what he knew was to follow.

His bride was neither a virgin, nor was she his precious lover, and he wasn't about to stir his cock for this travesty of a union. He wasn't an animal ready to breed at a moment's notice—nor would he play the fool.

In perfect silence, he carried Lianae up the tower steps, and the higher he climbed, the more the voices faded away.

He could feel her nails prick the back of his neck, so tight was her grip upon him.

At last, he reached the suite his sister had assigned to them—the same room he'd occupied five years before when he'd come to live, save that tonight, the chamber had been lavished with little luxuries. He pushed open the door to set loose a myriad of scents. Rose petals. Roasted almonds. *Vin*—the King's favorite, or so he'd claimed—a gift from the sovereign of Scotland, hand chosen from King Henry's cellars in Lyons-la-Forêt in France.

Keane had the briefest moment of ill humor over the notion—wondering if in fact the *vin* might be poisoned. *A gift of death for Scotia's remaining sons and daughters.*

Wouldn't that serve David well? He could keep the crown for himself, without any fear of reprisal—not that Keane had any use for Scotia's bloody crown.

Then again, he realized Jaime loved the man, and he trusted his sister's judgment without fail. She'd said she'd come to like the man—far different words than she'd spoken ten years past.

Once inside, Keane kicked the door closed, carrying his wife into the cozy chamber. Halfway inside the room, he set her down on the floor—well away from the bed—and marched straight for the carafe of *vin*.

"H-have I done aught to displease you?" she asked, incredibly.

Had she done aught to displease him?

Keane coughed, a sound that was part laughter, part something else he could not define. He poured himself a cupful of *vin* and then met Lianae's gaze. "Truly? You have the gall to ask such a question?"

CHAPTER NINETEEN

Lianae froze where she stood, impaled by her husband's hard, glittering gaze as surely as though it were a killing blade. They must have told him everything by now and he might loathe her for the rest of her days. But at least she trusted him not to harm her—which hardly relieved her terrible sense of guilt.

What a choice to be made?

Impugn an innocent man, or suffer like her sister Elspeth?

That was no choice at all.

He was titled now, landed—something for which he might be grateful, but there was nothing of the look of gratitude in his posture or in his gaze. If she were flammable, the fire in his eyes would have easily set her ablaze.

Uncomfortable with her husband's scrutiny, Lianae turned to examine the grandiose bed. It was overlarge—more befitting a king, with elaborate gold curtains that hung like festoons from a rich dark frame. The bedding itself was made of golden velvet. She made her way over to the gilded monstrosity, and ran her fingers across the soft blanket, marveling over how well King

David's earls seemed to live. To the contrary, she and her family had lived simply.

Images flashed before her eyes—of Elspeth on her wedding night—her final moments of life. The look of dread on her sister's face as she'd taken her vows and then later, as she lay so still upon her marriage bed, the bruises ringing her neck… the sheets stained with her blood…

Lianae swallowed convulsively, her throat thickening uncomfortably as she waited for Keane to make his move. Now that they were here, she didn't know what to do. In contrast to the cacophony down below, the room was unbearably silent. And when finally, it seemed he would never speak, Lianae turned to face him and asked breathlessly, "Shall I undress for you, my laird?"

"Nay!" He eyed her distastefully and poured a bit more wine, quaffing it down in a single gulp.

Lianae was confused. "But… the bedding. Will they not expect—"

One dark brow arched malevolently. "Blood?"

Lianae nodded, and he smiled thinly, slamming down his cup upon the small table. "Dinna fash yourself," he said. "I have a solution for that." And he marched toward her, reaching into his belt for an ornate dirk he had sheathed there.

Lianae gasped, and seeing the flash of his blade, she took a frightened step backward.

He came only as far as the heel of the bed and ripped away the blankets, exposing the white bedding beneath, and then he held out his hand, palm side up.

Was he asking her to join to him now?

How could he expect her to come to him so easily when he was looking at her so furiously? His green eyes glinted as sharply as did the steel of his blade. He stared for a moment, his mouth twisting ruefully and then he sliced the blade across his hand, cutting a fine, deep gash across the pad beneath this thumb. Lianae cried out in horror as blood spilled from his wound, into the palm of his hand. He turned it then, and let the blood trickle down over the white sheets.

"If blood is what they want," he said. "Blood is what they'll get. But we both ken verra well that ye'll no' be bleedin' for me tonight, *Maid of Moray*."

❧

CONSTANCE FOUND herself standing near the entrance of the cave, screaming at the top of her lungs. Ash filled her throat and nose, making it difficult to breathe. The mountain rumbled all about her and she stumbled to her knees. "Help," she cried, frozen with fear where she knelt. "Help me!"

Lachlann was the first to arrive. His post was the closest on the mountain, but Aidan's captain could barely hear the girl wailing over the rumble and din of a mountain collapsing.

Una remained somewhere below. It was impossible to imagine how anyone could escape such a catastrophe from deep in the belly of the ben. The caves were decimated, the entrance barred with enormous, immovable boulders that were three times the size of a man.

"The light," Constance sobbed. "I saw light! Now I see naught," she cried, bursting into tears. She covered her face with trembling hands. "I canna see," she said over and over again. "I canna see!" Until the words became a litany.

"I canna see!"

Grief stricken, Kellen escorted his disconsolate wife to his old chamber in the crannóg, where she would be safe. All able-bodied men gathered on the hill, moving stones as best they could, tugging relentlessly and in vain at others that refused to budge.

There was scarce more than a crack large enough to send a fly into. And for all that he was the laird of his clan, Aidan worked hardest of all, with tears burning his eyes, unashamed to weep. All about, there was nary a pair of eyes that were not veined with red and no cheek to be found that was not salted by tears.

It should have been impossible to escape the shower of stone—impossible, and yet, somehow Constance had managed to do so. Until Aidan discovered how, he refused to stop searching for Una. Men and women worked tirelessly into the evening, by the light of pitch torches, and every so oft, a man broke down and fell despondent to his knees, sobbing without constraint.

The Stone of Destiny was buried half a league down beneath the cold, hard ground. But far more importantly, so was their beloved Una—for Aidan and his brethren, the only mother they had ever known. The old woman birthed their babes, as well as nearly every single man and woman present. She had tended their wounds. Loved their aged. She'd guided Aidan and his father and his father before him. She'd cursed their enemies, taught their children, loved their bairns. She was more a part of the dún Scoti clan than any living being. But the love they bore her couldn't save her. She never emerged from the cave—not that night, or the next morning, and it soon became apparent Una was lost.

And still, every kinsman available moved stone after stone, stubbornly seeking a way in and cursing amongst themselves every time they reached a dead end.

In the snow and freezing rain, they tried everything —attempted to breach the cavern through a crevice they'd sealed some years past, but that too was unbreachable now. No matter where they attempted to dig, they made little progress, reaching solid granite at the end of their spades. Two long days they labored without rest, until their hopes began to dim. Tired and hungry, and soaked to the bone from ice-cold rain, they crowded together in the crannóg's long hall, taking turns by the pit to warm their frozen bones. Filthy from a hard day's work, Aidan emptied the cabinets of *uisge* and set the jugs out for anyone to have. The mood in the hall was doleful and there was little appetite for food, but the mind-numbing *uisge* would be welcomed.

"*Cha bhithidh a leithid ami riamh,*" Lachlann offered after a moment of silence, raising a cup to Una. *Her equal will never be among us again.*

Aidan was not yet ready to let her go, and yet he drank a toast with the rest of his kin, his throat too thick to utter a single word.

Sorcha sat at the table, her head cradled within her arms, weeping softly. With red-rimmed eyes, Cailin patted her youngest sister on the shoulder. Lìli sat beside them, cradling the newborn babe—a child Una would never know.

With skinned legs and bloodied fingers, Kellen had retreated to his chamber to console his poor wife, who had yet to recover her sight.

No one could quite make out Constance's story, but as best as they could decipher, she had gone down into the tunnel below Una's grotto, after finding the door ajar. She found Una lying prayerfully upon the ground, next to the altar bearing the Stone from Scone. She read aloud from the plaque, she'd said—a scripture Aidan knew by rote.

Unless the fates be faulty grown
And prophet's voice be vain
Where'er is found this sacred stone

The blood of Alba reigns.

AND THEN LIGHT EXPLODED, blinding the girl, shattering the caverns like glass. Like their beloved kinswoman, the stone called *clach-na-cinneamhain* was now lost. It was once the destiny of his people, but now they would be guardians nevermore.

Swallowing the contents of his tankard whole, Aidan slammed his cup down on the table, and poured himself another, tears stinging his smoke-red eyes. "Lael, Cat and Keane must be told," he said to no one in particular.

"And Cameron," Cailin added. "He may not realize his sister has wed our brother."

Another moment of excruciating silence.

"We'll send a messenger to Keppenach," Lìli suggested. "The winter has been mild enough. The road is not yet unpassable."

"I'll go," Lachlann offered.

"As will I," Auld Fergus said.

"Just the two of you," Aidan agreed, his throat scarce allowing words to pass. "We will need every pair of hands to continue the search."

Lìli gave him a look filled with sorrow and tears spilled down her cheeks. "Aidan... we have heard not a sound from the caverns below. The tunnels are sealed, my love."

Sorcha said softly, raising her head, "She canna live without..." She swallowed the rest of her words.

Auld Fergus stood and raised another toast. "What's that she oft said?"

MAY those who mùirn us mùirn us;
And those who dinna mùirn us,

May the Cailleach *turn their hearts:*
And if She wadna turn their hearts
May she turn their ankles,
Sae we'll know 'em by their gimp.

"Here's to us," toasted Lachlann, with a throaty voice that sounded full of gravel.

"Wha's like us?" added Sorcha sadly, in the absence of her youngest brother, who would often say the words.

And Aidan, with glassy eyes and a gruff voice, finished the toast for the rest, "Damned few," he said. "And they're all dead."

Auld Fergus sighed wearily. "Guess she weren't no Cailleach, after all."

With the first light of morning, Keane rose from the chair he'd slept in and wandered close to the bed.

She hadn't had any true notion what to expect from the marriage bed, but this was not it. The look Keane had given her last night had turned her flesh to ice, and the tone of his voice engendered tears she'd refused to shed. Whilst he'd sat staring into the brazier during the long night, alone in the bone-chilling darkness, she'd lain in the bed they were meant to share, curled up as far away from the stain of his blood as she could possibly get.

For a moment, Lianae could *feel* him standing there, a shadow behind her lids, but she daren't open her eyes to see what he was doing. He lingered but a second before turning and walking out the door and in his absence, the room felt colder and more barren than before.

Confused and uncertain how to proceed, she lay abed now, reluctant to rise—not the least for which she was still wearing her accursed wedding gown, never having bothered to undress. But she had no wish to wear it again today. She'd had enough of wedding gowns for an entire lifetime!

Had she dared to hope for more? What could she expect? That he would simply overlook her many lies and find himself enamored enough to love her as his wife?

Her fabrications might have sent him to the gallows; it was no wonder he loathed her so much. If any one thing had happened any differently, she might be laying here this instant, listening to the din outside her window as they waited for the executioner to appear.

But nay. Somehow she had known it would not come to that... hadn't she?

She must have known.

Remembering the way Keane had looked at her only two days past, standing beneath that precious white-beam tree, she felt a pang in her heart and desperately wanted him to come back as he was.

Would he never forgive her?

The kisses they'd shared—every one—gave her reason to believe. Even the one he'd given her at the altar... it made her tremble merely at the thought.

After a long while there came a knock on the door, and Lianae's heart skipped a beat. She sat upright in the bed. "Come in," she said.

The door opened and a lovely young woman pushed her face into the crack of the door. "Good morn, Lianae. I am Kenna—Jaime's sister."

Embarrassed to be caught in the state she was in—tear stained and fully dressed, Lianae scrambled from the bed. "Oh, please... come in."

The woman smiled and came into the room, and

Lianae saw the resemblance nearly at once. Their eyes were the same as the laird of Keppenach's, that odd steely blue.

"The maids will be along soon," the girl said. "In the meantime, I brought you these."

In her hands there was a stack of folded garments—a generous pile. Only belatedly did the girl seem to realize that Lianae was still wearing her wedding dress. Surprised perhaps, she averted her gaze from the bed, blushing profusely. "The lady Lael would have you keep your wedding gown," she explained. "And these…" She pointed a chin at the stack of garments she held, all without meeting Lianae's gaze. "They once belonged to a lady she once knew. She said to tell you that Aveline would have wished to share them with you."

"Who is Aveline?"

Kenna shrugged. "I barely knew her," she said. And Lianae didn't press, because there was something in the girl's expression that didn't welcome any more discussion along that vein. Coming forward a little nervously, Kenna dropped the stack of clothing on the edge of the bed, her gaze automatically scanning the bedding, and discovering the blood, she appeared confused, once more averting her gaze, to peer over at the chair by the brazier.

If it were possible, Lianae sensed Keane's warmth in the chair, ready to decry her a failure as a bride.

Watching the girl, Lianae considering the emotions that flitted across the woman's face. Relief perhaps? "I trust you slept well?"

"Quite well, thank you."

A knowing smile touched the woman's lips. "I must say, there's nae been a lass belowstairs who dinna swoon over *that kiss*."

The one at the altar, Lianae realized and tried to smile. Somehow the thought did seem to improve her mood. He could scarce loathe her so much if his lips spoke a different tale.

"You're a lucky woman," the girl said, and her ensuing smile was genuine.

"You admire him?" It was perhaps a fortunate guess on Lianae's part, and the girl's answer might have given her dread, save that there was little in her tone or expression to give Lianae pause.

Kenna's cheeks bloomed with color. "I do… er did," she confessed. "But that is neither here nor there. Alas, but Keane never once looked my way, and certainly not the way he looks at you."

"Me?" Lianae asked. Her fingers plied through the stack of garments Kenna had placed upon the bed. After all, she chose the one on top, a soft, golden-yellow wool dress without embellishments.

"I would give my legs *and* my arms for a single heartfelt glance like that," the girl confessed. And when she sighed, it came from the very depths of her soul.

Lianae hid a tiny smile—not for Kenna's heartbreak, but for her own burgeoning sense of hope. After all was said and done, there *must* be something between them. And for the manner of their marriage she would beg his forgiveness evermore, but before she could do that, she must win his favor again. She would make Keane a good wife, she vowed, or the effort would kill her. One way or another, she would make it up to him. And even despite everything that had occurred, she had more hope for the future than just a few days before.

Aye, then—unfurling the dress, she decided it was time to win back her new husband. Whether or not she ever found her brothers, her place was now by Keane's side. She held the dress up to her breast, testing the length of the hem. "'Tis pretty," she said, and looked to Kenna for confirmation.

"That one will be lovely," the girl said. "It matches

your eyes. But 'tis too long!" She came forward then and chose another—one from the bottom of the pile. This one was pale green, made of wool as well, but with a golden girdle. "Try this," she said. "It will fit you best, and we'll mend the others together."

CHAPTER TWENTY

Keane spent the entirety of the next few days in council with the king—a welcome distraction despite the matters to be discussed.

In Aidan's absence, he was asked to represent the dún Scoti clan—a fact that he might have told them was entirely pointless. Aidan would never agree to aught that was discussed here. His brother would not acknowledge Scotia as his sovereign nation, nor would he kneel before David as his king. And yet, the more Keane heard, the more he found wisdom in David mac Maíl Chaluim's words, and he was becoming conflicted —a dilemma that did not bode well for his relationship with his brother. Little by little he was beginning to understand why Lael had embraced the man, and although he himself struggled to honor his vows, one day in witness to the king's counsel and he could no longer view the man as a raging madman. He was civil, fair minded and held the wellbeing of his people in every word he spoke. Even the sentence he'd given Keane—a seat in Moray and a bride—was far more generous than he might have deserved were Lianae's accusations even remotely true. Alas, but it was her word against Keane's, and Keane counted himself fortunate that he had witnesses enough to vouch for his character. Elsewise, his head might now be adorning a pike, and Lianae would be...

With William fitz Duncan... who, by the by, was suspiciously absent from the king's council. But he was not the only one yet to come. Broc Ceannfhionn remained at Chreagach Mhor, along with MacKinnon. But although Broc would join David without question by virtue of his sworn vows, MacKinnon had sent word that he would support David's campaign in Northumbria, only so long as David acknowledged his son as Aldridge's rightful heir. It was agreed. And by the end of the day, despite the last failed attempt by King Duncan to take Northumbria, David had garnered support from all the barons present, with assurances that he had more allies in the north.

Along with Carlisle, they now intended to secure Wark, Alnwick and Norham as well, and they would engage within the fortnight—as swiftly as they could gather the necessary troops and make the journey south. Stephen would be too pre-occupied with securing his throne. It would be months before he could turn his attentions to the North. By then, David would have secured the entirety of Northumbria.

By the time they were finished detailing the entire campaign, Keane was more than ready for respite. And yet, the tensions awaiting him in his chamber were far greater than in the place he left—if one could believe it. He climbed the tower steps, hoping Lianae was otherwise occupied, for he sorely longed to stretch in the bed. Even as comfortable as it was, the chair was a poor substitute.

Kenna and Lael had kept his wife pre-occupied, and he was grateful to them both, and still, he longed to see her—if only for an instant. *Why* he had no clue. She was a cunning little vixen who had wormed her way into his thoughts. He rued the day he ever met her.

To his surprise, he found the room cozy and warm, with a brazier burning and a steaming, herb-filled bath in the center of the room.

Lianae met him at the door, with a sweating flagon in her hands. "Ale?" she asked, raising the tin. "Or would ye prefer warm spiced mead?" She waved a hand toward the small table by his chair, the look in her eyes filled with apprehension.

Keane would have liked to say neither, but at the moment, a cup of ale was precisely what he needed. And the bath was more than he could have hoped for.

"Ale will be fine," he said, peeling off his gloves and setting them down upon the table, his eyes scanning the treats she had gathered: crispels, tiny pastries basted in honey, along with herbs and spices.

Without a word, Lianae poured him a cup of ale. She handed it to him. Keane took the cup, his shoulders tense, and his body aching with repressed desire.

She was as beautiful as she was treacherous, he decided. Simply because he shouldn't want her didn't mean he didn't...

"Would that I bathe you?" Lianae asked sweetly as though she would serve him with a willing heart, and he had to remind himself that she was a very, very good liar. If she would woo him, it was because she wanted something from him. What it was, he couldn't fathom and didn't care. He would not play her fool.

"Nay," he said, but there was less resolve in his tone than he would have hoped.

She came forward anyway, stubborn as she was. "I would aid you if you'd but let me, Keane."

She was dressed today in plainer clothes—a soft green wool that clung to her curves, outlining the high rise of her ample breasts. His eyes hungrily devoured her, famished for the sight of her after two days of coming and going, in the dark, whilst she slept.

Keane struggled to deny her. He took a final sip of his ale and set the cup down in silence, stripping himself before the brazier. He shrugged out of his gambeson and tunic and then began unlacing his trews, not daring to acknowledge the other occupant of the room. Without the barrier of clothes between them, it would be his undoing, because even now, he found himself stirring at the thought of them together in this room... *their room...* in which he had been expected to bed the woman he'd taken to be his wife.

The warmth he felt now as he undressed had little to do with the fire burning in the brazier, and he could almost imagine that his skin was steaming not unlike what emanated from that tub.

Without a word, he climbed into the large wooden tub, turned his back to his wife, and sank down into the water, grateful for the cleansing warmth. But no sooner had he settled his head against the rim, did he suddenly felt Lianae's fingers in his hair.

"I will help you," she offered stubbornly.

Closing his eyes, swallowing his protests, Keane laid his head back and prayed for strength. When he said nothing, she took it as an invitation to continue, and Keane felt the blood begin to simmer through his veins. He pulled the washcloth over his lap.

Without a word, she took an empty cup from the table and dipped it into the water, bidding him to close his eyes so she could lave his hair. But they were already closed, and she knew they were, so he adjusted himself a little so she could wet his head without soaking the entire room. If she was so determined to help, he might as well allow it.

But his heart beat a little faster as she worked her fingers through the long strands of his hair, wetting it fully, before lifting up the soap and lathering his hair. The feel of her fingers massaging his scalp felt heavenly. He could hear her breathing behind him—panting softly and he monitored his own breath, trying not to think of her lovely breasts rising and falling with each and every breath...

He was beautiful.

His body was firm, his belly tight. And his bare arms —they were nearly as wide as his thighs. God save her, Lianae had no thought but to stare.

She wanted so desperately to make Keane understand. She had never meant to bring him any harm. He, more than anyone had been kind to her and she wanted desperately to prove she could be a loving wife—if only he would allow it. She wanted to tell him she was still untouched, but the words simply wouldn't emerge on her tongue.

Instead of feeling joyful over the truth, would he consider it more of her lies? For that, in truth, was what it was. She had lied about nearly everything from the moment she'd met him, and now the truth came more difficult than her lies.

Spilling through her hands, his long hair was… soft, like ebony silk. She had visions of him turning to see her—truly see her. As she was. Merely a wife, wanting her husband to love and forgive her, though for now, his silence was enough.

Resting in the tub, he appeared for the instant as though he hadn't a care in the world and Lianae wanted to forever smooth his worried brow and brush her fingers against his shadowed jaw. Lathering the soap in his hair, she poured her heart into the task, wanting him to feel her remorse with every caress of her fingers. And once she was done with his hair, and still he hadn't protested, she moved to his shoulders, working the soap into his flesh. His skin was dark, a color achieved through a lifetime that could scarce be faded by the passing of months.

Realizing that he had pulled the washcloth down to drape over his lap, she reached over to grab it and Keane stilled her hand.

"Nay," he said.

"But…"

"I will finish on my own."

Her cheeks burning with chagrin, Lianae released the cloth and stood, moving away from the tub. "I-I am sorry," she said, and swallowing her tears, she hurried out of the room.

KEANE HEARD the door close and only once Lianae was gone, he removed the cloth from his lap, snarling at his traitorous cock. He was prepared to raise her child as his own, but he would not allow himself to mingle his seed with that of William fitz Duncan.

However, the last thing he needed was to leave his *old chap* unattended. The tension was insufferable. As hard as he was, as long as he'd been denied, he didn't need much coaxing to find his release… and in the moment when he did, it was Lianae's face he saw.

NOTHING SHE DID SEEMED to please him.

For the remainder of the week, whilst her husband avoided her, Lianae occupied herself with Kenna and Lael, learning from each woman. Having been raised on a farm in the bitter north, where men and women both tended their duties together, Lianae was only now learning how to sit and sew, beginning with the adjustment of her new gowns. A few were too short. A few too tight. All, save one, had belonged to a young lady from the border lands—a daughter of the laird of Teviotdale, who'd perished some years past, although none of the women present seemed overly inclined to reveal how.

From Kenna, Lianae gleaned everything there was to be known about Lael's mysterious brother. It was curious to hear the girl speak of Keane, because Lianae had met a very different man—one who was not so aloof and who had taken Lianae under his wing from the instant they'd met. She longed to see that man returned.

"I will never forget the first time I saw him," Kenna confessed, with rosy cheeks. "He was newly arrived and I thought to myself that he was the epitome of male beauty, so dark and handsome. But of course, the ladies were all half in love with him from the instant he rode through the gates."

Lael laughed. "Dinna speak such things in front of my brother," she forbade Kenna. "His head will grow overlarge, and Lianae will suffer his arrogance all the more."

"I dinna find him arrogant," Lianae demurred.

Kenna smiled. "Aye, well, until you, if wasna made of metal, feathers or horseflesh, Keane did not see it. One day, I thought I would come to sup dressed as a shield, with feathers in the front my head and a horse tail behind." The ladies present all tittered over the image.

Lianae might have told a different tale, but she didn't wish to make Kenna feel bad. There were many things she might find to call her new husband, but inattentive was not one. Blind was not one. And neither was passionless. Despite that they had yet to consummate their vows, she knew this for a fact, for she'd certainly not missed that *lump* beneath his washcloth. Her cheeks heated over the memory.

But the bath had been a pointless endeavor. Now, even more than before, he would come to bed in the wee hours, whenever he thought Lianae was fast asleep and he rose early, long before she could chance to open her eyes. She took her frustration out on the cloth she was sewing, shoving her needle furiously through the hem. There was only so much she could say, for today Lael's daughters were all present in the solar.

Some of the ladies in attendance were the daughters of neighboring lords. Others were the wives of Jaime's wards. And some were lowly maids who served the lady of Keppenach. Lael seemed prepared to invite anyone within, whether or not they were ladies in truth. All were welcome in her solar, with the hearth fire blazing and the candlelight sparkling overhead. A beautiful carpet had been laid out upon the floor, with enormous, brightly colored pillows tossed hither and thither—a style, Lael had explained, was inspired by her husband's travels to the land of the Saracens.

"I have never traveled overmuch," Lianae confessed.

"Mayhap you will now that my brother is sworn to David?" Lael suggested, smiling as she worked her needle through the hem of one of Lianae's new gowns.

"Mayhap," Lianae replied. Although, as of now, her *husband* was like to carry her back to Dunràth and leave her there ever more. *Alone.* "Green was the Lady Aveline's favorite color?" she asked. It certainly seemed to be so, for nearly all the gowns she wore were some shade of green.

"Aye, but if the color does not please you—"

"Oh, nay!" Lianae reassured. "They are all lovely and I have never seen their like. My own gowns have always been far plainer. I am grateful for *all* you have done, m'lady."

"Mine as well," Lael confessed.

"And mine," Kenna added. "But it surprises me that yours would be, Lianae."

"Me?" Lianae asked, with some bewilderment.

"You are a princess!" one of Lael's ladies interjected.

Lianae blushed. "Ach! A princess of *what*? Ye must have a people to rule to be a princess, and Moray is no longer what it was."

Both Lael and Kenna shared a glance. "I ken what you mean," Lael confessed with a sigh. "Neither is Dubhtolargg."

Lianae's needle stilled, remembering suddenly what King David had called her husband. *Dún Scoti.* "Dubhtolargg?"

Lael continued to sew, nodding, as though her revelation were ever so mundane.

Like Lilidbrugh, Dubhtolargg was a place only spoken of in whispers—the mountain stronghold named for the murdered king of the Southern Pechts. It was said that, upon Black Tolargg's death, his blood ran in rivulets down into the mountain streams and flowed red all the way to the mountain loch where the mother of winter lay slumbering in her cave. Drawn forth to mourn the fallen king, her tears transformed the glen into a bounteous place surrounded by the roughest terrain known to man. It was there, to that glen the last of the Pechts had flown to more than two centuries past, and there supposedly remained—in the red hills, stained crimson by the blood of Black Tolargg.

Lael was a dún Scoti. Certainly, that would explain their coloring, for they were darker than most Scots—in both complexion and hair—and their eyes were a peculiar shade of green as well. Considering this, Lianae pushed her needle through the thick material of her gown. On this particular dress she had adjusted the neckline, so that it would reveal the moons of her breasts. *Let her husband ignore her then,* she thought to herself.

Kenna cast her a knowing glance, for they were fast becoming friends, despite their adoration for the same man. No matter that she tried to deny it, Lianae could see the heartbreak in Kenna's eyes every time she spoke of him.

There was a sudden knock at the solar door. "Ailis?" Lael inquired of the well-rounded woman who appeared behind the door.

"M'lady... we've a messenger..." But the unhappy servant refused to meet her mistress's gaze.

"Do we know from where?"

The servant nodded, staring at her feet.

"Who, Ailis? Speak up!"

At last, Ailis met her mistress's gaze. "I shouldn't say, m'lady. But my laird Jaime bids ye come at once."

Commanding her daughters to stay, Lael leapt to her feet at once, leaving everyone staring after her as she hurried out the solar door.

RIDERS DELIVERED news of the death of a dún Scoti kinswoman.

Thankfully Keane would not refuse Lianae the chance to stand beside him in his time of sorrow. Together, they were bound for Dubhtolargg, and from Dubhtolargg, they were meant to travel north to Dunràth in Moray. Lael and Jaime would go as well, though Jaime's sister was asked to remain at Keppenach along with Lael's daughters. With Elspeth gone, Lianae would sorely miss the sisterly companionship, for while Keane's sister was kind and sweet, she was not nearly so affable as Kenna.

The king himself intended to make the journey too,

but from Dubhtolargg, he would ride south to Northumbria instead of traveling north to Moray. So whilst the king lingered to ready his troops for war and collect his remaining liegemen, he sent the grieving family ahead. Jaime Steorling remained to accompany the king into the Mounth, while Keane, Lael, Lianae, Cameron, and the messengers Fergus and Lachlann rode with all due haste.

Lianae attributed the hurry to Keane's and Lael's desire to be at home with their kinsmen in their time of grief, though it was a grueling pace they'd set, putting more and more distance between their party and that of the king's. It was as though they meant to make certain they arrived long before David mac Maíl Chaluim.

Along the way, Keane was far too distracted to trouble himself with their quarrels. He was neither angry, nor solicitous, but rather brooding, given to long stretches of silence that left Lianae feeling like a stranger amidst her new kin.

And yet, being ignored by Keane dún Scoti was by far a better fate than the one she might have had at William fitz Duncan's hands. She shuddered to think what William might have done to her by now. And still… she found herself wishing Keane would only turn to look her way… if only but once. She held an apology ready in her gaze, and prayed with all her heart that he might see it.

But he did not. And the mood of the party remained glum. They made their way through pinewood forests and valleys that sliced through precipitous cliffs. As they climbed the hills at last, the hillside forest thinned, and finally, the path wandered down a hillside, into a snow-blanketed valley that was bordered on three sides by corries and on the fourth by an icy loch. As they entered the vale, the sound of a horn blast filled the air.

This, at last, was the legendary Dubhtolargg.

In the valley below, protected from the winds and encircled by bare-limbed rowan trees, sat row upon row of cobbled stone cottages topped with snow-covered thatch. Out on the loch sat an enormous wooden island, connected to the beach by a long wooden pier.

Hidden away like a precious gem, the sight of the tiny village stole Lianae's breath away, for despite that it appeared as some visage from their past, a sense of something portentous assailed her the minute she entered the glen... something undeniably ancient and powerful.

From their vantage on the hillside, they could spy Keane's kinsmen down below near a raging bonfire. From its center, smoke curled upward into a bleak sky. Long before they neared the village, a welcome party came forth to greet them.

With nervous fingers tapping at the inside of her belly, Lianae followed her husband to the stables, where they abandoned their mounts and then made their way toward the bonfire on the beach. Hugs were exchanged along the way, and more tears shed, but Lianae was not among the ones embraced. Her heart aching for these people, she bided her time, standing near her husband like a good and dutiful wife.

Presently, a young woman came to embrace Keane —a beautiful girl, with bright red hair. The two hugged, embracing as though the world was coming to its end.

Jealousy reared its little beast eyes, and Lianae glanced away, unable to bear the sight of their embrace. Remembering how Keane had taken her wounded feet and wrapped them with so much care, she swallowed over the loss of his affections.

What had she done?

Saved herself, in truth, but she'd made her husband cold. A sorrow to match her husband's grief seeped down into Lianae's bones.

After a moment, the woman broke free of their embrace and folded herself into Cameron's arms as well, and seeing the two together, Lianae was at once reassured.

If the girl's hug for Keane was fervent and heartfelt, her embrace for Cameron was tender and full of longing. Lianae noted the fingers that looped through the curls at Cameron's nape, and at once she sought her husband's gaze.

Clearly, Keane noted the gesture as well, for he turned to look at Lianae at long last, and gave her a tentative smile—the first such smile in weeks. Her heart did a painful flip inside her breast.

Judging by the look upon her husband's face as he watched Cameron with his sister, Lianae dared to hope that he, too, craved more than the fief he would receive as payment from his king.

And then there was this: Any other man might have taken the king's bribe, and in order to secure the alliance between their houses, he would have forced Lianae to lie with him by now. Keane had yet to even touch her… and even now, if she chose to, she could declare herself unwed, for she was a maiden still in the eyes of the law.

But she *wanted* to be Keane's wife in truth.

Alas, he thought her defiled, and worse, he suspected she carried another man's bairn. Another lie—the greatest lie of all—one Lianae longed to bring into the light.

He stood so close now—so very close—and yet they might as well have been standing leagues apart. Longing for the merest brush of his skin, Lianae moved closer, and once the initial greetings were done, her husband drew the woman aside, introducing her to Lianae.

"Cailin, greet my wife," he said without flourish.

The girl's eyes widened. Her gaze snapped to Lianae. "Wife?"

Belatedly, he took Lianae by the hand, but the gesture seemed perfunctory. "Lianae, this is my sister Cailin. She will see to your comfort and I will join you anon." He bent to place a chaste kiss upon Lianae's forehead and she pressed her face into the warmth of his lips, but he broke free and moved away, abandoning her to his sister.

Cameron was quick to follow at his heels.

"Where are you going?" Cailin called after them. When Keane didn't reply, she turned to give Lianae a strange look.

"David comes," Lael said, and bolted after them.

Cailin opened her mouth to speak, but closed it again and merely watched her brother and sister take their leave, seeming to comprehend something Lianae did not. Though she had the immediate sense that whatever it was... it had everything to do with David's imminent arrival in the vale.

CHAPTER TWENTY-ONE

Auld Fergus stood guard at the crannóg door whilst the men all circled the pit, warming their frozen fingers. The dancing flames cast a capricious light over each of the surrounding faces. In the shadows, near the long table, Lìli quietly rocked her newborn babe, listening with trepidation to their discourse. Along with the elder Lachlann, Aidan, Lìli, Sorcha, Cameron, Keane and Lael had all closeted themselves to discuss what was to come. Sorcha and Lael stood arm in arm, grateful to see one another after so many years, but their attention remained riveted on their brothers. For more than two hundred years the dún Scoti had not called attention to their vale—for a good cause—and now, the king and his men were on the way.

"How many ride with him?"

"Five hundred, now." It was Cameron MacKinnon who provided that information. "He intends to meet another two once we leave the vale, and the rest will join us in Northumbria."

Keane more than anyone understood the coming confrontation in Northumbria was not Aidan's primary concern. "Five hundred of the king's men will convene *here*?" his brother asked, his tone clearly displeased. His gaze narrowed on Keane, clearly holding him responsible.

"I encouraged him to forgo the journey," Keane said. "He insisted. What would you have had me do?"

The two brothers locked gazes, Aidan furious and Keane unflinching. He well knew his brother's fears, but after all was said and done, what difference would it make now?

"We all ken David mac Mhaoil Chaluim isna come to pay respects," Aidan suggested. "So, tell me, what does he want?" He was angrier now than Keane had ever heard him be—more so than he was on the day Lael rode out from the vale. The fact that his voice was calm did not conceal his fury. It was there in the glint of his steely eyes.

The only man Keane had ever knelt before was his own brother, but not today. Unaccustomed to Keane's diffidence toward anyone, and sensing a row, Cameron moved to diffuse it. "I believe he means to ask you to join the campaign. If we are to succeed in Northumbria, we need all the men we can get."

Aidan's pupils dilated as they met the MacKinnon's cousin, until his green eyes were overshadowed by the black. "We?" he asked carefully.

"Aye," Cameron said.

His brother's temper was barely contained. "Northumbria is *not* my concern, it is not *my* war," he snapped.

For all the talk he'd heard from outsiders—that Aidan coddled their women too much—Keane had never met a man yet who wasn't ready to piss himself when faced with his brother's wrath, including King David himself. But for the first time in all the years they'd known each other, Cameron MacKinnon stood his ground, straightening his spine, facing Aidan squarely. “Neither is it the MacKinnon’s fight, and yet I am told he will join.”

Aidan took a step toward Cameron. “Regardless, *you* have no business in my council, Cameron MacKinnon.”

“Aidan,” Lael interjected, moving between them, and splaying a hand upon Aidan’s chest to shove him back. “Come now,” she said. “He is our guest and we have lost too much already. Let us not fight,” she pleaded.

It took Aidan a long moment to compose himself, but when he looked again at Cameron, there was new respect in his gaze. “Chreagach Mhor lies in ruins,” he informed him, somewhat more calmly. “It will take months to rebuild what they have lost.”

“Even so, Aldridge Castle lies vulnerable now that FitzSimon is dead, and I dinna believe my cousin will allow his wife’s patrimony to be so easily remanded. He will come.”

“Aye, well, whatever Iain MacKinnon does is Iain MacKinnon’s concern. I will not lend good men to defend a crown we have not supported in more than two hundred years.”

“And we are in mourning,” Lìli interjected from her seat by the table, her tone fraught with worry. She rocked her babe, eying Keane pleadingly, as though he were the one now at fault. But there was more, and there was no sense in putting off what must be said.

“I mean to join him,” Keane announced.

Every pair of eyes snapped to meet Keane’s. He felt them more acutely than he did the heat of the fire pit. Brother stood glaring at brother, green eyes clashing over the dancing flames. Only Lael had ever defied Aidan so, ten years past, and she alone could comprehend what Keane felt as he stared Aidan down, more than prepared to stand his ground.

He had given his word to David, and despite that he was a dún Scoti long before he was a king’s man, he had long suspected that auld slab of stone hidden in the belly of their ben would prove a curse to his kin—as much as it was a curse to men. It was a slaughter waiting to happen—a fly in the web. If Keane had had his druthers years ago, they would have buried that rock so deep beneath the mountain that no man would ever lay eyes upon it again. That the gods themselves had seen fit to do so was a blessing in disguise.

The silence endured.

"And... I have taken a wife."

Silence.

Uncomfortable with the growing tension, Cameron MacKinnon crossed his arms, peering down at the floor, and his sisters and Lìli all remained quiet as well.

Aidan allowed him to continue without interrupting—or mayhap he was simply too angry to speak. "In return I swore David my fealty," Keane said.

The separation between them had never been more palpable.

Keane measured his words carefully. "I have not come to fight, Aidan."

The muscles in Aidan's jaw twitched as he, too, crossed his arms as though to temper his reaction to the news.

"*What* did you come for?"

"Una. She was my kinswoman, too."

And again there was silence, along with a tension so heavy one could slice it with a blade. His brother eyed Sorcha meaningfully, nodding subtly toward Cameron.

She caught his meaning at once and took Cameron by the arm, pulling him away from the pit. "Come," she said sweetly, "I have news to share..." And she drew him out of the room, speaking in gentler tones once they were out in the hall. Keane heard them exchanging words as they walked away, but Aidan had yet to utter a sound.

"I would know what happened to Una," Keane demanded, sending a pleading look toward Lìli. "I did not ride all this way to argue about David."

Tears filled Lìli's eyes. "It was Constance who found her," she said, but quickly looked away, unable to continue.

"Constance?"

"Cameron's sister."

Keane lifted both brows, surprised to find that she was in Dubhtolargg. His brother must have brought her back from Chreagach Mhor. Why was a matter to be discussed another time, for Aidan sounded defeated when he spoke again. But his tone lacked the anger it bore but moments before.

"The girl has seen more than she should have."

Keane waited with bated breath. Not even his brother would be so cruel as to kill a woman for the sake of that sacred stone. But for the first time since his arrival, Keane felt a moment of dread, for he realized that he had yet to spy Cameron's sister's face, and then he realized Sorcha had pulled him away to tell him news. "Aidan? What did Constance see?"

No one dared speak.

A muscle ticked at Keane's jaw. "If aught has befallen the lass, Cameron has a right to know."

For a long, long moment, the crackle and pop of old wood was the only sound to breach the thickening silence. His brother seemed momentarily unable to speak. Suddenly, a trembling hand went to his face as though to conceal his grief. Three days' worth of whiskers darkened Aidan's jaw, and suddenly Keane understood what Una's death had cost him.

"She is with Kellen now," Lìli explained, and it was she who rose to the occasion, explaining what happened.

As best as anyone could say, Constance came across

Una in the Stone's chamber, down below her grotto. There, she saw the Stone of Destiny and read aloud the words on the ancient plaque. According to Constance, Una struck at her like a viper. There was an explosion of light, followed by a terrible thunder and she had no inkling how she came to find herself standing outside the caverns. But there they found her, trembling in the cold… and blinded. Una remained below. Now everything was gone. The upper chamber where they'd happened to store their wares, Una's grotto, as well as the Stone's cavern were all now mounted with layer upon layer of debris. It was as though the mountain collapsed upon itself. No one could survive such a catastrophe.

Keane heard his brother's breath catch, and he was yet unable to speak. "Ye dinna retrieve the body?"

Aidan shook his head, looking wearier than Keane had ever seen him.

"It was not possible," Lìli said.

The funeral bier was merely for show. It held but an effigy made of straw. Luckily, Fergus had ridden ahead to alert Aidan to the incoming horde. They did not want the king to ask where Una was interred. It was better that they did not know precisely what had occurred. And so Aidan instructed Kellen to keep Constance preoccupied in their bower while the king remained in the vale. If at all possible, Cameron must not be told about the stone. The fewer people who knew, the better, even despite that the Stone from Scone was gone. Neither man nor beast could disinter it, but no one would have liked to see them try. Somehow, with Una gone, it seemed to be the will of the gods that the stone be forever lost.

"What is this I hear; you've taken a wife?" Aidan asked gruffly.

"A daughter of Óengus."

"The Mormaer?" Aidan leveled a disbelieving look at Keane.

"Aye. King David would see peace come to *all* of Scotia," Lael defended. "He wills it with this union. He could have hung our brother; and yet he did not. Instead, he sought an alliance with our people, even despite that it will bring him grief once William Fitz Duncan learns the truth."

Aidan swore softly, his anger returning. "What else should I know, *brother*?"

Keane peered back at Aidan with hard, glittering eyes, unwilling to speak ill of his bride, whether or not Lianae deserved it. She might not be standing here at his side, and he didn't entirely trust her himself, but he dared to hope that someday he might... and if she carried another man's babe, no man but Jaime and the king would ever hear of it whilst Keane lived. "I love her," he said, and realized only in that instant that it was true.

Aidan lifted a brow. So too did Lael. Keane met each of their gazes and willed them to understand. But he thought he saw Lael smile, though she hid it with a hand.

"But this is joyous news!" Lìli exclaimed, jumping up from the bench and coming forward. "Isn't it Aidan?"

Aidan jaw remained taut, his eyes glittering as hard as diamonds.

"Aidan please," Lael begged.

The hall remained silent as they awaited the laird of Dubhtolargg's response. Finally, he conceded. "Aye," he said. "'Tis good news... we welcome your Moray bride."

Having remained quiet long enough, Lachlann cleared his throat. "Much as I loathe to interrupt so much talk of love, shall we go and light the bier before the king arrives?"

❧

"LIGHT THE BIER! LIGHT THE BIER!"

Responding to the panicked voices of her kinsmen, Cailin dún Scoti abandoned Lianae upon the beach to light the funeral bier. Her red hair burning as brightly as the flames she meant to burn, she climbed atop the dais, commanding the torches all be lit, and then she accepted them one by one, tossing them unceremoniously atop the pyre.

As five hundred mounted soldiers marched down the mountain, flames tore across the wood, like a bone-dry field of grain.

Pushing back her cloak over her shoulders, Lianae succumbed to the heat as she watched the flames consume the cadaver, burning through it as though it were made of nothing more than straw.

But why would they burn an effigy?

Remembering the smell of burnt flesh as they'd burned her father's body, she knew beyond a shadow of doubt that the old woman they'd spoken of was not there on the bier. And still there was no belying the sense of grief Lianae noted amongst these folk, for there was not a dry eye amidst the lot. Some wept openly, disconsolately. Others were more stoic, but with bloodstained eyes that gave lie to their quiet sorrow. And yet surrounded by heart-rent people, she had never felt more alone.

Who would weep for her once she was gone?

Ewen and Graeme were very likely already dead, and at the moment, she felt the loss of hope most acutely. She had no proof either of her brothers had survived the battle at Stracathro in Forfarshire. Elspeth was gone. Her mother, gone. Her father, gone. Her brother Lulach, for all intents and purposes, he was gone as well.

Lianae stood alone, watching the fire burn, mesmerized by the leaping flames, as inch by inch, the hillside gave birth to dozens of campfires.

From the instant they'd arrived in the vale, there had been an air of apprehension amidst the people of this sleepy village, and now that David had marched into the vale with five hundred armed men, a hush fell over the kindred.

They were hiding something, but Lianae didn't know what—and, still, even if she'd known, she would never tell David aught, for she had more in common with her husband's kinfolk than she did with the Scots. Like the Moraymen, these dún Scoti people were now in danger of being extinguished like a candle swallowed by a dark night.

David mac Maíl Chaluim was on the verge of uniting all the clans, but in the process, their legacies would all be lost. Rather than be bolstered by the sight of them, the king's army felt more like an infestation upon the land—a plague of Scots, with drunken, overloud voices that disrespected the dún Scoti dead. And in the midst of them all stood the king's tent, an elaborate silken edifice striped in gold and red. For all that Lianae felt like an outsider, she knew instinctively that whatever it was that these people were holding close to their vests, it was not something they cared to share with the *King of Scotia.*

But for so long, she had considered David to be her enemy. It was by his command her father was butchered. And yet... if the king had sensed she'd been lying about Keane, he had nevertheless shown her a kindness by not returning her to the Earl—a judgment he might have found justified, for William fitz Duncan was not a man anyone wished to cross. Instead he'd given her to a man who, Lianae had since learned, was not entirely David's ally. According to Keane's sister Cailin, who claimed to know Keane best, her husband had donned the king's livery as a matter of circumstance. Cailin was equally as certain he would never have accepted a gift of land and title—unless he believed there to be a greater cause.

It was that greater cause that had Lianae thinking now, although she didn't fool herself to believe it could be love. She was so deep in thought, considering what it could have been that motivated Keane to wed her, that she didn't hear anyone approach.

She started at the sound of a female voice. "There are so many," Aidan's wife said and Lianae had no need to ask what she meant... it was the king's men she referred to—the endless campfires winking amidst the dark night.

Lianae turned to smile at the woman who'd wed Keane's elder brother. She was childless at the instant, though it was the first time since their arrival at Dubhtolargg that Lianae had seen her without her newborn babe in her arms.

"The babe is sleeping?"

She was lovely, with dark chestnut hair and stark violet eyes that seemed to peer straight into Lianae's soul. "Aye, at last. The hour has grown late."

Lianae turned to look over the hillside. "I was... waiting," she confessed, but she didn't wish to say for what.

For her husband to forgive her, in truth.

"Of course," the woman said. "You are newly wed."

Lianae blushed hotly. "Oh, nay," she protested. "It isna like that."

But it was. Whether her husband would bed her or nay, she had no desire to spend the night alone in the little cottage they had been assigned. She was driven to seek him, even if she didn't know why. He was her touchstone now—her center.

Keane was all that remained to make sense of her world. She had no one but him, and as angry as he was with her, she still trusted him to keep her safe.

The woman's eyes twinkled as she studied Lianae, as though she knew something Lianae did not. But then she couldn't know that Keane wanted naught to do with her, and rightly so, for Lianae had bungled everything so very thoroughly.

But what would she have done differently if she could?

Certainly not return to the Earl.

Never that.

Naught, Lianae realized sadly. She would do naught differently, for if she had played her hand any differently at all, the king may have well returned her to the Earl. She swallowed her grief over the truth and stood, hugging herself against the chill of the night, staring out into the hills.

"He is quite pleased with your marriage," the laird's wife remarked.

Lianae's gaze snapped to the woman's face. At first, she thought it must be a question, because it certainly couldn't be true. "Keane?" she asked, thinking she must be mistaken.

She nodded, and long moments passed where Lianae simply didn't know how or what to respond. She opened her mouth to speak and closed it again.

"I ken what 'tis like to be torn between worlds," the woman said, surprising Lianae with the insight.

There was an air of familiarity between them already, though it wasn't an affiliation Lianae could readily explain. She'd felt the same kinship with Kenna, and a little bit from Lael. But not a one of them must realize what Lianae had done… or they, too, would despise her as surely as Keane did.

"When I first came to Dubhtolargg," she confessed. "I wondered how the fates would allow that I should wed the man whose people cursed my very existence."

"Aidan?" Lianae asked with surprise.

She smiled. "Aye, 'tis true. My husband's people loathed me once upon a time. In fact, it was Una herself who cast me the evil eye. Perhaps you've heard of the Caimbeul's curse?"

Lianae's eyes widened. Even in the north, they'd heard the stories of how the mountain folk cursed the Caimbeul's daughter for his sins. This, then, was Lìleas MacLaren.

Lianae's gaze slid to the bier. "Una was the one?"

Lìleas's throat constricted visibly. "The very one."

"And still you mourn her loss?"

Lìleas's eyes filled with unshed tears. "More than words can say. You are a daughter of Óengus, so they say?"

Lianae nodded. "Aye, but he is now gone... along with my mother and my sister... I am alone."

"Nay," Lìleas contended. "Not so long as you have us. We are your family now, Lianae. The dún Scoti men are loyal to a fault and I tell you now that if Keane loves you truly, you will want for naught as long as he remains at your side."

Lianae said naught to that, unable to reveal the things she'd already done to put their marriage asunder. Feeling glum, she turned to stare out over the hillside, at the dozens and dozens of twinkling fires... like stars that fell to earth.

Both women stood in perfect silence. After a time, Lìleas spoke again. "I will share with you what Una once told me when I needed to hear it most. She said, 'Trust your instincts, and whatever ye do, do it with all your soul.' I sense you will need this advice in the days to come, Lianae."

Willing away tears, Lianae turned to blink at her.

"Be true to your heart, not so much your head," Lìleas offered with a smile, and there was something about her violet eyes that made Lianae want to believe.

And then she turned to find Keane standing behind her, and her heart ceased to beat…

CHAPTER TWENTY-TWO

Faced with his brother's challenge, Keane spoke the words as a matter of consequence, though now he feared they must be true.

For all that he'd pined for it, he didn't give a damn about Lilidbrugh anymore, or Dunràth for that matter. Lilidbrugh was but a broken link to their past, a long forgotten symbol of the history of his clan. Lianae was his future... wherever it should lead.

But could it be love if there be no trust?

Nevertheless... it was past time to put their trials behind them. For better or worse, Lianae was his wife now and he must find a way to learn to trust the woman he intended to love.

Lìleas spoke first. "We were marveling over the sight of so many..."

"Outliers?" Keane said, finishing for his brother's wife.

They both shared a private look that conveyed so much—things that Lianae would never know, things he could not trust her enough to reveal.

Lìli crossed her arms against the chill. "Would ye e'er have imagined Aidan would allow it?"

"Not in a thousand years."

But of course, they no longer had the Stone of Destiny to defend. What did it matter who came to the vale now that the Stone was out of their hands?

Lìli eyed them both, and sensing Keane had not come for idle chatter, she excused herself at once. "By your leave," she said. "I am certain you two have much to discuss." And without awaiting Keane's reply, she made her way back toward the crannóg, where Aidan and her children awaited her. For a long uncomfortable moment, Keane watched his brother's wife walk away, feeling the weight of the world descend upon him.

Not only was the Stone of Destiny gone—the entire purpose of their clan's existence for more than two centuries—he had come to bury the woman who'd raised him from birth. And if that were not enough, his wife was a liar—and she had nearly cost him his life. After all that had been said and done, it wasn't easy to overlook his wounded pride. Still, he held out a hand, inviting Lianae to take it. "Come," he demanded.

For a moment, she merely stared at him, and then she reached out, and her touch was like a bolt of lightning to Keane's heart.

It was an arrogantly worded command, but Lianae recognized his vulnerability in that moment and swallowed her complaint, giving him her hand. Without a word, he pulled her gently along, away from the beach and the bonfire. Along the way, they passed his sister Cailin speaking low with Cameron in the shadows.

The night air held an unmistakable chill, but the heat emanating from Keane's hand made her palm sweat. Doves flew amuck inside her breast. "I suppose 'tis good to see your people, even if the circumstances aren't supreme?"

Keane nodded, though he didn't elaborate and

Lianae found herself craving knowledge about the man she had wed. Marveling at the great size of his hand, she imagined him as a child. "You and your brother Aidan are close?"

"Aye," he said, and fell to silence once more. The overwhelming sound of it squeezed Lianae's heart. Was this how it was to be between them now? She missed his easy banter—and even the haughty curve of his beautiful smile.

They neared the cottage they'd been assigned and Lianae struggled to keep up. "Una was much loved?" she asked, scrambling more for words than she did to keep the pace.

He squeezed her hand almost imperceptibly, as though he meant for her to hush. "She was."

Ach! Lianae would do anything to change what she had done—anything save give herself to William fitz Duncan. Forsooth, but she could not find any regret for that—not when her lies had garnered her this... But what was *this*? she berated herself.

And where was he taking her now?

There was something different in Keane's demeanor tonight, and it gave her a terrible flutter of anticipation as they neared the cottage they'd been assigned.

Struggling to keep up with his long, hurried strides, Lianae scrambled for something more to say that would help mend their wounds. "Well, I am sorry for your loss, Keane."

"As am I. She was like a mother to me," he said, and he changed the topic almost at once. "You are still favoring your left foot, Lianae."

Without warning, Keane swept her up into his arms, hushing her so easily. She could scarce breathe much less talk as he bore her into the cottage, across the threshold, and then another few short steps to the bed.

Inside, the cottage was warm and cozy. Lianae had

left the fire burning in anticipation of their return. They had ridden long hours and she had arrived weary and ready to repose.

A small table sat in one corner, flanked by two simple chairs. A cot sat in the other corner, along with a small table. Atop that table was an empty ewer and a bowl.

Without a word, Keane set her down upon the cot—a much smaller bed than the one they'd shared at Keppenach—and set about inspecting Lianae's feet once again, removing first one shoe, then the other. They were still sore, but not nearly as much as before, and Lael had given her a sturdy pair of boots to wear.

As he knelt to inspect the soles of her feet, Lianae wondered how they would sleep. He could not possibly slumber in those chairs, and the bed was so small in comparison to the one they'd left that they wouldst need sleep on top of one another in order to fit.

The thought tripped the beat of her heart, even despite of the fact that they'd slept far closer than this upon his pallet. "I am fine," she reassured him.

In truth, she was. Compared to but a few days ago, she was quite well in fact. Aside from the grueling pace of the day, the husband who would have little to do with her, a dead sister and long lost brothers, Lianae was perfectly fine.

But as she watched Keane tend her feet, his actions were not those of a man who would loathe his wife, and the realization made her heart beat a little faster...

"'Tis healing," he said gently. "Ye must keep them clean. Tomorrow, I will ask Lìli to prepare a balm."

"She needn't trouble herself for me," Lianae said breathlessly. Truly, her feet were her very last concern. "I ken there is much to be done."

To that, her husband peered up, brows askew. "Ye dinna behave much like a princess," he said.

Lianae arched her own brow, unable to hold her tongue. "Aye, well, aside from your officiousness, neither do ye."

"Ach, lass, that would be because, in case ye ha'nae noticed, I am *not* a princess."

Realizing only belatedly what she had said, Lianae choked on a well of laughter.

"Ye're a pawky wench," her husband accused her, but if the fact displeased him, it didn't appear to be so—not judging by the laugh lines that formed around his sensuous lips.

Lianae's heart squeezed a little at the return of his good humor.

She was desperately alone and wished not to be anymore. She had ruined everything with her lies... and still he'd managed to show her kindness and affection.

"I would be a wife to you in truth," she blurted, surprising herself with the request—for that's what it was.

She was a virgin still, but that didn't mean Lianae didn't know how a proper bedding was supposed to be done. She would see their vows consummated rightly, despite that he still believed she carried another man's child. She wanted so much to say it wasn't true. But she didn't know how—not with her mouth. Fire burned in her cheeks at the thought of speaking the words aloud. But she no longer wanted him to look at her the way he did on their wedding night—as though she were unclean. Nay... she wanted him to look at her the way he did when they'd first met... the way he was looking at her now...

But the warmth in his gaze vanished the instant she spied it.

Keane released her foot, and made to rise.

Lianae seized him by the arm, silently begging him not to go.

. . .

KEANE WANTED MORE than anything to stay... he wanted to kiss her again... but there was a deeper longing that couldn't be appeased—not now.

Not yet.

Not whilst she carried another man's bairn.

There must be no question in his mind whose child she would bear. He would raise a son of fitz Duncan, but he would not confuse the truth in his head. If he bedded Lianae now, he would make himself believe the child could be his, and this, he could not do.

"Please," she begged, and he could see the desire writ upon her face. The unabashed plea tugged at his heart. She was his wife, he reasoned, and after all, if she had wanted to be with the Earl, she would never have lied to the king.

Instead, she had made Keane complicit in her stories, accusing him of things he had only coveted—and aye, he was guilty of it all inside his head. He *wanted* to bed her that morning in Lilidbrugh.

Who was he fooling?

He wanted to bed her now. And that look upon her face... it made him want to believe she had done everything for the very same reason he longed to kiss her right now...

Because she wanted him.

He could see the truth in her eyes. And suddenly Keane couldn't hold back—not when she gazed at him with those liquid amber eyes. Surrendering to his desire, he lifted a hand to her cheek, willing Lianae to push him away. But she did not. Instead, she slid her arms about his neck and Keane bent to claim her lips. She kissed him back... ever so sweetly... and he could no longer think of any reason to stop...

But nay... nay...

Desire warred with his pride. If he loved her now, he would always wonder if the babe could be his...

"Lianae," he begged, and yet, he needn't please himself in order to please his wife, he realized. He could give her what she longed for. And later, much later, once he was alone by the loch, he would please himself, and remember the taste of her lips, the silky feel of her hair...

CHAPTER TWENTY-THREE

If she could not speak the words, Lianae could think of only one way to prove her innocence. Feeling like a wanton, she unlaced the bodice of her gown, freeing her breasts to her husband's gaze, searching for proof in his eyes that he wanted her still…

"Art beautiful," Keane whispered, and she gasped with delight when he finished peeling open her gown and placed a warm hand upon her breast.

"Art beautiful," he said again. "Do ye know what I would give you?"

Lianae nodded.

"Would ye have me, Lianae?"

Lianae swallowed. "Aye," she said. And just to be certain he continued, she lay back upon the bed, pulling him down along with her, grasping him by the tunic so he couldn't leave. And then, Lianae dared something she had never dreamt of doing before… she slid a hand between them, cupping him *there* as he'd cupped her breast.

"Ach," he said with a groan, and his body shuddered violently. His male anatomy pulsed against her palm.

He pulled her hand away and Lianae arched beneath

him, a bold invitation more suited to a courtesan than a virgin or a wife. But she was not a prude. Nor was she unwise to the ways of the world. She'd heard her parents, upstairs in their room, loving each other unabashedly. And although she'd never dared allow her mind to wander to such places, she sometimes couldn't help but envision the way it might be when she was wed. And now she was, and no one could shame her for what she wished to do…

"Lianae," he begged, and she followed his lead, placing her hands at his hips where they could wander free… exploring the hard lines of his body, his hips, his chest…

He seized her hands, pinning them above her head, unfurling her fists beneath his so they rested palm to palm. "You are like a flower," he murmured. "Opening to the heat of the sun. I would spread your petals wide," he whispered, "love each one."

Lianae trembled beneath the promise of his gaze.

"Show me…"

KEANE WAS a man famished set before a great, heaping feast, but the dish she would tempt him with belonged to another man first. And still, like a traitor, his cock strained against his belly, greedy for all that she would give. After so long without a woman, he nearly spilled himself at her bold touch, and then again as she arched her body in supplication.

Someday, he would show her the pleasures that awaited her in his arms, but he was unwilling to share her body with another man's bairn. And still, he would not leave her this way, for that would be cruel.

Trying desperately to clear the fog of lust from his brain, he slid a hand beneath her skirt, searching for the sweet flesh beneath. He found her wet and ready, and the soft silky nectar nearly unmanned him once again. Gently, Keane pushed a finger inside her body, parting the silken petals. But it took him a foggy moment to realize what it was he'd encountered... and then another to recognize the warm flow of blood spilling over his fingers. Like a man wounded in battle, and now in shock, Keane withdrew his hand and stared at the bright red stain that trickled into his palm.

The jagged wound beneath his thumb—the one he'd made himself on the night of their wedding—was already healed. He was dumbstruck. "Ye're a virgin?" he said with no small trace of surprise.

Lianae nodded, her cheeks deeply flushed. But if Keane had hurt her, there was little evidence of that in her expression. He took one look at her full, lovely breasts—fevered pink, the same color as her cheeks—and the widened pupils darkening her amber eyes, and knew he would not deny himself—or Lianae—this night. Trembling with desire, he stood and stripped, staring possessively at the bed. "From this day forth, you are mine, Lianae of Moray."

Lianae nodded.

"I would hear you say it," he demanded and hurled his tunic at the floor.

"I am yours" Lianae whispered.

He was beautiful—a golden idol, his skin aglow by the light of the fire. He shrugged out of his trews, and then stood, nude, and unashamed, his green eyes filling her with promises his body meant to fulfill.

She would have no barriers between them this night. All that he would take, she would provide willingly... Desperate to be shed of her own garments Lianae removed her gown, and lay back upon the bed all the while he watched her, his green eyes glittering like twin, gems.

"What is mine, is mine," he said quietly. "I will kill to defend it."

"I am yours," Lianae repeated once more.

A look of fierce satisfaction came over her husband's face, and Lianae held her breath as he climbed atop her, pressing himself gently inside her body. Instinctively, she wrapped her legs about him, embracing him eagerly as a lover.

She nuzzled her face against his cheek. "But if I am yours," she dared to whisper in his ear, nipping softly at his lobe. "You are mine, my prince."

"Aye," he swore, rearing back his hips. "Aye," he said again. "I am yours." And he thrust so deep that Lianae felt him straight into her breast. Crying out over a stab of pain so intense it bordered on pleasure, she gave him back equal measure, their bodies fusing and moving in perfect accord.

Keane returned a fierce moan of pleasure, claiming his bride for his own.

He loved her until they were spent, and then, afterward, they lay together in the small bed, naked and unashamed, painted gold by the firelight as he explored every inch, committing the feel of Lianae to his memory and purging all others from his heart and mind. If he would leave her soon, he would have her take a piece of him north...

His babe, in truth.

She may not have been pregnant before they'd arrived, but she damned well would be by the time they left, and the thought of this pleased him immensely—more than he might have supposed. Before she could fall asleep in her quiet languor, he pulled her to him once again, insatiable now that she was his, and only his.

❧

DURING THE DAYS TO FOLLOW, the mountain village bustled with activity.

The dún Scoti men bided their time, wanting to return to the caves in order to attempt once more to retrieve Una's body. But so long as the king remained in residence, no one dared mention the grotto. The bier stood blackened and half consumed by the beach, a charred wooden skeleton left standing to remind them of their loss. And still no Una happened down the hill.

She was gone.

At sunrise on the third day came a summons from the king. Keane's brother was invited to join him in his tent. Aidan refused, but he agreed to meet the king in a more sacred place—the boulder his people called Clach Tolargg, in honor of their fallen ancestor, Black Tolargg. His kinfolk believed the stones were the leavings of the gods, and the bigger the stone, the greater the spiritual connection. So they held all their counsels by the biggest one of all—had been holding counsels in that place since the day his people first arrived in the vale. If they would speak of the future of their clan, Aidan would only do so where he would be guided by their forefathers—where he could be closest to the woman who'd counseled him since the day his father died. *Una.*

Loathe to take orders from a petty king like Aidan dún Scoti, David mac Mhaoil Chaluim nevertheless agreed to the request. They met mid morning, whilst the women were preparing to break the fast. Keane leaned against Clach Tolargg, watching the exchange, and hoping he would not be forced to intervene.

His place had always been by his brother's side, but now that he had a wife, he meant to keep her. Decisions were no longer quite so clear, though if he had his back against the wall, and was forced to draw his sword, he would not shed his brother's blood...

The king came with five of his personal guards, Jaime as well—his champion. But considering that Jaime was wed to Lael, his part in this discussion was still unclear—as much so as was Keane's.

Lael was present today as well—because no man had balls enough to make her leave—along with Lachlann and Fergus as both were elders on Aidan's council.

David mac Mhaoil Chaluim was not the overeager young king he had been when he and Aidan first met, and there was, despite his grizzled pride, a certain respect between the two men. At fifty-one, David's girth was no longer so lean and his hair not so dark, but his dark eyes were canny and clear with purpose. "I would have you join the campaign in Northumbria," he said without preamble. "I can use all the good men I can get. Carlisle will open her gates to my men, but Stephen will ride north as soon as he has word I have taken the border city."

"As I have said... I will not lend my men to battles that do not concern us."

The king's calm scarcely hid his anger. "Since when does keeping the king's peace not concern you, Aidan dún Scoti?"

"I'm *no* Scot," Aidan argued. "I have told you this as well, and yet ye insist upon claiming my people to your realm. We are no' dún Scoti!"

"What are ye then?"

Ri against *Righ Art*—petty king against high king—stared at one another, fists clenched, neither willing to cede. Not many would understand how little sway David had in this vale—against his brother and laird. Only Jaime and Lael could possibly comprehend—but Jaime not nearly as well. His people purposely kept themselves apart from Scotia's *politiks* and nothing would ever persuade his brother to change his mind, not after all this time.

"My place is *here...* in the vale."

Keane could feel the tensions coming from his sister, and despite her ladylike attire, he more than anyone recognize the warrior beneath her gown. He would be willing to bet she had a knife hidden beneath her skirts... the question was, where would she put the blade... if push came to shove? She had four children with Jaime Steorling and Jaime swore his fealty to the king.

As did Keane...

For one terrible moment, he wished he were back in his youth, when times were simpler and choices were all clearer. Pushing himself away from Clach Tolargg, hoping to avert disaster, Keane announced, "I will go in my brother's stead."

Aidan shot him a look filled with contempt.

Lael might have done so as well ten years ago, but the look she gave him now was filled more with relief. Had she been a man, she might have spoken the same words he did now.

Because she loved her husband.

As Keane was coming to love Lianae.

Cracking his knuckles and stretching the chords of his neck, the king considered Keane's offer, and finally nodded. "You were *always* meant to come, Keane, but if Aidan will agree to it, and if he will recognize me as the rightful sovereign over Scotland, I will leave it at that." David mac Mhaoil Chaluim would not leave the vale without some small victory and more careful words had never been spoken. He was not asking Aidan to kneel before him, and he clearly understood that it would be asked in vain. But he simply wished Aidan to recognize him as the sovereign over Scotland—a nation to which Aidan did not subscribe.

There was not a man present who did not comprehend the war of wills. After a long stretch of silence, his brother sighed. "Very well," he agreed, aware of the dance of words. "I will recognize you as the rightful sovereign over Scotia."

Before they could come to an agreement, Keane spoke up again. "All I must ask is to see my wife to Dunràth myself."

"Nay." The king said, shaking his head. "There isna time. If you would serve me, you will ride out from the vale at my side."

Keane clenched his fist. "Nay! I willna allow *my wife* to traipse into the north lands unescorted, without protection." Foremost in his mind was to keep her safe from the likes of William fitz Duncan. If the man should lay a hand on his wife now that they were wed, he'd gut him from belly to throat.

"We have wasted too much time already," the king lamented.

Keane was treading on dangerous ground and yet he could not accept this decree. "*You* have wasted your time, *Your Grace*. *I* have come to mourn my kin, and in truth, ye werena asked to join us in the vale."

David mac Mhaoil Chaluim's face turned red, and then purple. Whatever charity Keane had witnessed in the man before now was lost in the bile of his expression. They were at odds here, and so were their interests. Lianae was not like Lael. She was not a warrior. She was a gentlewoman to her soul, prickly though she might be. What good was a castle or land if he lost his wife?

"I will take her," Lael announced.

"You?" the single word exclaimed in unison, was an echo from every man present: Jaime, the king, Aidan and Keane as well.

"Aye, me!" Insulted now, Lael stood at her full

height, unbowed by the air of disapproval. "There is not a *dún Scoti* lass who canna best the lot o' your men." She directed this declaration to the king. "*I* will take Lianae, along with Cailin and Sorcha. Give me but one of your men—not even your best—and I will make do. Then my brother may ride south in good conscience when you leave."

The king remained silent, unmoved.

Lael persisted. "Would you deny him—your servant—the peace of mind to serve ye unburdened, Your Grace? Or would you have him preoccupied o'er his pregnant wife whilst he must guard your back?"

More silence followed Lael's outburst.

Over the hillside, there was much chatter as men rose to break their fast, but here around the ancient stone Clach Tolargg, not a man save one dared to speak and deny her.

"Lael," Jaime said, meaning to reason with her.

His sister turned to give her husband a quelling look. "Dinna think to argue against me, Jaime. I *am* your beloved wife, but long before I was your wife, I was a dún Scoti maid. I am more than capable and betimes more so than you!"

It was a challenge no man in his right mind would embrace.

Angrily, Lael shoved her cloak behind her shoulders and marched away. It was only once she was gone that there was a titter of nervous laughter amidst the men, and the king broke the silence, confessing as he scratched his head, "That woman scares the piss out o' me. You've some bollocks, Jaime," he announced, to which, every man present barked with anxious laughter.

But Keane was not appeased. "Will Lianae be safe at Dunràth if fitz Duncan will not join the campaign?"

The king eyed Keane with a gleam in his eye. "I am

not witless enough to leave *any* stronghold of import without men enough to guard her." And by *her*, Keane had little doubt he did not mean Lianae. "I will send a writ along with your lady to ensure my men will heed her command. The better question then might be… is Dunràth safe with your lady wife in command, Keane dún Scoti?"

Despite the past few days, Keane was unable to defend or impugn Lianae—not with all that had transpired. But so long as she was safe, that was his greatest concern.

"Would you wed my brother to a woman who would betray kith and king in the same breath?" Aidan challenged.

The king answered after but a moment of deliberation. "Nay," he said.

"So that's that," Jaime agreed. "Lael will take Lianae north, and if it please you, Your Grace, I will send Luc along with them. The man is loyal to a fault."

"So be it," the king said. "Enjoy yourselves whilst ye can. We ride for Northumbria two days hence."

CHAPTER TWENTY-FOUR

It was the first of January, and the Mother of Winter had not yet come to stay. Unseasonably warm for the ides of winter, it was easy to take to the bed, in particular for those who would not be alone.

Later that same evening, Jaime and Lael lay down their arms… and their gowns and shoes and trews and gambesons, and left them all upon the floor.

Outside, on the hill, the din continued—raised drunken voices, ribald jests and laughter—but in the room the lovers shared, there were only heartfelt whispers.

Jaime laced his fingers into his wife's hair. "Promise me you will take care, my love?"

"Dinna worry, Jaime. My people have traversed these northlands long before the Scots arrived. I ken how to take care of myself as you well know," Lael reassured her husband.

But still he was not appeased. Gently, he brushed the hair from Lael's face. "I will not be there beside you to be certain others realize your worth to me, and you would sentence me to a lifetime of vengeance were I to lose you. I bid you take good care, my lovely wife."

It was difficult to remain angry with the man, when

he gazed at her just so. "Dinna fear. I will come back to you, if only you promise me the same: You will come back to me." It was only now that it was sinking in: After five long years of heightened tensions across their nation, her husband would again go to war, as men were ever want to do. "I tell you true, if women ruled this world, there would be so little bloodshed."

Jaime lifted a brow, as though he did not believe her. "Would you pull each other's braids until the enemy surrendered?"

Laughing despite her irritation, Lael warned him, "I will pull *your* braid!" And she reached beneath the covers.

Jaime moved out of his wife's immediate reach. "Why do you think I wear no braids, wife. In any case, ye canna say such things, when you're as fierce as any. You have shed your share of blood in all your thirty-two years."

"Only when I am forced to," Lael argued sweetly.

"And how many times have you been forced to?"

Cast her head back upon the pillow, Lael rolled her eyes. When other men might concern themselves more about whether their wives bedded other men—or how many—her husband only cared about how many she might have killed. She peered up at the ceiling, watching the shadow-play of the firelight as she tried to form a truthful answer.

On the day her father died, she might have killed at least one, though she was only ten. There were a few men who'd thought to infiltrate their vale, and she'd wielded her swords against them, but Aidan was the one who dealt those killing blows. There were two she'd killed up on the ridge the night Rogan MacLean thought to steal her brother's wife away. So that was three. And then three more on the day they took her, bound and gagged, from the gaols beneath Keppenach.

But then, of course, there were all those men she'd faced in battle on the day before they'd put her on the gallows. "I don't know," she confessed. "And you?"

Jaime lay there, staring at the ceiling, his hands behind his back. "I don't know," he admitted readily. "I stopped counting too long ago." He sighed wearily. "What say we try not to shed anymore?"

Lael rolled over and lay her head upon her husband's chest. "That is not a promise either of us can swear to keep. You will go to wrest Northumbria from king Stephen, and I will ride to Dunràth soon."

Either direction, north or south, there was unrest. In the north, the Earl of Moray kept the king's peace, but should he ever decide to cast away his oath… well, he was a rightful claimant to the throne, and in the end, it was the mightiest who would rule these lands.

Lael was devastated to have lost Una, but the loss of the Stone itself could be no more fortuitous right now, for while David held the sword of kings, if it were ever to be known he took his crown while seated on a false stone…

It was for that very reason they'd kept Constance away from the guests, so she couldn't inadvertently betray the Guardians' secret.

But Lael didn't wish to think about such things at the moment, not when there was a sweeter victory to be won right here in her bed. Smiling, she climbed atop her husband, naked and proud to be his lover. Jaime's blue eyes pierced her, like an arrow to the heart.

She bent to kiss him lovingly, taking not a single moment for granted; tomorrow was never promised. "I love you," she whispered into his mouth as his hands reached for the moons of her breasts.

"I love you," he returned, and they melted into each other's embrace, joining their bodies as one.

❧

THE PAST TWO days had been a dream Lianae did not wish to see end.

With mere hours remaining before the king's men were set to depart the vale, she waited impatiently for Keane to return to the cottage. Again, at sunrise, his brother had roused him from his bed, and Lianae had scarce had a moment to speak to him ere he left.

Once he was gone, she was afraid in her heart that she might never see him again, for Stephen would never cede the border lands so easily. Some part of her prayed that Aidan dún Scoti would talk him out of it—or command him not to go—despite that she realized it wasn't possible. Keane had sworn his oath to David. And even if he should wish forfeit Dunràth and Lilidbrugh, Lianae was part of that bargain. He would have to forfeit her as well. And then he would be tried for treason, for he was David's sworn man.

Pacing the small one-room cottage, she ran her hand over the furniture curiously, considering her hosts. The house itself was finely kept, with nary a speck of dust to be found and the ashes in the pit were freshly swept. In one of the coffers, she'd found stacks of gowns folded neatly, and another smaller coffer held clothing belonging to a man. By all accounts, whoever lived here valued their abode, and yet they'd so graciously abandoned it for guests. As a thank you, perhaps Lianae might leave them one of her stones? Despite the sorrowful occasion, they had welcomed her with open arms.

Waiting for Keane to return from his counsel with his brother, Lianae unfastened the silk purse from her girdle and brought it to the table. She sat in one of the chairs to work the knot and once the knot was freed, she widened the cinch and emptied the contents on the table. Five charm stones remained.

Were they worth anything at all without the entire set of twelve? Lianae hadn't any clue. And yet, it was all she had to give...

Each of the stones bore a similar mark—two moons, with a lightning rod betwixt. She turned them over, one by one, fingering each of the deeply etched marks. The instrument of such artwork was unclear, since it would have taken a needle finer than the one she'd used to sew Aveline's dresses, and yet they would have had to have been razor sharp to cut the quartz stones like butter. Marveling over the fine craftsmanship, she studied the stones all laid out upon the table, thinking that come spring, she would ask Keane to take her back to Lilidbrugh for the rest. Even if she could not use Uhtreda's charm stones to buy news of her brothers, they could sell them to resupply the hallhouse. After so long without a thane or a chatelaine, Dunràth would be in sore need of provisions—

There was a rap at the door. Startled, Lianae swept the stones back into her purse, cinching the bag. "Come in," she said.

"Pardon," a young girl said. She was barely more than a child.

Discomposed, Lianae hid the purse in her lap. "May I help you?"

The girl's face fell. "Have I come to the wrong house?"

"I-I don't know," Lianae said, and only then did she realize the girl's eyes had yet to focus on her face. *Because she couldn't see.* Further proof came when she produced a crude stick from behind the door and began to tap it on the floor in front of her. "I beg pardon," the girl said brokenly, and the words came out as though on the verge of tears. "I came for a change of clothes."

Lianae bolted from her chair, discarding the purse upon the table. "Let me help you," she said, rushing to the girl's aide. "You ought not be alone!" Lianae chided, but it was the wrong thing to say, for the sweet lass folded to her knees and began to weep there upon the floor.

"I wanted to be a good wife," she cried, and Lianae stooped beside her.

She rubbed a hand on the girl's back, trying in vain to soothe her. "Now, now," she crooned. "'Twill be alright..."

HER NAME WAS CONSTANCE. But Lianae hadn't time to consider the fantastic story she had told, for no sooner had she returned the child bride to her husband, freshly dressed in a new gown, and calmer for the talk they'd shared, when Keane came to bid Lianae goodbye. He kissed her sweetly and with an aching heart, Lianae followed him to the hillside where five hundred mounted warriors waited for the king's command to go.

Already, David mac Mhaoil Chaluim had placed himself at the head of the cavalcade, his gold and red banners the only splash of color against a bleak and grey sky. Silver mail and long swords winked along the hillside as a few men scrambled to gather their belongings and ready mounts.

Desperate to prolong the final moments, Lianae clung to Keane even after he was mounted, loathe to see him go.

She was terrified she would never see him again. There was so much she wished to say, but with so many ears around to overhear, she held her tongue. Resting her cheek against her husband's thigh, he reached down to lift Lianae's face by the chin. "Dinna worry. Lael will see you safely home, and I will join anon."

"Promise me!" Lianae begged.

He slid his gloved hand across the pate of her head, gently cradling the back of her head. "Lianae, my sister is as capable as any man, and once you have arrived at Dunràth ye will have the king's writ. Dinna fear, my love."

My love...

They were the sweetest words Lianae had ever heard. But it was happening all too quickly. Voices screamed inside her head. She couldn't bear for him to leave now. She wanted to plead with him to stay but the insistent sound of a horn blast held her tongue.

"Keane," she cried softly, grasping at his hand. His green eyes compelled her to speak now, or forever hold her tongue, but the words caught in the back of Lianae's throat. Confused by her own emotions, she stared up into her husband's twinkling eyes.

And then all too swiftly, her chance was passed. A runner bore down the hillside from the front line. "We ride!" he shouted. "Fall in line! Fall in line!"

Reluctantly—she could spy it in his eyes—Keane peeled Lianae's fingers from his hand, and then he spurred his mount, turning his back to her and taking up the rear of David's cavalcade. Lianae felt the separation as acutely as though they'd rent her arm. With her throat too thick to speak, she watched him leave, and once the troops had filed out, the vale appeared a desolate place, the hillside ravaged and trodden, with burnt spots along the tattered snow. The air itself smelled scorched.

Keane looked back only once to give Lianae a short wave, and then never again. She had no inkling how long she stood thereafter, but she could no longer see the king's troops by the time Lael came to drag her away to begin the task of packing their own saddles for the journey north. With a heavy heart, she allowed Lael to lead the away.

Most of Lianae's belongings—what little she had to her name—had been sent ahead to Dunràth, straight from Keppenach. She'd brought little in her saddlebags, save for a change of clothes and a purse full of stones. Everything she had had in her life before Keane was lost now—forfeit to her brother Lulach and his wife. She would start again, raised from the ashes of her past.

In the end, Lianae decided against giving any of her charm stones to Constance since the poor girl could not even see them to appreciate them. Later, when she had the opportunity, she would sew Constance a brand new dress. And mayhap, she would find someone to fashion the girl a staff, so she could more easily find her way about.

In the meantime, a simple thank you would have to suffice. All too often, life wasn't fair. But then again, Lianae herself was no stranger to this truth. At twenty-three, she'd had more than her share of trials and loss. And yet, if she'd thought herself hardened by her circumstances, she was ill-prepared for the dún Scoti sisters, who, judging by their dress, were far more hardened by life than Lianae could ever think to be.

Painted in woad, similar to the markings Keane had worn, they came dressed as seasoned warriors, like Boudicca, the queen of the long-ago Iceni tribe. For all her gentleness while at Keppenach, today Lael was transformed, equipped like the fiercest of warriors, covered in leather, fur and blades from her head to the tips of her toes. She wore woad across her cheeks and forehead, and her rich, black hair was bound in braids, so that, in the event of a battle, her long silky tresses would not interfere. She'd traded her silk gowns for leather, and her knives were all bound with skins, which she explained, kept the cold from icing them to her fingers and hid the glint of metal from the enemy. Unlike the English, who donned silver-coifs and twinkling mail, a true Scots understood intuitively that to survive the Mounth, a man—or woman as the case may be—must be at one with the land. The sight of Lael gave Lianae a private smile, and she wished for a moment that she might be so brave.

If only she and all the women of Moray had banded together with the men... they might have been ten thousand strong. But, "Women dinna lead armies!" her brother Graeme had said one day, when he'd caught Lianae admiring her father's sword. "'Tis naught but fantasy, Lianae! Like the raising of the corries, and ye dinna believe Cailleach dropped them stone by stone?"

"Aye, but it could be so!" Lianae had argued.

And her mother's gentle voice came back to remind her: *There are more things unknown under the heavens than men can suppose, Lianae. Anything is possible—anything.*

Including the love of a husband for a wife he'd never mean to have.

Lianae must endeavor to believe it.

From Dubhtolargg, they would have but sixty miles to travel as crows flew, but over mountainous terrain, with thick forests and swift, foaming burns. This far north, there would be no inns or alehouses to be encountered, and no one anticipated the comforts of a bed along the way. At least this time Lianae had a horse and a good pair of shoes.

Altogether they were six riders, the women atop snow-white mares that were born to the terrain. Sleek and sturdy, Lael extolled their virtues. Unlike the *destriers* the Normans rode, with blood lust in their eyes, they kept their wits while in battle. Lianae prayed she would never bear witness to that fact. And despite Lael's boast that she needed only one man to join them,

Aidan insisted Lachlann join the party as well. Not only would it ease his mind to have his trusted captain along to protect his sisters, on the return journey, Luc could return straight to Keppenach along with Lael, and Sorcha and Cailin would have Lachlann to escort them into the Mounth.

"Keep to the shadows along the crags," Aidan advised, constraining Lael's mount by the bridle. He cast a meaningful glance toward Lachlann. "Avoid the auld road, keep to the woodlands 'til you are well north o' the Spey."

Lael grinned down at her brother. "Dinna fash yersel', Aidan. We'll take good care of your captain, and ye worry more for the fool who would dare impede us."

Lianae could well believe it for Lael was frightening in the saddle.

Releasing her bridle, Aidan shared another meaningful look with Lachlann, spared a good-bye for Luc, and then he turned to Lianae. "Your father was a good man," he said.

Lianae nodded. "He was and I thank you."

There was sincerity in the man's gaze. "I would that you'd come at a more pleasant time, Lianae of Moray, though we will expect to see you again soon."

"I shall look forward to that day," Lianae said. "And I thank you kindly for your hospitality, laird."

Aidan reached out to pat her horse's mane. "This was Una's mare though she never once put her arse in the saddle," he said. "She will serve you well."

"Thank you," Lianae said again, and then, "And I am sorry for your loss."

"As we for yours."

Tears pricked at Lianae's eyes.

"Look after my brother is all I ask."

No matter what tensions had been roused between

them, Lianae could see the affection in his eyes. She nodded, her throat too thick to speak.

Flanked by Cailin, Sorcha, Lachlann and Luc, Lael took the lead to guide the way out of the vale and Lianae waved good-bye to Keane's brother, and then, with a last look toward the mountain where Una met her fate, she fell in line behind them.

CHAPTER TWENTY-FIVE

Dunràth was nothing at all like the scabrous Norman creations that had risen along the southern border of Scotia. No walls surrounded this coastal city, although the tower itself had been erected upon a *motte*, near *An Cuan Moireach,* with a network of sturdy tunnels descending to the beach. Lianae knew this despite that they could not be seen. For centuries, it was the way the lords of Moray had used the coastline, much of which had been formed by the capricious North Sea.

Surrounded by mostly wattle and daub homes, with brown thatch roofs covered in snow, the hallhouse itself soared high on the hill, attached to a single tower of the type that could be found throughout much of the northlands, made of field stone and mortar.

Gold and red, David mac Mhaoil Chaluim's lion rampant standard flew from the rooftop—one to match their own—a reminder that no matter what their history here, their future would be determined by the reigning king of Scotia.

But from the time Lianae had first learned to walk and talk, this was the land she'd called her home. She felt her strength renewed as the cavalcade came to the journey's end.

As the mesnie rode through Dunràth, the chapel bells began to ring, luring villagers out from their homes. The people waved as Lianae passed by, or stopped and stared, and what a sight they must have presented, with three war-clad women in their midst, a burly Highlander, and a Lowlander, garbed in Norman mail.

Mingled with the salt spray of the ocean, the moorlands held the very scent of green, even beneath a mantle of snow. At this time of the year, it was not unheard of to see snow swirling in the sky, even beneath a bright blue sky. And Ailginshire was close by, not more than a half-day's walk along the shore.

Dunràth's thane had been a Morayman, who was loyal to Lianae's father, but he too perished that day at the battle at Stracathro in Forfarshire. It was a kindness that fate placed her here, amidst these people who would surely welcome a daughter of Óengus.

Simple as the place might be, Dunràth filled her with awe. It wasn't Ailginshire, but now it was hers, and in her saddlebag she held the chatelaine's keys along with a writ from the king to command a garrison to keep her people safe.

Her people—even more than Keane's.

Trying not to think of her husband—waging another hopeless war—Lianae took the lead now, cantering all the way up the hill. And the higher they climbed, the more of Moray she could spy. Sandy beaches. Fishing huts dotting the horizon as far as the eye could see. The rich, snow-covered moorlands, the blue-grey dolphins surfacing close to shore.

Once, when Lianae was three, they'd found a whale stranded in the shallows along the inner Moray Firth.

The neighbors all shared the spoils, and the whale's fat lit their homes for years thereafter. The sight of her home shire took Lianae's breath away, and judging by the way Keane's sisters all gaped, they too were instantly enamored of the place.

Neither Cailin, nor Sorcha, nor Lael had ever set their jewel-green eyes upon the great North Sea, and a sense of pride filled Lianae as the cold wind whipped through her golden hair.

"Tis the lady of Dunràth!" Luc announced to one and all. "Make way," he commanded a wee boy with a goat.

Lianae and the dún Scoti sisters all shared a smile, for Luc had taken to puffing up his chest in a prideful manner, and, in fact, seemed quite enamored of Sorcha.

"Make way for your new lady," he shouted as they approached the top of the hill. "'Tis the lady of Dunràth ye'd behold!"

Keane's sisters, all three, surrounded Lianae protectively, but there was little need. Lianae was home. There were no gates to admit them, so she dismounted before the hall, where a pair of armed men stood guarding the entrance to the hall.

"I am your new lady," she announced, addressing a tall, lean man with silk-white hair. He was not a Norman, nor was he a Scot and she recognized the auld thane's faithful servant.

His blue eyes were sharp and wary, but held a spark of recognition. "Lianae of Moray," he said, clasping her hand. "Welcome, m'lady," he said, his eyes brimming with tears. "Welcome!"

Built upon the ruins of an old Roman fortress, the city

of Carlisle was a strategic stronghold for Scotland. William Rufus raised it, but David intended to keep it and make it Scotia's southernmost capital. Understandable that he should wish to, for even when the countries were not at war, the Border Reivers were a pain in David's arse. Controlling them, even more than controlling the new cathedral, was his ultimate design.

Three thousand men marched on the city at sunrise, and ill prepared for siege, the gates opened swiftly. There, in the name of the Empress Matilda, David mac Mhaoil Chaluim sent splinter troops to seize Wark, Alnwick, Norham and Newcastle. MacKinnon would descend upon Aldergh within the fortnight. Only once Carlisle was secure, David took Keane aside, and gave him the news about Lianae. The words he spoke sent cold shivers down his spine.

Bolting out of the king's court, leaving a sour-faced sovereign in his wake, Keane told Cameron on his way to the stables, "We ride for Moray *now*!"

"With David's blessing?"

Keane shot Cameron a quelling glance. "I go with or without it!" God's truth, if they had told him what Lianae would discover at Dunràth, he would *never* have let her go alone.

With all due haste, Keane gathered the men he'd been promised—only seven. Forty more would follow once David could spare them. The rest awaited him at Dunràth—all under Lianae's command!

Angrily, he secured his saddle, while Cameron watched. "What if she has found them?"

"I canna say what Lianae will do, but *you knew—you knew,* damn it. And yet ye dinna say—*why*?"

"I will break no more oaths," Cameron said simply.

Despite Keane's fury, both men understood what it meant for Cameron to keep his vows. He struggled now to live a life of honor, in order to redeem himself in the eyes of the world—in the eyes of Aidan and his sister most of all.

But this was the one thing Cameron had yet to learn: If you were not fighting for the ones you loved, who the devil would you be fighting for?

"Damn you," Keane said, and turned on his heels. "Stay and fight for *your king*," he commanded him.

"I will come—"

"Nay!" Keane shouted. "I'llna ride with a man whose loyalty I must question." In one easy leap, he mounted Beithir. To his men, he commanded, "Ride!"

Even if he rode day and night, without rest, it would take them a sennight to reach Moray at best.

He didn't care whether Cameron joined them. Furious beyond reason, Keane led his men through Carlisle's open gates. Once the last man had passed over the bridge, he heard the groan of metal as the portcullis lowered. He did not look back.

❧

THE DÚN SCOTI sisters remained at Dunràth only a few days—long enough to see their horses rested and procure a few nights' rest. But they did not go before Lianae escorted them down to the beach and let them touch their toes in the ice-cold surf. She cajoled them to return in summer, when they would enjoy the warmer weather. Lael spoke of bringing her daughters and mayhap sending Kenna along. "It'll do her good to get away from Keppenach," Lael said.

Lianae couldn't be happier to hear this. She felt more at ease than she had in years. In fact, she had little to complain about, save for the sudden bouts of sickness she couldn't quite explain. It was Cailin who asked before she left, "Might you be with child, Lianae?"

The possibility hadn't even occurred to her. Despite

her lies to the king about Keane, Lianae hadn't truly considered how quickly it might happen. She and Keane had spent nearly every waking moment in Dubhtolargg... *getting to know one another.* So it was certainly a possibility, and the notion pleased her.

A child?

With Keane.

How different her life would be. As close as they were, she wasn't even concerned about the possibility of seeing Lulach again, or William fitz Duncan, for she had the king's writ in her possession and a prince of Scotia at her side. Not that she had ever aspired to such things, for Fitz Duncan was a king's son, after all. But Keane dún Scoti—even as modest a man as he was—was worth ten of fitz Duncan.

In fact, she had little doubt that if Keane's brother had not lost *Clach-na-cinneamhain*—and she was quite certain now that's what it was, the *Stone of Destiny*—the dún Scoti might have wreaked havoc with this knowledge alone. If what she suspected were true, King David was never crowned upon the rightful stone. Therefore, his coronation would not be sacrosanct. If *anyone* should glean this knowledge, Lianae had very little doubt there would be a race to the vale to recover the true stone and crown a new king. And, for that, there might be any number of contenders, all with more right to succession than David mac Mhaoil Chaluim, including William fitz Duncan, Aidan dún Scoti and her brother Graeme.

On the day the sisters departed Dunràth, Lianae was sorely tempted to ask them about the stone, and about the accident that blinded Constance, but despite that they had grown closer along the way, there was a way about the dún Scoti sisters that discouraged any such questions. For all that they'd seemed like normal siblings, with sweet, freshly washed faces, they clearly were not.

All three hugged Lianae before mounting their white horses, and even before they had returned to the saddle, their looks were stern and backs were straight. Once again they were bedecked for war.

"You!" Lael said to Lianae's steward. The elder man looked terrified all at once. "Take care of your lady," she demanded from her saddle, and the old man nodded quickly.

Smiling to herself, Lianae crossed her arms, battling yet another wave of nausea. Forsooth, it must be exactly what Cailin said. *A child.* The very thought made Lianae's heart hurt. A child, but what if his father never returned? She had not seen Keane now for weeks, but she had the king's writ, she reminded herself. And she had Balloch, the old steward.

But she would not think this way. There was much to be done before her husband's return: take stock of their supplies, and find out how much remained before the spring planting. She must wash the hallhouse from top to bottom, give it the love of a home. There were grievances to hear, and bread to bake. She had heads to count and animals to see to. And most of all, she had a nursery to shape.

The old steward would help her, but out of everyone, she believed he would be most pleased to see the dún Scoti sisters go. For all that the man appeared to be her greatest ally at Dunràth, he was as timid as a church mouse.

Of course, goodbyes were never easily said, and Lianae had voiced them now more oft than she would have liked, but, of course, it was only meet that they should leave. Lael had her daughters to return to, and Cailin and Sorcha were expected in the vale.

"Godspeed, my sisters. May Cailleach be merciful and put the wind at your backs."

"And you, Lianae... have a care," Lael said, eyeing each of her guards, and once again the steward with a sharp, cutting glance. For emphasis, Lael placed a hand to her sword and gave each man a terrifying nod.

Lianae tried not to laugh at the looks the guards passed to one another. They might be afraid of the sisters, but Lianae herself was not afeared.

She had more than fifty men, with loyalties to her alone by writ of the king. So long as she remained vigilant, they would be more than enough to defend the hallhouse. As a daughter of Óengus, she knew every last villager would raise arms to defend her, even the smallest child. But soon after the sisters' departure, they had a chance to test her theory. An envoy arrived, with riders bearing fitz Duncan's blue and silver banner.

Lianae was eyeballs deep in the ledgers, for she could read, and she would have them settled before her husband's return. Her father had never managed their accounts. It was her mother who'd kept the books. The old steward appeared in Lianae's solar, standing there with wide, round eyes. "The lady Uhtreda bids an audience w' ye m'lady."

At hearing the name, Lianae's shoulders tightened. "The lady Uhtreda?"

Had she come to retrieve her stones?

The steward nodded, as though he'd read her thoughts. But nay, he could not know she had them... nobody but Keane knew she had the charm stones. Lianae furrowed her brow. "Does she come alone?"

"Nay, m'lady. She comes with six of fitz Duncan's guards."

"But not fitz Duncan himself?"

"Nay, m'lady."

Relaxing a bit, Lianae put her quill down upon the table and pushed the ledgers away, reminding herself that she had fifty men—plus a houseful of servants who were loyal to the old Moray thane. Not even fitz Duncan would dare defy a king's writ. She was lady of the manor now, and she refused to be cowed by fitz Duncan in her own home. At any rate, Lianae no longer had the majority of the stones, nor did it behoove her to confess herself before a woman who'd raised a monster such as William fitz Duncan. "Let her in,' Lianae allowed.

"Art certain, m'lady?"

Lianae sat straighter in her chair. "Dinna worry, Balloch. If she dares to challenge me, it will be the same as challenging her sworn king. Show the lady Uhtreda into my hall."

"Very well, m'lady," Balloch agreed, though reluctantly, but then he stood, his lips parting as though he meant to speak again. It was a look she was coming to know well, for the man always seemed to be on the verge of telling Lianae something more. But he shut his mouth again and turned to go.

Lianae let him leave, and once he was gone, she went to change her dress.

Despite that she was far more accustomed to wool than silk, it was a message she meant to send to the lady Uhtreda. *She* was the lady of Dunràth now, and as such, Lianae would look the part to face her accuser. For a moment, she considered leaving the small silk purse behind, but as they went with her everywhere now, she did not wish to leave the charm stones unguarded, not even in her own house. Fastening the purse to her girdle, she made her way toward the great hall.

The Lady Uhtreda herself had once been the consort of a king. Her father Gospatric was Earl of

Northumbria, but Lianae was a daughter of Moray—the true Moray heir.

Dressed in one of Aveline of Teviotdale's mended gowns—a pale rose samite surcoat, with a white tunic beneath and a gilded girdle—she arrived in the great hall to find the long-faced woman seated calmly at her table, without her guards. Having left them outside, she sat alone, blinking innocently at the sight of Lianae.

To the contrary, there were at least four of Lianae's guards present—two at the hall doors, one each at opposite ends of Lianae's long table. Intrigued that the lady would come without her hateful son, Lianae approached the table and sat down, facing the older woman.

"What brings you to Dunràth, Lady Uhtreda?"

Lianae couldn't quite give the woman the deference her title commanded. It made her stomach even more ill than the haggis she'd consumed this morn—and she longed for a bit of her husband's whitebeam tea.

Uhtreda smiled cannily, with hooded eyes. For an older woman, Lianae must admit she was still lovely, with dark hair and bright blue eyes, though her face was marked with even more wrinkles than Lianae remembered. She wore her hair in braids, much as a young maid would, laced with golden ribbons. Her dress, as well, was finely sewn, woven with tiny threads of gold. "I had a visit from an auld crone a few days past… she wore a patch over one eye," she said at last.

"What has some auld woman to do with me?" Lianae asked her. The stones at her belt seem to weigh a little heavier.

Uthreda's eyes twinkled with a certain knowing. "Ah, well, she was passing through on her way to the Isle of Skye," she said.

"And?"

"She assured me I could retrieve the remainder of my stones... from *you*."

Lianae's breath caught over the blatant challenge, and the two women assessed one another across the table. Lianae felt the edge of her dirk cut into her thigh, but Uhtreda did not lose her temper, nor was there any true imputation in her tone.

After a moment, the woman reached for a small purse attached to the girdle at her waist—a purse not unlike Lianae's—and Lianae heard the hiss of steel leaving a scabbard as she reached for the pouch.

Lianae lifted a hand to stay her guard as Uhtreda lifted the purse from its clasp. Calmly, unconcerned about the guards, Uhtreda opened the small purse and dumped the contents upon Lianae's table.

Lianae stared, aghast.

There were seven stones laid before her; some landed on their backs, displaying two moons, side by side, with a lightning rod betwixt. It was the very same symbol on the stones Lianae had lost. Slowly, after meeting Lianae's gaze, the woman turned her charm stones over, one by one, until all were displaying the finely etched moons on their backs.

They were the same stones.

Even the rare white quartz was precisely the same color.

But it was not possible, for Lianae had lost the other seven charm stones in the brambles at Lilidbrugh—beneath a mountain of snow.

It was near twilight now, and Lianae had yet to light the candles in the hall. Uhtreda's charm stones appeared to glow with the same strange pale light she recalled from the ruins at Lilidbrugh—ever so slightly, almost imperceptibly.

As though they grew in weight yet again, she felt the heaviness of the five stones attached to her belt... as though they longed to be reunited with the stones laid out upon the table. Self consciously, Lianae put a hand to the purse attached to her belt, lifting her face.

Both women locked gazes.

Uhtreda smiled yet again—but this time, it was a weary smile that was neither cold nor cruel, nor was it warm and loving. She seemed merely tired—like a woman who'd long weathered the whims of men. "You see… she brought me these stones," she explained, "and assured me *you* would return the rest." She fingered the runes, one by one. "Do you see these marks?" She continued to pet the stones over the moons, and they seemed to shiver slightly, like tiny living creatures. "So finely etched. There are none remaining of their like. These in particular were branded by Taranis, the thunder god himself."

"And who is this woman who claims I would return your stones?" Lianae asked, unwilling to part with the ones she had. If, indeed, it was true that they were special, she didn't relish the thought of leaving them in fitz Duncan's hands.

The lady Uhtreda shrugged. "She is known by many names, I hear. Some call her the great white witch. Others call her The One. Still others have named her Cailleach." She narrowed her eyes, peering straight into Lianae's soul. "My grandmother knew her by another name…"

"And what name is that?"

Uhtreda's grin revealed straight white teeth. "She was known to my kinsmen as… Merlin. It was she who helped restore my great, great grandfather Uhtred to his seat as Bamburgh's Earl. I am named for him, ye ken?"

Her eyes seeking proof of her stones, Uhtreda glanced over the table at Lianae's purse. "You are drawn to keep them close, are you not?"

Lianae tapped her fingers upon the table. "If you believe I have wronged you, lady Uhtreda, why is it that you have come alone, without the aid of your son? I am quite certain if William raised his standards he could decimate Dunràth in but a day."

"My dear child, I have no delusions about my son. Any mother worth her salt kens the worth of her men. William is not fit to rule, and neither was his father."

"And still you wed him?"

Uhtreda arched a brow. "As did you with one you ought not love?"

Lianae swallowed the words that longed to emerge. Whatever it was she did or didn't feel for Keane, it was none of Uhtreda's concern.

"Lucky for you. Not all women are fortunate enough to wed for love," Uhtreda said. "And for such a coupling, ye ken, a woman might be branded a shrew?"

As a matter of courtesy, Lianae averted her gaze, for she herself had sometimes spoken ill of the lady. There were not many who'd been spared Uhtreda's biting tongue—Lianae and her sister included. It galled her more for Elspeth's sake, for now her lovely sister was dead. Lady Uhtreda had opposed their marriage vehemently, but only this moment did it occur to her to wonder why. Perhaps she'd known something more about her son. Or, she might have simply been a shrew, but she was neither shrewish this moment, nor unkind, and the look in her eyes was empathetic.

"I would wager my son did not mean to harm your sister," Uhtreda said. "He was born with the same affliction his father had. To put it rather indelicately, my child, neither could produce proper seed… without a bit of bed play. I fear your sister Elspeth was dealt a mercy by Bhrìghde herself."

While Cailleach was the mother of winter, Bhrìghde was her summer sister, whose smile could raise up saplings from the ground by its warmth alone. But not even Bhrìghde could raise her sister from the dead. Lianae's heart wrenched.

Before she could harden her heart, the woman claimed, "I have a gift to give you in return for my stones... a bit of news..."

The older woman watched her, studying Lianae's expressions.

"I trust you have not yet visited the tunnels below your keep?"

"Nay," Lianae said. There had been little reason to visit them as yet. They were mostly used by the men, for they were dark and deep and too dangerous for a woman to venture into alone. They were mostly used for access to the sea, and to house the gaols...

"Why should I trust you?"

Uhtreda shrugged. "If it makes any difference, I come without William's knowledge."

"But not without his men?"

The older woman shrugged again. "There are those who would see the Mormaerdom returned to its rightful state. I would not dare travel alone." Her eyes fairly gleamed, piercing Lianae with their incredible intensity as she lifted her chin and peered down her nose. If there was aught about her that reminded Lianae of her son, it was that gesture.

"Your gift?" Lianae entreated.

Uhtreda stabbed a finger at the air in the direction of Lianae's purse. "My charm stones, if you please, then I will tell you what I came to say..."

There were only five remaining, after all.

What good was one without the rest?

Curiosity needling her, Lianae sat back a moment to consider the offer. Only once she realized it was no offer at all—that her curiosity was worth the price of her few remaining stones—she pinched the purse from its clasp and set the purse upon the table. Uhtreda reached for her stones at once, her long lean fingers snatching the silk into her palm.

For an instant, she merely squeezed the purse with a look of quiet contentment on her face, and it was odd, for when Lianae blinked, it seemed that a few of the tired lines receded from her face...

CHAPTER TWENTY-SIX

The guards would have preferred to deny her, Lianae realized. Wielding her chatelaine's keys before her, she forced her way past two guards, and then lifting one of the pitch torches from its brace upon the wall, she descended into the ancient tunnels below Dunràth. *Alone.* If by chance they didn't already know what awaited her there, she wanted no one present to witness what she would find.

Dark and cold, despite the glow from her torch, the scent of salt permeated the dank air. The walls themselves wept, leaving the rock stained and crusted with an age-old scab of white. Icy drafts swept past her legs, but she pinched her cloak together and continued boldly in her descent. Somewhere, beyond the confines of the walls, she could hear the surf pounding furiously against the cliffside. She met another guard along the way, but the instant Lianae met his gaze, the man fled before she could speak a word—*because he knew.*

She was her father's daughter, she told herself, a daughter of Moray. She would not cow before usurpers. Whatever it was that awaited her below, she was not afraid.

Brandishing her torch before her once again, Lianae

inhaled a breath and continued the drafty descent. A rat scurried past her feet, startling her and she gave a little yelp, but not even a fear of vermin could stop her now. Were she told she might meet Viking marauders at the end of her journey, Lianae would refuse to turn back now.

She heard a crunch beneath her feet and felt the crack of bones. The remnants of another small rodent lay in pieces in her path.

If it were true what Uhtreda had said, all things were subject to change… especially with Lianae's knowledge of the Destiny Stone.

Despite the woman's uncanny sense of knowing, not even Uhtreda knew about that lost Stone from Scone. And yet… if Lianae betrayed confidences, if she spoke the words out loud, her life with Keane would lost with the very next breath. Alas, she must consider the good of Scotland, not simply her own welfare, or that of her babe's.

Along the midway point, Lianae reached a forked passage, each tunnel descending further into darkness….

Which path to take?

Forward, ever forward, she decided and chose the darker of the two—the one that promised the deepest secrets. Holding her breath against the stale, cold air, she moved past cobwebbed corners and putrid smells.

What would Óengus do?

At last, Lianae came to a recess in the tunnel, wherein they had carved four cells into the stone walls, each barred by heavy iron doors.

Here, even the sound of the ocean was quieted by the thickness of the earth. Inhaling sharply, Lianae thought about Keane and tears stung her eyes. Producing the chatelaine's keys from her belt, she located the key meant to open the cell doors.

Three of the doors were already unlocked and slightly ajar, the fourth was shut tight against what lay on the other side…

The bars were too high to peek inside, but Lianae understood this would be the one.

She held her breath as she lifted the key to the rusted old lock, turning it quickly, before she could lose her nerve. For a long moment, she stood by the closed door, half expecting that whoever was on the other side would come barreling through at the turn of her key, but they did not. Somehow, Lianae sensed they were holding their breath as did she... Placing a hand to the cold iron, she pushed the door open. And there he stood.

Graeme.

Beaten and half starved, with a gaunt face that was dirtier than a chimney, her eldest brother stood staring at her through bloodshot eyes.

❧

EVEN THE TREES WEPT.

It was a strange winter they were passing, far warmer than any Sorcha could ever recall. It was as though the Mother of Winter herself had somehow abandoned them forevermore.

Betimes she missed Una more than she could bear, but the sojourn away from Dubhtolargg had managed to distract her from her grief.

Sorcha liked Lianae. And the simple fact that she liked her only served to prove that her brother was wrong to keep them all so secluded in the vale. People were mostly the same, no matter from whence they hailed. In the end, their bodies would all feed the earth altogether, and a new generation would arise again and pass.

"We are all merely passersby in this life," Una once said.

Fleeting breaths, through impermanent lungs. There is an unseen life who dreams us... one who knows our fate...

As they sat watering their horses near a wide spot in the burn, Sorcha ferreted out the crystal Una had given her from her saddlebag, inspecting the bauble in the palm of her hand.

Una had been such a curious woman, and betimes Sorcha witnessed things in her grotto that could not be explained—like the color of her eyes now. One was violet, one was green, and she only realized it because Ria had asked. In fact, Sorcha felt changed after that morning in Una's grotto—but the change was not so telling as the color of her eyes.

Tell me what you see...

Sorcha heard the auld woman's voice even now, like a gentle whisper rifling through the ancient trees, and she studied the crystal in her hand, the milky white stone that once graced the hilt of Una's staff—that punishing staff that so often found the pates of their heads. And yet Sorcha remembered it fondly, tears forming in her eyes.

The bruadar is yours alone to decipher...

They must be near Lilidbrugh by now; Sorcha could feel it in her bones—the same way Una's crystal had called to her from her bag.

Lael had promised to stop and explore the old ruins along the journey home. They belonged to Keane now, but Una had often spoken of the birthplace of their clan—the pale stone towers that had once risen high into the pinewood trees, the cobbled courtyard made of the white quartz culled and hauled from the lands near River Ness. It was the same kind of stone some referred to as coldstones, used by the blessed to cure sickness and bring peace to the dead.

Charmed by faeries, they were said to float like lilies on the water.

The fountain in the courtyard at Lilidbrugh had once been filled with coldstones, enough to provide blessings for every man and woman in Scotia. But, alas, it was as though the white city had decided it did not wish to be found, for they'd been searching for half the day and Lael was growing impatient. She had daughters waiting for her at home.

Thinking about Lael's daughters, Sorcha studied the small crystal in her hand. Made of the same lucent stone as Una's *keek stane,* the glass was smaller in size. It fit neatly in the palm of her hand and looked a bit like the one Una had kept upon her table—the one Sorcha had peered into the day before the old woman died. The *keek stane* was lost now—like the Stone of Destiny—but on the very day Una died, Sorcha had discovered this smaller stone lying upon her bed. It was as though Una had left it for her there… a gift.

Like the book.

The collapse of the mountain had not been the work of mortal men. The gods themselves had seen fit to take Una and her grotto, along with the Stone from Scone, with the sweep of a godly hand. Only *this* now remained…

Far more solicitous these days, with four girls to look after, her eldest sister came to check the bridle of Sorcha's mare. "What is that?" she asked.

"Una's crystal."

Touched by a ray of watery sunshine, the glass seemed to wink in Sorcha's hand.

Curious as to what they might be looking at, Cailin wandered over as well. "The one from her staff?"

"Aye."

"Una gave that to you?" both sisters asked at once. That damnable ash wood staff had never left Una's hand, and the thought of her prying out the stone from its hilt was inconceivable... and yet she must have, for here it sat.

"When di' she gi' that to you?" Lachlann asked. "I saw her with her staff the night before she died. I took the last watch on the hill."

Sorcha shrugged. "I discovered it lying upon my bed..."

For a moment, whilst the horses drank, they all stood peering into the crystal as Sorcha cradled it within her hand, rolling it gently back and forth. And then she stopped and froze, peering inside. But neither of her sisters saw what Sorcha saw, for Lael and Cailin soon grew bored and walked away. Cailin stood chatting away with Luc.

"I say we leave off searching," Lael said.

"Oh, nay! Ye may go," Cailin argued. "We dinna need for ye to stay."

Barely listening, Sorcha blinked, studying the crystal.

"I would not leave you," Lael replied, her tone more snappish yet. "If I go, so do you—both o' ye. I'llna give Aidan yet another reason to forsake me, do ye ken?"

"It isna your place to see to my welfare," Cailin argued. "I am a woman grown! We are scarce twenty miles from the vale. Lachlann and I will see our Sorcha home!"

"Over my dead body," Lael argued. "When I go, the rest of you will leave as well. There is naught for us here."

Much like the *keek stane* in Una's grotto, the crystal in Sorcha's hand suddenly appeared to glow. The forest fell to silence, and the mist about them seemed to flow deep into the crystal. Inside the crystal, shapes began to coalesce, and Sorcha's heartbeat a little faster. Mesmerized, she studied the changing shapes.

"Well?" Cailin prompted.

"What is wrong wi' ye, Sorcha?" Lael asked. "Ye look like ye've seen a ghost. And by the by, what the devil's happened to your eyes?" she asked, as though she'd only now noticed the different colors in the glow radiating out from the crystal.

But Sorcha couldn't pry her gaze away. She spied the same tower rise up—the one she saw in Una's *keek stane*. Only now she recognized it all the better.

Because she had been there.

Dunràth.

The blood drained from her face. There in her crystal, before the *motte* and tower raged a blue, four-legged bird, its beak dripping with blood... and then a wounded and bleeding wolf... *Keane would be that wolf.* Even as Sorcha tried to make sense of the images, she knew it for truth. The four-legged bird... it was the sigil of William fitz Duncan.

White-faced, Sorcha peered up at her sisters. "We must hurry back to Dunràth!"

❧

LOOK TO YOUR HEART, *not to your head.*

Una's words echoed in Keane's head. Logic told him he should stay and fight beside his king, but his heart said he must go.

With the sweep of a hand, he could lose everything: Lianae. Dunràth. Lilidbrugh, and perhaps even his kinsmen, if Lianae had betrayed them. All for what? For a chance to hold his own seat under a sovereign his people never recognized?

But nay, that was not why.

He'd done everything for Lianae—for the woman who held his heart.

He had been willing to lie, to accept the sins of another man, to eschew his best friend—because, in truth, it should have been Cameron to hold Dunràth in his stead. If only Keane had not taken command of their men. And still, Cameron had stood beside him. The man's greatest sin had been to withhold the news that Lianae's brothers were awaiting sentencing at Dunràth, and this was why Murdoch fled as well.

Keane would not fool himself into believing that Lianae had chosen him for love. All she needed to do now was to free her rebel brothers and then hand over the keys to Dunràth to them—a stronghold from which they could mount a new rebellion against the king. There was no way to tell what might come thereafter, for half of Moray remained loyal to Óengus the Mormaer, even unto the grave.

For five years, David had held those lands per force. Why would he now put the Kingdom of Moray at risk? The king had pushed his pieces around his chessboard, marrying this laird with that lady, assimilating rather than conquering, despite that his armies grew and grew. But, then, he ought to know by now that you could not force Highlanders into subjugation. Even in death, the sons of Óengus would plague him still. Unless…

And suddenly he realized…

It was a test.

A test Lianae must not fail.

She held the keys to Dunràth and David's writ. David mac Mhaoil Chaluim had placed them knowingly into his wife's hands, and he must have known she would find her brothers—and what then?

Did he have men at the ready to crush a rebellion? Did he mean to ferret out the rebels using Lianae? Even now, was fitz Duncan preparing to ride on Dunràth under the king's command?

Alas, but the one piece of this puzzle that David

could not have anticipated was the Stone of Destiny, and Keane realized that Lianae knew. He spied the truth in her face the day he'd ridden out from the vale.

Aye, she knew.

When he arrived, would her brothers put an arrow through his heart the instant they spied him? Would they open the doors for the new laird of Dunràth? Would Lianae hand over the keys to Dunràth willingly? Would the king's men turn on her if she chose the wrong path? She had fifty good men at her disposal, but how many of those men were loyal to David and how many remained loyal to Óengus?

I am not witless enough to leave any stronghold of import without men enough to guard her, he remembered David saying. And he knew instinctively it would be true.

Heartsick, Keane picked up his gait. He could smell it now—the salt fury of the ocean, and he prodded Beithir faster, faster, eager to arrive—eager to set eyes upon his wife—eager to know whether his life would be crushed as easily as the Destiny Stone had been removed from their grasp.

❧

"Riders, m'lady!"

Lianae peered up from the house ledgers she'd been studying for the majority of two days. If she was not mistaken, there were discrepancies in the accounts. Cartloads of their supplies had been requisitioned by Kinneddar. What this meant, she hadn't any clue, but she wouldn't put it past fitz Duncan to empty the coffers and pantries of all demesnes under his control. "Do they bear the royal standard?"

Balloch shook his head. "If they fly any, m'lady, we canna see it."

Lianae worried the pen in her hand, unaccustomed

to making such decisions, and just now, the moment of truth had come. She could read and write and keep the ledgers as well as any man, but could she hold Dunràth against invaders?

Here, there were no ramparts to hide behind, no rooftops from which to set loose missiles. The hall-house itself sat high enough on the *motte* that any men firing from the three-foot rampart surrounding the keep would have an advantage for but a *very* short time. There was little time to prepare if they meant to fight and hold what was theirs. Even if she were inclined to, it was too late to send riders to Kinneddar, and there was little assurance fitz Duncan would aid them anyhow. For all she knew it could be him out there, though she wasn't about to lose what she'd fought so hard to win.

"The men to arms," she commanded the steward. "Women and children to the hallhouse. Gather everyone straightaway." If the attackers should ascend the *motte*, they would protect themselves by setting fire to the ditch. "Go and tell my brother—quickly!" she urged Balloch.

"Aye, m'lady!"

By the rood, if Lael and her sisters could dress themselves for war, so then could she! Bound to protect her people, Lianae raced up the tower stairs to the lord's chamber to don the lord's armor—not much more than a boiled gambeson and tunic, but the tunic bore Dunràth's sigil so that her men might easily recognize her in battle.

She knew little about how to wield a sword, but she would try nonetheless—if only as a show of strength. Alas, but she tried to lift the heavy claymore displayed upon the wall, and it sank to the floor with a mighty thud, hacking pieces from the floor. Muttering curses beneath her breath, Lianae abandoned the sword where it lay, cursing it to rot, and snatched up her trusty little blade from the bedside where she'd left it.

Hurrying over to the cold brazier, she dirtied her fingers with ash. It wasn't the same as woad, but this too would have to do. She swiped two fingers across her cheeks and brow and hurried out into the courtyard, shouting for the men to bring around her mare.

Cailleach have mercy, she would soon discover how well Una's horse could handle blood and gore. But then suddenly, before she had the chance to mount, she peered down the *motte* to spy the approaching horde.

At the foot of the hill, twenty men riding without banners spilled from the woods and fell upon a smaller band of eight. Of those eight, she recognized the leader at once—his hair black as midnight and his coat dark against his snow-white mare.

Keane.

HAVING FLED CARLISLE SO SWIFTLY, Keane had abandoned more than half his promised men. He was ill prepared to meet more than twice his number on the field of battle. But the attackers came not from the *motte,* he realized, unsheathing his sword, and placing himself between his men and the assailants, to give his men precious seconds to prepare. But seconds was all the time he could buy, for they flew at Keane, one by one.

"To the laird!" his men cried, rallying themselves to fight.

"To the laird!"

The clash of swords rang against the twilight. Metal struck metal. Sword against axe. Axe against sword. Men shouted battle cries unto the heavens and Keane felt the cold bite of steel pierce his shoulder...

. . .

"To the laird!"

"To the laird!"

Riding hell-bent through the pinewood forest, the dún Scoti sisters heard the cry to arms and spurred their mounts to greet the battle, with Lachlann and Luc close at their heels. They reached the melee as the battle engaged.

There were no banners flown, but Lael had no need to know whose blood she would spill to defend her brother. "To Keane!" she shouted, unsheathing her great sword along with a nine-inch blade from her belt.

Standing in her stirrups, Cailin drew her crossbow, slamming the butt against her shoulder.

Crying out in vengeance, Sorcha, drew her sword.

Together, the dún Scoti sisters shouted the dún Scoti war cry. Painted in woad, and ready to die for their kin, they joined the battle at the foot of Dunràth's hill.

By the gods above—every last one—Keane had never been more relieved to see three women in all his days! He recognized the war cry of their ancestors and grinned—for the sound was no less terrifying coming from a woman's tongue. He heard Lachlann's shout as well and knew the battle would be turned.

If he'd been surprised by his sisters' arrival, the assailants were all the more so and their momentary stupor was their undoing. Keane felled one, and cut down another as Lael came galloping by, wielding her long blade alongside him, cutting down another.

Already, his arm was covered with blood, making it difficult to wield his sword. He gritted his teeth and fought through the pain, struggling to retain command of the heavy blade. Lachlann flanked him on one side,

Lael on the other, and together they fought, parrying every blow. Cailin's arrows came whizzing by. Unlike Keane's hunting bow, hers was made for war. Each and every arrow met their marks with deadly thunks. He lost two of his numbers before another thirty warriors came marching down the *motte,* and another ten circled, attacking from behind. "To the laird of Dunràth!" they shouted to a man.

"To the laird!"

Like rats before a torchlight, the assailants fled into the woods.

So swiftly, the battle was done. But in the space of minutes, more than twenty men were felled—a few of his own. The mottled snow was strewn with bodies and peppered with blood. Dismounting, Keane saw to his fallen men. Only one of the assailants remained alive. He lifted the man to his feet and hurled him toward Lachlann. His brother's captain held a blade to the man's throat before he could take a step. "Take him to the gaols," he commanded. "Find out who sent the bastards and why."

And then he turned and saw her.

His wife.

Mounted upon a snow-white mare, like the ones his sister rode, she trotted down the *motte,* with ten more men at her rear. She wore a heavy gambeson over a bright green dress, but the look did not suit her. And still, she was lovely to behold. Overcome with emotion and relief, Keane sheathed his sword and went to her. Without a care that his men—and sisters—might witness a grown man cry, he went to greet his Moray bride. Spilling into his arms from her saddle, Keane swung Lianae jubilantly, covering her with his blood.

She didn't seem to care. Her amber eyes were liquid. "Ye're hurt!" she cried.

"Nay, Lianae, I am whole again," he said; and only

now did he know it for truth. She was the piece of him he'd been missing most of his life.

Lianae wept unabashedly, soaking his blood-stained coat with her tears. "Welcome home," she sobbed, hugging him fiercely. "Welcome home, my prince!"

"Ach, my love… what good is a prince without a princess?" he asked, and set her down upon her feet, falling to one knee, bloodied though he might be. "From this day forward, Lianae of Moray, I pledge my troth to ye… to the bairns we'll make together, to the land we'll keep and serve."

Weeping as she reached for him, her hands smeared blood and sweat across his whiskered face, but it was the most tender caress Keane had ever known. "My heart is yours, my laird of Dunràth," she said. "I love you truly. And if ye can see it in your heart to forgive me, I will be your faithful wife."

"I forgave ye before I left ye," Keane confessed, and it was true. He had known from the first time their lips met that she was the only woman he would ever know again. To keep her, he realized he must trust her, and to trust her he knew he must love her.

The people shouted huzzahs, but neither Lianae nor Keane heard them. The world fell away as they kissed once more… one last kiss to change the fates.

EPILOGUE

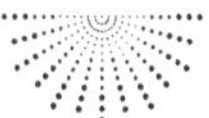

DUNRÀTH CASTLE, 1137

Some would say that Lianae had had the Kingdom of Moray at her fingertips and she threw it away.

But Lianae had won herself so much more that day. Praying by the rood that she would choose love over all, David mac Mhaoil Chaluim gambled and won.

So had she.

In retrospect, all of it had been no more than a calculated risk, for David mac Mhaoil Chaluim must have seen something more than Lianae or Keane had realized at the time.

And yet, David must have also known that Lianae would never allow her brother to hang and some day she meant to ask the king why he'd shown her brother such mercy, when his own brother Edgar had blinded their Uncle Donald and sent him to work as a scullion in the kitchens, for much the same offense.

In fact, now that she considered it, perhaps that was the reason, for it was said that David's brother Edgar had died a miserable man, wasted with guilt for what he had done to his own kin. Say what they would of him, David mac Mhaoil Chaluim was smarter than that. He conquered less by the sword and more by his wits.

The wind whipped at Lianae's skirts, tussling her hair. Summer was here and the chill of winter was long gone, but, like the lands themselves, the Highland winds could not be tamed. They blew as they blew, and if a man could not embrace the wildness of the North, it was simply not in his blood. Lianae lifted her face to the wind and smiled, enjoying God's caress.

Alas, her brother Ewen was dead—perished of fever soon after coming to Dunràth. With Graeme's help, she moved his grave to a spot high on the hill, beneath an elderberry tree. Whatever David's reason for sparing Graeme, she couldn't profess to know, but she was grateful nonetheless, and her brother no longer had any will to fight.

She made her way to the beach, bouncing their ten-month-old son in her arms. She'd named him Angus, after her father. Cooing sweetly at her ear as she made her way down to the beach where Keane was busy at work on a new boat, she held Angus close.

Keane had said he'd always meant to learn to fish, and now that he had the sea to challenge him more than the loch in Dubhtolargg, he found great joy in the thought of sharing a sail with their son—but not until Angus was old enough if Lianae had any say in the matter. In the meantime, he must be contented to share his time with her eldest brother.

She waved at the men, and Angus clearly said, "Pa-pa!"

"Aye!" she exclaimed, excited by her son's first word.

Fat and happy as he should be, Angus clapped his chubby little hands.

"'Tis your papa! Hi papa!" she said, waving again at Keane.

Almost in answer, the north wind lifted a briny scent to Lianae's nostrils and she inhaled deeply of the scent as she made her way to the water's edge, much as the women of Dunràth had been doing for centuries long before her.

She never saw her charm stones again, but she didn't need them.

Uthreda's son was a cruel snake, but no one could ever prove he was the one who'd beset Keane that day at the foot of Dunràth's hill, so he continued to serve David as Moray's Earl, denying aught to do with the treachery. The man they'd captured died later of his wounds, so they lived with a snake in their midst, keeping him at arm's length.

As for her brother Lulach, he'd come around but once. Though even if the loss of her blood kin dampened her spirits, she had Graeme. And she had Keane… and the future of her clan right here in her arms…

"Pa-pa!" Angus said again.

"Pa-pa," Lianae repeated with a smile.

Ready for Sorcha's story? Turn the page for a preview of Maiden from the Mist, a July 2017 release.

MAIDEN FROM THE MIST

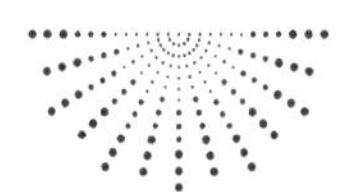

PROLOGUE

DUNRÒNAIGH KEEP, THE ISLE OF RÒNAIGH, APRIL 1135

Caden Mac Swein seized his grandfather's halberd from its brace upon the wall and stepped back to swing the heavy weapon, recalibrating its weight. "How many?"

"Fifty, near as we can see," Alec said.

Caden swung the halberd again, cursing roundly beneath this breath.

Made of sturdy ash wood, the haft of the great axe was more than four feet long. The blade was a solid thirty-three inches of black iron edged with fine steel. As a whole, the weapon measured six feet long and weighed more than two stone. Only a man of Caden's size and strength could ever hope to wield it, and anyone within arm's length of his swing could attest to his prowess with the weapon.

If they still had a head to speak.

He ran his fingers across the blade. Far more than the great sword, the Viking relic was his weapon of choice, for it once belonged to his great, great-grandsire, Swein of the North, whose aim was always true. The Beast, it was called, and once he set The Beast in motion, it unerringly met its mark.

Just then, Wee Davie rushed in, bearing their father's great sword. At thirteen, Wee Davie was petite for his age, and the length of the claymore was nearly as tall as him. "They're gatherin' near the Giant's Cave," he announced. "Let's go smite them from our land!"

Caden's brow furrowed. The Giant's Cave was a natural sea cave, with a ceiling so high it formed an echo. It was, in fact, deep enough to conceal at least fifty men. If any were hiding within, their numbers could easily be misjudged, and it was critical they know precisely how many men they would face today. So soon after the last raid, he had fewer able bodied men to join the fray.

"Have they gone inside?" he asked his brother, realizing that Davie probably spied them from the tower. Built by the ancients, Dunrònaigh Keep was "laird of the Minch." Its enduring presence defied even the storm kelpies—the Blue Men—who ruled the waters of Scotland's Firth. His people, his land, his tower, were guardians of the Minch, the tempestuous sea his ancestors once called Skotlandsfjörð.

"Nay," his brother said.

"Good." Caden nodded. To their good fortune, that cave by the shore was haunted and cursed. Most living souls would never venture inside, where bones of hapless men and women still clung to stalagmites near the ceiling. Trapped by the rising sea, their bodies had been borne too high to retrieve them. Now, clinging to their berths, even in death, they awaited with shivering bones for the sea to return and claim them. And claim them it would, for the Minch was a vengeful sea. No man who'd traversed the fjord could claim the kelpies weren't the fiercest of foes. The Scots of the Western

Isles feared them, though not enough to keep their filthy feet off Caden's island. And likely because he who controlled Rònaigh and Dunrònaigh, also controlled the trade between.

"I am ready!" Davie announced, but then he struggled to lift up their father's great sword.

Eying his youngest brother with displeasure, Caden said, "Nay ye're no', Davie."

The boy's helm fell over wide blue eyes. "Aye, Caden, I am," he argued. "Ye canna keep me from it! No' this time!" He cast a glance at Alec, hoping to win the captain's aid, knowing full well he was the only man Caden might listen to, but Alec wisely turned away. "I will fight like a mon aside my brethren!" Davie maintained.

Caden softened his voice. "Nay, Davie boy. Ye're of better use to me here."

Inside the keep. Away from so many bloodthirsty blades.

Once upon a time, Caden had been the second of five strapping sons, but only he and Wee Davie now remained. Their forefather, Conn Cétchathach of the Hundred Wars, had been a high king of Erin, but Wee Davie was little more than a boy. Already, during his scant years, they'd seen a quarter of the battles Conn had, and one of them—either Caden or Davie—must survive to see the end of these days with all their limbs and head intact. Caden aimed to see it would be Davie.

The youth pouted, his jaw set firmly in a freckled face.

"Davie," Caden reasoned. "One of us must stay and guard the keep."

"*Gonadh*! 'Tis a woman's job ye would leave me to," Davie complained, his voice cracking.

Caden laid a hand upon his shoulder. "To guard the chieftain's seat? Nay, my brother. 'Tis a task befitting only a chief."

Unconvinced, Wee Davie screwed his face. "Then do it yourself!"

Caden's fingers tightened about his brother's shoulder. "*One* of us must lead this fight, and until the day ye can wield this halberd in my hand, ye'll no' be the one to do so. D' y' hear me?"

Wee Davie lifted his chin. "Please," he begged. "Please, Caden. I'm a mon now!"

"A mon need never say he's a mon, Davie. My resolve remains." By the eyes of Conn, there were not even women remaining of their blood to strengthen alliances. This decision was not open to discussion. His brother would *not* fight today. He would remain safely within the keep.

He and Davie met eye to eye. To make his point, Caden handed the Viking halberd to his brother and it dropped with a thud to the floor, the iron spikes chipping the stone beneath. It barely missed Davie's foot, and the clatter it made rivaled the echo in the Giant's Cave.

No more need be said. Davie scowled, but allowed Caden to lift the halberd from the floor. He was still glaring as Caden turned and made for the door.

His captain hurried to keep step beside him. Only once they'd quit the hall, Caden turned and said, "See that he remains safe."

"I will try."

"Nay!" Caden said, his voice snapping like thunder. "You will do it. If my brother comes to harm today, I will take *your* head."

It was a bold threat, one Caden Mac Swein would never carry out on his most trusted friend, but Alec understood his laird's resolve better than most. At all costs, he would protect his youngest remaining sibling from the evils of this war. He, himself, might bear a dozen scars from chin to toes, but rather Caden should bear them than Wee Davie. In the end, it would be Davie Mac Swein who'd lead their clan, and Caden wouldn't bear the loss of yet another brother.

Outside, their ancient standard whipped in the breeze from Dunrònaigh's single tower—a tiger rampant ermine holding an arrow. The cat's powerful jowls snapped, and the wind was a roar from its toothy grin.

Down by the sea cave, a throng of usurpers waited to be ousted, their steely weapons glinting maliciously against a waning sun. Three more boats navigated the foaming surf, their numbers growing by the hour. It was better not to wait. Their advantage today would be a swift course of action.

"Di' ye spy their banner?"

"None."

"Greedy buggers," Caden said. "I warrant tis Angus Macleod again. He craves this island more than he does his firstborn son."

"Who would want that fork-tongued eegit anyhow?"

Seventy of Caden's men awaited outside the keep. He raised his grandfather's halberd to the heavens. "For Dunrònaigh!" he cried.

"For Dunrònaigh!" they returned, and together they marched down the hill, toward the beach. The sky was blue, and the sea churned with a ferocity born of the North wind. Caden shed his cloak, and with it, the last vestiges of his civility.

His men all followed suit, wanting nought to impede their movements in battle. Like their Viking predecessors, they welcomed the berserker lurking deep in their souls, each man prepared to defend this land and their people until their dying breath.

As they marched, they shouted war cries, and cut their weapons through the air, calling down the fury of the Blue Men of the Minch. Their every step was made easier by the pitch of the land, spilling them down and down the hill, like a deadly flow of silver. From the highest vantage point, atop Dunrònaigh Keep, it appeared as though a human wave plunged toward the sea.

By contrast, the usurpers came trudging up the hillside, weighted in their every step, but greed and blood lust fueled their march. "For Dunrònaigh!" Caden shouted one more time.

"For Dunrònaigh!" his men returned.

The sun glinted off helms and swords as the two forces collided on the hill.

The battle engaged. The roar was deafening, the clang of metal relentless. Blood sprayed the land, a macabre rain that covered every new blade of grass and turned the hillside red.

Battling tirelessly, Caden deflected incoming blades, swinging his halberd like a man possessed, felling all who came within his reach. The battle raged until all who remained were the fiercest of the lot.

Caden fought until his arms grew heavy, until he felt cold metal slice through his shoulder. Pain shot like lightning through his brain. Black rage overtook him. If he failed today, Wee Davie would be the one to pay. He would not fail his brother.

When he might have taken yet another blow, Alec came to save the day. The tip of Alec's sword entered the base of the man's skull, protruding through his nostrils. The man fell lifeless to the ground, his blood mingling with those who fell before him.

Caden roared his vengeance, raising his halberd yet again, finding strength in his brother's fate. By God, they would cut him down limb for limb before he stopped. And yet, even as he fought, two more long boats arrived upon his shore. Warriors trampled up the hillside to join the battle.

Realizing how swiftly the tide could turn against

them, Caden renewed himself, strengthening his resolve. With a war cry to the heavens, he moved through the melee, striking wherever he could, aiding his men one by one, and each life he took fed his madness.

Blood ran in rivulets down his arms, oiling his grip, but Caden embraced the axe as an extension of his being, swinging with all his fury and all his might. He felt another stab at his calf, and stumbled forward, howling in pain. The halberd turned before him, alive with a vengeance of its own.

The sun shone down, glinting off the metal of a helm, blinding him, but the halberd swept a deadly path before him, cutting flesh and bone. He heard a sound that gave him pause, his brother's voice, but he was not quick enough to ken from whence it came.

Davie's blue eyes met his for the briefest instant—prideful in his accomplishment. He'd felled the man who'd pierced Caden's leg. He'd stabbed him through the breast with their father's great sword, and the man fell short of his intended aim—Caden's heart. But Caden's halberd had no understanding of this. His brother stood before him, grinning, waiting for Caden's blessing... waiting for him to see that he was, indeed, now a man grown. *Waiting.*

Precious seconds passed in slow motion. Davie did not ken to step aside. Caden could not top the fateful swing of his axe. Once more, his halberd crushed through flesh and bone, severing Wee Davie's head in one fell swoop. The boy's body folded to the grass. His head flew. But Caden never saw it land. A curtain of black swept before his eyes, and he stood imprisoned in darkness, listening helplessly to the screams of men dying all about him.

HIGHLAND SONG

WANT TO READ CATRÌONA'S STORY?

Find out what happens when a fey, flame-haired beauty, wearing nothing but woad, turns her hand to captivating the last of the Brodie men…

The Highland Brides series continues with Gavin Mac Brodie's story.

Read Highland Song now

AUTHOR'S NOTE

Dearest reader,

If you've been following this series, you're probably wondering if this is the end. In a word, NO.

While the story of the Stone from Scone is complete, thus ending the trilogy, we still have many questions left to be answered. For one, we still have Sorcha's story to be told. You can find her story in my July 27, 2017 release, Maiden from the Mist.

Then, Malcom's story will take us in another direction entirely—smack dab in the middle of King Stephen's rebellion and a brand new connected series. The publication date is yet to be decided, so be sure to stay tuned for more news!

While reading, you might also have recognized a few names from history, most notably MacBeth (spelled Macbeth in literature), who was much maligned by Shakespeare, though he was, by most accounts, a fairly wise king, who ruled Scotland for seventeen peaceful years. On the other hand, Duncan I of Scotland was supposedly a selfish man whose six years of kingship brought no peace or glory to Scotland. The northern lords actually rebelled against him for invading Northumbria, and he was slain by MacBeth in a skirmish at Bothgouanan.

You also might also have noticed a few other names, like Merlin (hey, why couldn't *he* be a *she*?), and if you are a major history buff, Uhtreda, who was Uhtred the Bold's (or if you're watching The Last Kingdom, Uhtred of Bebbanburg's) great, great granddaughter.

Throughout Scotland's rich history, *magik* was an undeniable element in the Scottish culture and, of course, the "real" Stone from Scone was returned to Scotland after resting under the English throne for centuries, but there *is* a legend to the contrary, and maybe, just maybe... . I hope you enjoyed the Guardians books and that in reading these tales you might believe... if only for a moment... it could have happened just this way.

Happy reading, my friends!

GAELIC DICTIONARY

Provided for better reading enjoyment. For Gaelic words not included here, the meaning has been worked into the story itself. Look for both the Gaelic words and the English translation in italics.

Am Monadh Ruadh: the Cairngorms, but literally the red hills distinguishing them from Am Monadh Liath, the grey hills

Aurochs: large wild cattle, now extinct

Bean sìth: banshee

Ben: mountain

Breacan: short for breacan-an-feileadh, or great kilt

Brollachans: ghouls

Corries: mountains, or hills

Crannóg: wooden dwellings the early Picts used as homes, often built over a body of water

Dwale: a drink made of nightshade or belladonna, often used for anesthesia

Keek stane: a scrying stone, or crystal ball

Loch: lake

Mormaerdom: Gaelic name for the Kingdom of Moray

Mormaer: Gaelic name for a regional or provincial ruler

Quintain: a piece of training equipment used for jousting, often formed in the shape of a person

Reiver: raider on the English-Scottish border

Scotia: Scotland, also known as Alba

Sluag: God of the Underworld

Targe: a circular shield used for defense

The Mounth: range of hills on the southern edge of Strathdee in northeast Scotland

Trews: close-fitting tartan trousers

Uisge-beatha: whisky, literally means water of life

Vin aigre: vinegar or sour wine

Woad: a dye extracted from the woad plant

ALSO BY TANYA ANNE CROSBY

A brand-new series

Daughters of Avalon

The King's Favorite

A Winter's Rose

Rhiannon

The Highland Brides

The MacKinnon's Bride

Lyon's Gift

On Bended Knee

Lion Heart

Highland Song

MacKinnon's Hope

Guardians of the Stone

Once Upon a Highland Legend

Highland Fire

Highland Steel

Highland Storm

Maiden of the Mist

The Medievals Heroes

Once Upon a Kiss

Angel Of Fire

Viking's Prize

The Impostor Series

The Impostor's Kiss

The Impostor Prince

Redeemable Rogues

Happily Ever After

Perfect In My Sight

McKenzie's Bride

Kissed by a Rogue

Mischief & Mistletoe

A Perfectly Scandalous Proposal

Anthologies & Novellas

Lady's Man

Married at Midnight

The Winter Stone

Romantic Suspense

Speak No Evil

Tell No Lies

Leave No Trace

Mainstream Fiction

The Girl Who Stayed

The Things We Leave Behind

Redemption Song

Everyday Lies

ABOUT THE AUTHOR

Tanya Anne Crosby is the New York Times and USA Today bestselling author of thirty novels. She has been featured in magazines, such as People, Romantic Times and Publisher's Weekly, and her books have been translated into eight languages. Her first novel was published in 1992 by Avon Books, where Tanya was hailed as "one of Avon's fastest rising stars." Her fourth book was chosen to launch the company's Avon Romantic Treasure imprint.

Known for stories charged with emotion and humor and filled with flawed characters Tanya is an award-winning author, journalist, and editor, and her novels have garnered reader praise and glowing critical reviews.

Tanya and her writer husband split their time between Charleston, SC, where she was raised, and northern Michigan, where the couple make their home.

For more information

www.tanyaannecrosby.com
tanya@tanyaannecrosby.com

www.ingramcontent.com/pod-product-compliance
Lightning Source LLC
Chambersburg PA
CBHW051008180726
48291CB00006B/2024

* 9 7 8 1 9 4 7 2 0 4 2 1 8 *